Falling for Mister Wrong

LIZZIE SHANE

DEDICATION

For my mother, who shared with me her love of music, and Mrs. Rios, the best piano teacher ever.

CHAPTER ONE

Her hands were shaking. That was normal, right? After all, it wasn't every day a girl had a fifty/fifty shot of getting engaged or getting dumped on her ass on national television.

Caitlyn curled her flawlessly manicured hands into fists to still the trembling, wincing a little when the nails bit into her palms, but grateful for that nip of pain. She'd been drifting, floating in the surrealness that had become her life, until that pinch gave her something to focus on. Something real.

Real was in short supply lately.

She squeezed her fists tighter, wondering how far she could go before she broke the skin. She wasn't used to wearing her nails so long—as a former child-prodigy pianist, her nails were always neatly trimmed to prevent clacking against the keys. She was probably already leaving marks—would one of the production staff notice and stop her?

As if on cue, Miranda—the producer the other producers feared—appeared over her shoulder, crossing to stand behind her, both of them facing the mirror.

"Lovely as ever, Caitlyn. How are you feeling? Excited?"

Caitlyn decided the question was rhetorical as Miranda pointed out a red lock that had come loose from Caitlyn's up-do and a hairstylist rushed forward with a comb to tuck it away. Miranda's gaze evaluated every inch of her, scrutinizing every seam of the designer fabric that hugged her figure, pausing for a moment on her fisted hands—she didn't miss much—and Caitlyn forced her fingers to straighten.

"You're doing great, hon." Miranda's hand came to rest on Caitlyn's bare shoulder, giving it a gentle squeeze. "Not much longer now."

Caitlyn nodded, unable to make her vocal cords form words. She almost hoped she was the one Daniel decided to ditch. At least then she wouldn't have to croak out a response to a proposal.

No. That wasn't what she wanted. She loved Daniel. Jitters. That was all this was. Stage fright. She'd had it before and never let it defeat her. She would master this.

Caitlyn vaguely heard the crackle of voices through Miranda's headset, then the producer gave her an eager smile and another shoulder squeeze. "Are you ready?"

No. Please God, don't make me do this.

She wondered what the producers would do if she made a run for it. Just up and bolted, sprinting out of the hair and make-up suite and not stopping until she was curled up on her couch at home, swaddled in her favorite comfy PJs.

They'd probably follow her with cameras, trying to get the best angle on her freak-out. This was reality television, after all. And they were good at what they did.

"Caitlyn?"

"I'm ready." Huh. Her voice sounded so normal. How did that happen?

She didn't remember getting to the beach. Only the vaguest impression of a long stone staircase and circling cameras penetrated her haze.

The setting was breathtaking. The producers would have made sure of that. The scent of tropical flowers in full bloom permeated the air and Caitlyn's nose twitched as she sniffed back the urge to sneeze. A wooden walkway had been built over the sand so she wouldn't sink and break an ankle in her heels. Every detail had been seen to—even the weathering of the brand new walkway so it blended in with the rusticity of the secluded tropical resort. The walkway stretched the last twenty meters to the dock that thrust out over the lagoon.

He would be waiting there, surrounded by the still Tahitian waters. Daniel.

Caitlyn's stomach clenched painfully and she stopped at the foot of the steps up to the dock. One of the production assistants rushed forward to help her lift her skirt and then faded back to let her navigate the steps herself—lest the PA be caught in the shot and ruin the magic of the moment.

Her chest felt tight and heat pressed against the backs of her eyes—she'd promised herself when she came on the show that she wasn't going to cry. Unfortunately she'd broken that promise three weeks ago and once the seal had been broken couldn't seem to stop weeping at the drop of a hat. She wasn't even sad. It was the pressure. All the stress seemed to push against her tear ducts with an alarming frequency.

She swallowed thickly, refusing to cry today. He was either going to pick her or he wasn't. He was going to propose or he wasn't. There was nothing she could do about it now. The score had already been written—all that remained was for her to play her part.

She flexed her fingers, moving them in the opening

bars to *Flight of the Bumblebee*. The music playing in her head calmed her and Caitlyn stiffened her spine, lifted her chin—and saw him.

Daniel. Movie-star gorgeous Daniel. Waiting for her at the end of the dock, surrounded by tropical flowers and a single high pedestal. A pedestal that would hold a ring.

Prince Charming couldn't have been more handsome. He smiled, and even though she was too far away to see it, she knew his blue eyes would be sparkling. His dimples would be flashing, emphasizing his air of boyish sincerity.

Mister Perfect. Sure, it was the title of the show—*Marrying Mister Perfect*—but she hadn't expected him to actually be perfect. That he would want all the things she wanted, and say all the right things. Caitlyn really hadn't thought she would get this far, but she'd been swept along, caught up in the fairy tale of dream date after dream date until here they were. The finale. The moment of truth.

She'd wanted this, dreamt of this. It was the reason women auditioned for the show—the promise of that elusive prize, true love. And Caitlyn had more reason than most to crave it, but this might not be her happily ever after. She might just be the obstacle to Elena's dreams coming true.

Her stomach rolled. She forced her feet to keep moving toward the end of the dock. One heel caught on an uneven plank and she wobbled for a fraction of a second before righting herself. *Don't fall into the ocean. Don't be that girl.*

In the water to either side, cameras were set up on strategically placed platforms, so they could capture every angle without ruining the illusion that it was just the two of them, alone in a Tahitian lagoon.

Illusion. She felt the weight of the cameras pressing on her, bearing down on her shoulders until it became a battle to keep her spine straight. At first she had been one of many Suitorettes and it had been easy to blend into the crowd, but these last few weeks it felt like every eye in America was on her. Homebody Caitlyn Gregg, on display for all the world to see.

She'd had to fight her natural urge to shy from the cameras. For him.

Caitlyn lifted her gaze, eyes on the prize. Daniel.

He was worth it. He was. Mister Perfect.

He smiled and the buzzing in her ears receded. He took a half step forward, reaching out to catch her hands as soon as she was within range, and her heart rate dropped back down to non-life-threatening levels.

"Together," he mouthed silently and Caitlyn remembered how to breathe. He was her eye of the storm. The still oasis of calm that kept her sane amid all the insanity of the show. *We're in this together*, he would say whenever she confessed how much the constant attention wore on her, how often she thought about giving it up and going home.

She could do this. Just a little more. One last moment. One last scene. And then it would be done. Over.

The relief of that thought almost drowned out her fear that she might be about to become America's most famous dumped girl—until the next reality television cycle rolled around.

Daniel was speaking, she realized distantly. Okay, maybe she wasn't as together as she'd hoped. The words seemed to be passing through some sort of distortion tunnel before they reached her ears and all she could make sense of was the occasional snippet.

"...journey together...never imagined...feeling so strongly..."

She couldn't seem to focus on his face. It seemed broken into disproportionate pieces like a Picasso. A nose. A mouth. An eye. A cheekbone. An ear.

Caitlyn reminded herself not to frown as she concentrated on figuring out whether this was the pre-proposal speech or the pre-break-up speech. She'd seen enough of these shows to know those speeches often sounded almost identical to one another with the exception of one very crucial word.

But.

As soon as the but came, she would know she was getting ditched. She strained to catch the words swirling around her head, wondering if Daniel had any idea the depth of her panic at this moment. His hands were cool and smooth and strong. Hers were a hot, sweaty clench gripping him.

She realized she was holding her breath and forced herself to inhale. *Thou shalt not pass out on national television* had become a favorite mantra and she repeated it to herself now.

Christ on Crutches, how long could this last? Wasn't he done enumerating her many wonderful qualities yet? Didn't he know she couldn't concentrate on a word of it until she knew whether it was yes or no? Glory or heartbreak? Euphoria or national laughingstock?

"...all this time my feelings for you have been growing stronger, but—"

Caitlyn sucked in a breath so hard she nearly choked herself. There it was. The infamous *but*. Suddenly the words were crisp and clear and as loud as if they were coming through a bull horn.

"—I haven't been able to tell you how I feel. Thank

God, I can finally shout it from the rooftops. I love you, Caitlyn. It's you. From the very first moment I saw you, it's always been you. You're perfect."

Daniel sank down to one knee and released one of her hands to reach over and pluck the ring box off the pedestal. She blinked at him, confused.

Wait. You just said 'but,' she wanted to protest. *You're supposed to be breaking up with me.*

But he popped the ring box open one-handed and Caitlyn's heart rate accelerated rapidly back toward critical levels.

Beethoven's Sainted Ass, that was some rock. A massive emerald cut diamond caught the late afternoon sun, all but blinding her with bling.

"Caitlyn Marie Gregg, will you marry me?"

Oh shit.

She'd been so busy worrying about being dumped, she hadn't really thought about what she would say if he actually proposed. She'd thought if that happened she would just speak from the heart, but her heart was conspicuously silent—other than racing faster than Hussein Bolt.

She needed to say something. Yes. She needed to say yes. They'd talked about their future together. She'd hoped he meant everything he said, hoped he would get down on one knee. She had to say yes. Cinderella said yes to Prince Charming. That was how it worked. But now the words caught in her throat.

"I…"

Daniel gazed up at her, earnest, adoring and almost impossibly good-looking, his heart in his eyes and the world's biggest diamond in his hand. Tahitian water lapped against the posts supporting the dock. Tropical flowers crowded into her peripheral vision and filled the air with their intoxicating scents. It was the perfect scene, carefully crafted to get a single answer—but she couldn't speak.

Did she love him? Was that what this feeling was? It felt an awful lot like panic, but maybe the two weren't so far apart. If she might love him or even if she *could* love him someday, didn't she owe it to both of them to say yes? How could she hurt him by saying no when he'd only ever been good to her?

Caitlyn snuck a glance to her left out of the corner of her eye—to the large reflective panels angled just so to redirect the sunlight at the best possible angle. To the producers and production assistants and interns and lighting guys and make-up girls and stylists all lined up on the beach—most looking businesslike though one or two leaned against one another, sniffling and dripping sappy romanticism.

She felt the weight of America's collective desires pressing on her, urging her to say something. Anything. This episode wouldn't air for months, but she could feel them already. All those million eyes hungry for the drama of her life. Ravenous for it. They wouldn't care whether it was happiness or heartbreak, they just wanted the payoff.

But who would she be to them if she refused him? The girl who thought she was too good for the perfect man? He always said the right things. He was the man every woman in America had fallen in love with last season.

She saw Miranda—ever-present tablet tucked under one arm and headset mashed over her short, platinum bob. The producer seemed to sense the direction of her gaze and gave a slight, encouraging nod. An echo of a conversation they'd had a few weeks ago fluttered through her thoughts. *Don't be afraid to go with it.*

Was that what this was? Fear? Caitlyn had her fair share of baggage. In one of her teary moments, she'd confessed to Daniel—and the entire freaking home viewing audience—that she was afraid of love, afraid of making herself vulnerable to that kind of hurt, even as she longed for it desperately.

Was this her moment of truth? The moment when she would either overcome her fear or doom herself to a life alone? The perfect man was on one knee for her, all but *begging* her to say yes. The life she had always wanted was being handed to her on a silver platter. She would be a fool not jump at it. A spineless, pathetic, ungrateful fool.

This was her happily-ever-after. They didn't come along every day.

But what if it was just a carefully crafted illusion?

"Caitlyn?"

She met bluer-than-blue eyes. *Don't be afraid to go with it.* "Yes, Daniel, of course I'll marry you."

The collective sigh from the crew made it seem like even the island released its held breath.

Daniel beamed and the world which had ground to a halt kicked into warp speed again. The ring was on her finger, he was leaping to his feet, sweeping her off hers, swirling her around, kissing her, laughing, proclaiming his love—and then doing it all again on cue when one of the sound guys announced one of the mics was acting up and they weren't sure they'd caught the first take.

"We can get married on the reunion finale!" Daniel exclaimed and she felt herself nodding. Smiling.

Caitlyn held on tight when he hugged her, laughing, echoing the words of love, crying—with joy, she told herself, not relief—admiring the flash of the rock on her finger, and telling herself over and over again that this was it. Her husband. Her future. Her happy ending. It was real.

If she said the words to herself enough, she might even begin to believe them.

CHAPTER TWO

"Just think. In twelve weeks, we'll be on our honeymoon. Maybe even back here. Would you like that? It has a certain symmetry."

Caitlyn yanked her gaze off their interlocked fingers, gawking up at Daniel. "Twelve weeks?"

They stood in the Tahitian hotel suite they'd shared the night before, soaking in a last few precious minutes of togetherness before their separate cars arrived to whisk them away to separate planes, carrying them back to the U.S. where they would be able to contact one another only in the most secretive ways until the show finished airing.

"Two weeks until the show begins airing, nine regular episodes and then the finale with our wedding." His smile faded, blue eyes crinkling with concern. "That's still what you want, isn't it? We talked so much about wanting to dive right into our life together. I didn't think you'd want to wait, but if that seems too soon, I'll grab Miranda and tell her we need more time—"

"No, no, of course, I want to marry you," she heard some stranger with her voice saying. "It's just all the planning. Wedding dresses, flowers… I don't even know how we would do invitations when we can't admit to people that we know one another."

He beamed, instantly blithely happy with the knowledge that she hadn't changed her mind about saying I do on national television. "The network will take care of all that. You just have to kick back, relax, and watch it all come together."

The desire to protest again was strong, but she didn't even know what she would say. *I don't want someone else planning my wedding? Does everything we do for the rest of our lives have to be in the public eye? Can't we just wait a year or seven until I know for sure that you're the one?*

"You won't have to do a thing. Except of course, dream about me every night and miss me every day." He dropped a kiss on her nose. Caitlyn smothered the urge to sneeze. "The future Mrs. Pierzynski. Caitlyn Pierzynski. I like the sound of that."

I can't even spell it.

She tried to smile, but his movie-star gorgeous face was too close and her brain was doing the Picasso thing again. Ear. Nose. Why was she still so on edge? He was supposed to be her eye of the storm, but even though the cameras had left them alone for the last fifteen hours, she still felt the residual push of that always *on* feeling that had plagued her for the last weeks.

It must be the hotel. She probably wouldn't feel normal again until she got back to Colorado.

"Are you looking forward to getting back to Indiana?" she asked abruptly, digging for that connection, that moment of simpatico that would remind her he really was The One.

"Actually, I'm going to L.A. There will be so many media events and publicity appearances for the next several weeks—morning talk shows, late-night talk shows, guest spots on everything from cooking shows to medical advice programs—it seemed like it would be so much easier to manage all that if I was based in L.A. for a while."

"You aren't going home for Christmas?"

"They'll understand. It's such a busy time for me."

She'd loved his family. She couldn't imagine not wanting to spend the holidays with them. She was already fantasizing about next year when she could have a real family Christmas. "What about your students?"

"Oh, I already spoke with my principal. They know not to expect me back this year. It probably would be too much of a distraction for the kids anyway, being taught by a celebrity. And who knows? I might find something that suits me even better in Hollywood. Craig from last season is on one of those morning shows now." He grinned, all dimples and twinkling blue eyes. "Can you see me as a commentator?"

"What would you commentate on?"

He shrugged. "Who knows? If we're lucky, maybe we can afford a mansion next door to the Marrying Mister Perfect mansion in Beverly Hills. How great would that be? We could look out our window and see where we first met."

"I don't know if I want a mansion in Beverly Hills."

He grinned, lifting their linked hands and kissing her knuckles. "You're right. It's too early to be talking about all that. Right now all you need to be thinking about is going back to Colorado and packing up your apartment so we can start our new life together in twelve weeks."

He said it with such boyish enthusiasm, his eyes alight at the idea of her boxing up her old life to join him in his. And that was what she wanted, wasn't it? That was why she'd come on the show. Because she needed a change. She needed more than what she had in her lonely little Colorado apartment. Christmases by herself,

New Year's with no one to kiss. She wanted someone to come home to and the pitter-patter of little feet.

Daniel wanted all those things too. She couldn't count the number of conversations they'd had where they'd mapped out their life together. PTA and soccer practice. Who would change the diapers (both of them) and who would do the cooking (Daniel – Caitlyn was a disaster in the kitchen).

She wasn't losing her old life, she was gaining that new one. The one they'd planned. Even if they hadn't planned it in Los Angeles.

That wasn't such a big deal. It didn't really matter whether he was an elementary school teacher or a commentator. And she could teach piano lessons anywhere. She was still getting her happily ever after with the perfect guy.

A gentle knock sounded on the door. "Caitlyn," a familiar segment producer's voice called through the wood. "We're ready for you."

She smiled up at Daniel. "Probably won't be hearing that again for a while."

She wasn't sure Daniel heard her. He was too busy gazing meltingly into her eyes. "I love you, Caitlyn."

She tried to echo him, but the words got stuck in her throat, so she closed her eyes and tipped her face up for his kiss, concentrating on remembering the feel of him since it would be weeks, perhaps even months, before she saw him again. Her fiancé.

The Rock of Ages—as she'd come to think of her engagement ring—was safely tucked away in her carry-on bag. She couldn't be seen with so much as a tell-tale crease on her finger for the next three months. As far as the world at large knew, she might as well be another of the broken-hearted Suitorettes who had been discarded along the way.

Daniel opened the door and a pair of large crew guys swept in to collect her luggage. The show always shot strategically to make it look like each of the Suitorettes traveled with only one dainty roller bag, but the truth was they usually needed a separate SUV just to carry all the shoes.

Caitlyn squeezed Daniel's hand one last time before extricating her fingers, her hand feeling strangely light without his gripping it. She trailed the producer down the hall to the bank of elevators where Miranda was waiting, her tablet tucked against her stomach.

"Eager to leave all of us in your vapor trail?" Miranda asked, punching the down button with a single slender finger.

"Am I that obvious?" The engraved doors slid back and Caitlyn preceded Miranda into the car. The other producer and the two crew heavies with her bags continued on toward the freight elevators.

Miranda smiled her catlike smile as the doors shut. "Honestly? I consider it one of the great victories of my career that you didn't pull a runaway bride on us weeks ago. Some people have a harder time with the reality TV format than others and the girls who come on looking for love and family and happy endings tend to be the ones with the most disillusionment when the reality of reality TV hits."

"I guess I'm lucky it was Daniel then. I never would have made it without him. And now we really do get our happy ending."

Miranda blinked. "Lucky." But her tone didn't make it sound lucky at all.

Caitlyn frowned at the producer who had become the closest thing she had to a friend here in the last few weeks. "You know, as pep talks go, this one sucks."

Miranda grimaced as the elevator doors opened, waving her forward with one arm. "I'm supposed to be reminding you of all the non-disclosures you signed. No discussing the show—either in interviews or casual conversations with friends or family. No admitting to a relationship with Daniel—not even to the other Suitorettes, if they should contact you. Basically, the network will sue you into the ground if you do anything to spoil the ratings of the big finale."

"Understood."

"Telephone conversations between you and Daniel are permitted only if you use the cell phones we have provided for you for that purpose. You are not to use that phone except to call me or Daniel. You are not to be seen together—no matter how casually. At about the halfway point of the season, we'll arrange a weekend getaway for the two of you, but you aren't to tell anyone where you're going or who you will be seeing."

"Miranda, I get it. I read everything I signed."

They'd reached the black SUV waiting in the valet lane at the hotel—one of a fleet of such vehicles that the show used. Miranda stopped beside the rear passenger door, fidgeting with her tablet—which only reinforced Caitlyn's impression that Miranda was avoiding whatever she'd really wanted to talk to her about.

"It's gonna be fine," Caitlyn said. "The hard part is over."

The executive producer grimaced and glanced back toward the hotel, not meeting Caitlyn's eyes. "When you watch the show," she said haltingly, "try to remember that everything is exaggerated for dramatic effect. There may be times when things seem worse than they are. Try to focus on your experiences and trust your own memories."

Caitlyn frowned. Miranda had seen all the footage. She knew what kind of show it was going to be. Caitlyn only had her own little piece to go on. Love in a vacuum. "Is there something specific I should know? About Daniel?"

"No. Nothing like that. Just..." Miranda hesitated, flipping the tablet between her hands. "Well. You have my number. You can call me if you need anything. Travel safe, Caitlyn."

Miranda watched Caitlyn's car pull away, smashing down the flare of guilt that tried to rise. The girl was too delicate for this business by half. Too hopeful. Too trusting. And too damn sweetly optimistic. She actually thought the worst was over. Miranda cringed in spite of herself. Too naïve by half.

The filming was rigorous, but it was the airing of the show that really changed people. For the last several weeks, Caitlyn hadn't been able to walk down the street without a camera crew tracking her every move, and perhaps a few curious glances wondering why she was being filmed. In the next two months, as she became more and more of a featured player in the reality drama that was about to play out on national television, she wouldn't be able to walk down the street without being watched by every eye, pointed at, and stopped for her autograph or a photo. Camera phones would be sneaking pictures of her in the produce section at her grocery. Bloggers would discuss every minute detail of her life—on screen and off. Privacy was a thing of the past.

Not to mention the experience of everyone in

America watching her fiancé make out with half a dozen other girls.

And she thought the worst was over.

Miranda winced. She felt sorry for Caitlyn. For what she was about to go through. And she didn't like feeling sorry. She liked her job. She was damn good at her job. And she hated the stupid rumblings of her stupid conscience.

Damn Bennett anyway. It was his deep voice she heard grumbling in her head about the morality of using people like Caitlyn for America's entertainment.

Of course the griping was only in her head because he'd stopped speaking to her weeks ago. He'd been her mentor, then her lover—which had, in retrospect, probably been a colossal mistake, no matter how huge a crush she'd always had on him—but he'd been the one constant in her life and now he was… what? Her ex? It felt wrong to think of him that way.

Things had been so good at the beginning of the season. She'd thought they were over the disagreements about her work on *Marrying Mister Perfect* and his need to tell her what she should be doing with her life. She'd said the L word, for crying out loud, and he hadn't exactly said it back, but it had been implied.

But it hadn't been a cure all pill. Two weeks into the new season of *Marrying Mister Perfect*, he'd begun bugging her to quit and go back to work for him at *American Dance Star*. The fights had only gotten worse and when she'd decided to travel with the show again, rather than stay in Los Angeles with him… well, the result was predictable. Angry silence.

She swallowed back her anger at his abandonment. She'd told him she *loved* him, damn it. Not something she confessed lightly. And he'd just kept trying to turn her into who he wanted her to be.

And the worst part was, she still missed the bastard.

She hadn't been able to talk to him about her concerns for Caitlyn as the show progressed. She hadn't had anyone to talk to when she worried she was pushing Caitlyn too hard, coaching Daniel too much, or pulling too many strings to force the outcome that would get the best ratings. She missed her sounding board, but she wasn't about to apologize to him. He was the one who owed her an apology—

"A glorious day, isn't it, Miranda?" Daniel called jovially, jolting her out of her thoughts as he strode out of the hotel, golden and beaming.

"Glorious," she echoed direly, then grabbed hold of herself and put on her professional face. "Are you ready for the masses, Mister Perfect?"

Daniel grinned as another black SUV slid into the place Caitlyn's had vacated. "You know. I'm young, healthy and in love. Today I do feel like I deserve to be called 'perfect'."

Miranda laughed at his enthusiasm. "Save it for the interviews, you ham."

He winked and ducked into the SUV—and she scolded herself for worrying. The mild-mannered school teacher from Indiana might have morphed into a spotlight seeking attention whore, but he was still a good guy underneath it all. And she wanted to believe he really loved Caitlyn. If he did, maybe it wasn't naïve of Caitlyn to believe in their happy ending. And maybe Miranda wasn't the devil incarnate for throwing them together and exploiting their romantic drama on national television.

They just needed a happy ending. Miranda watched another SUV pull away, airport-bound, and vowed to do everything in her considerable reality-TV power to make sure Caitlyn and Daniel got their happily ever after.

If only so she would finally stop hearing Bennett's deep voice scolding her in her head.

CHAPTER THREE

After over fifteen hours of planes and airports and another hour's drive west into the mountains from Denver, Caitlyn watched, punchy with jet-lag, as the driver the show had arranged for her ferried her bags up to the shadowy second floor landing of her apartment building, neatly stacking them beside her door. This would be the last time for quite a while that anyone catered to her needs—a realization that met with an odd blend of nostalgia and relief as she pressed a tip into the driver's hand.

He said something about waiting to see that she got into her place all right, but she waved him off. This was Tuller Springs, not Manhattan. She was too tired to argue the point, but with a glance at his surroundings he seemed to agree with her, grinning and tipping an imaginary cap before heading down the stairs with an insulting amount of energy.

God, she was exhausted.

Caitlyn was tempted to sink down to the floor and just hang out there until she got her second wind. With all the travel they'd done over the last several weeks and her own jet-setting childhood, she ought to be used to it, but she still got off a plane and felt like she'd been flattened by a steam-roller. And that didn't even take into account time zones and sleep deprivation.

The dingy faded burgundy carpet on the landing looked remarkably comfortable. But her bed would be a thousand times better, so she forced herself to rummage in her carry on, feeling around for the apartment keys she hadn't needed in over two months.

The contents of her bag seemed to have done a full one-eighty rotation during take-off and landing. She fumbled for a good five minutes before her fingers brushed against a bit of metal and she heard the muted jangle.

Yanking out the keys, she unlocked and shoved open her door. Light immediately streamed onto the landing, blasting through the giant windows that dominated the apartment's main room. Her body might not know what time it was and all the clocks in the kitchen might be blinking from a power outage while she was away, but the angle of the sun told her it was early afternoon on this side of the world.

She'd dozed in the car, not really registering the familiar scenery, but now, with the sunlight greeting her, Caitlyn felt a weight lift off her chest. She could get a full breath again—and it wasn't until the weight was gone that she realized it had been pressing on her for the last two months straight.

Feeling lighter but still exhausted past reason, she began shoving and kicking her bags into the apartment, piling them haphazardly inside the door with just enough room for her to squeeze past and shut it.

The apartment wasn't particularly new or chic. Built at the base of one of Tuller Springs' three ski resorts back in the eighties when the town was trying desperately to compete with Aspen and Vail for tourist dollars, the A-frame chalet had been broken up into a pair of independent apartments over a decade ago. The lower-level featured a ski-out deck when the snow piled up in the winter, but Caitlyn got the giant triangular windows, exposed beams, and insanely gorgeous views.

The apartment was primarily one open room. She'd set up a little sitting area closest to the windows to capitalize on the views of the mountain and the warmth of the fat little potbelly stove. The kitchen was tucked into a corner on the wall farthest from the windows, home to a tiny café table and two chairs she'd picked up at a yard sale.

Where most people would have set up a proper dining room sat Caitlyn's pride and joy—a gorgeous sprawl of gleaming ivory, polished wood, and strings. Her Steinway grand piano. Her mother liked to brag about the Bosendorfer Caitlyn had been raised playing, but for her money nothing compared to the sweet bell-like tone of the Steinway.

Beyond the piano was the apartment's single tiny bathroom, always kept scrupulously tidy as her students often asked to use it as a stalling tactic when they hadn't practiced. Shower only, no tub, but those were the sacrifices one made for gorgeous views and heavenly acoustics.

Beside the bathroom door was the steeper-than-code staircase leading up to the loft. It wasn't large, just enough room up there for her double bed, a dresser, and a clothes-rack, but the loft was open to the room below and shared the view out the giant windows of the snowy mountain.

"Be it ever so humble," she murmured, automatically slipping the key ring onto the little quarter-note hook beside the door.

A fine layer of dust had settled over everything in her absence—more the impression of neglect than anything else. She hadn't been gone long enough for actual dirt to accumulate. Two months.

Time had been distorted on the show. A "week" in show parlance referred to an episode and was rarely an actual week, since some episodes were filmed over three days and others could take as many as ten, depending how far they had to travel. Everything revolved around maintaining the illusion for the home audience, and it was like being in a sensory deprivation chamber—no watches, no cell phones, no real sense of how long anything was taking.

But now, she was back in the real world, where two months had passed. Two months that changed everything.

Would Daniel be so quick to tell her to pack up her life if he saw how charming her little chalet was? If he had met her students and heard the promise of their burgeoning talent? Admittedly, the apartment was too small for two—it barely fit her and her Steinway.

It didn't matter what he might have thought if he'd seen the peaceful charm of Tuller Springs. Her "Meet the In-Laws" date—the one chance the show gave for him to see into her life—had been in Manhattan. Concert-for-one at Carnegie Hall, strolling hand-in-hand through Central Park, and a formal meal at her mother's posh, glacial Upper East Side apartment. The producers had loved it, Daniel had been enchanted, and even her mother had been on her best behavior—only throwing out barbed comments about her absent father twice.

She should call her mother, let her know she was back safely. Touch base with her father for the first time since she left for the show—if she could figure out where he was this month. Call her best friend Mimi and let her know she was back in town.

Her cell phone sat on the charger in the kitchen, right where she'd left it. But as soon as she picked it up, she'd be officially opening the floodgates to let real life in and she was too tired to even consider it. Caitlyn walked over to flop on the couch facing the window. Its cushy depths instantly enfolded her and she groaned with pleasure, toeing off her shoes.

Her entire body felt achy and grimy from the airplane—a shower would be heaven itself, but that would involve getting vertical and that was not going to happen. Caitlyn gazed up at the mountain—cloaked in white though scrubby bushes still pushed through the snow at the base and there weren't many skiers and snowboarders cutting tracks through the white. It had been surprisingly warm outside for December, she realized belatedly, which would be bad for the resorts and winter tourist revenues but would make the town quieter through the holidays. And it was still beautiful even with the patchy snow.

How many more times would she look up at this view?

She still had four more months left on her lease. Should she break it early? Or use the first two months of marriage as a transition time to pack up and move to L.A.

Marriage.

The word rang, huge and gong-like, in her head. She was engaged. Actually engaged. She raised her bare finger, trying to remember what it looked like with the Rock of Ages weighing it down.

It didn't feel real. Maybe because it had all happened so fast. Or because it seemed too good to be true. Or because she couldn't tell anyone.

Were you really engaged if you couldn't gush to your

girlfriends about how amazing your fiancé was? How was she supposed to pack up her life and get ready to move if she couldn't tell anyone she was packing up and getting ready to move?

She could call Daniel. He would have landed in Los Angeles hours ago. The unregistered cell Miranda had given her was tucked in her carry-on, right next to the Rock of Ages. But the idea of digging for it was as unappealing as the thought of calling her mother.

Maybe in a few hours. After she was rested. She needed to build up some reserves for both calls.

Caitlyn closed her eyes, resolved to nap where she had fallen rather than making the trek up the steep loft steps, but as soon as her lids fell a restless energy began to push them up again.

Freaking jet-lag. Here she was, too tired to be of any use to anyone—including herself—but her body clock was too out of whack to allow sleep.

There were a thousand things she ought to be doing. Her students wouldn't resume lessons until after the holidays, but she only had a couple days to get all of her Christmas shopping done, as well as any decorating she wanted to do.

A thousand things to do, but only one she wanted to do—the same thing that had gotten her through every other sleepless night in her life, when her restless thoughts chased her out of bed.

Caitlyn stood and stripped out of her plane clothes, tugging a random pair of yoga pants and a tank top out of the duffle next to the door. She swept her hair up into a pony tail while sliding the piano bench back with the practiced nudge of one foot. Seated, she slid back the cover over the keys and gently ran her fingertips over the smooth expanse of ivory, grateful she'd gotten bored on the first flight and filed her manicure down to a manageable length.

She mentally shuffled through her repertoire. Resting her hands lightly on the instrument that had been both her bane and her salvation over the years, she struck a single key. B above middle C. Letting the note resonate as the hammer hit the string. Listening for the sympathetic shivering of the strings beside it. Picking out the layers of sound in that one note until it faded into silence.

Chopin, I think.

She lifted her wrists, arching her fingers into position, and plunged into the Nocturne, starting with that same sweet B. And then she flew.

CHAPTER FOUR

Will woke up smiling as the music drifted down through the floor of the apartment above—something that hadn't happened in far too long. Both the smiling and the music.

She was back.

In the six months he'd lived below the piano teacher he'd never actually laid eyes on her, which was practically sacrilegious in a town the size of Tuller Springs where it seemed like everyone had to know everyone. Their schedules simply didn't match up—which wasn't surprising. Will's schedule didn't match up with just about anyone's.

As a volunteer firefighter-slash-ski-instructor-slash-river guide who worked nights at a bar a couple nights a week to pick up some extra cash in the slow season, he didn't have what most people considered normal hours. So he'd never seen his upstairs neighbor, but he'd always enjoyed the serenades, even when they interrupted his bizarre sleep schedule.

He stretched his arms above his head, joints popping satisfyingly as he tuned in to the music. Chopin, if he had to guess. Not that he was an expert. He'd only started learning about composers and classical music in the last couple months when he realized how much he missed his daily serenades and looked to replace them with CDs from the library. His thrill-junkie ski-patrol buddies would never believe how relaxing he found Beethoven.

He wondered if he could send a request through the mail slot for a little Moonlight Sonata.

He pictured his upstairs neighbor—Ms. Gregg, according to her mailbox—as a bespectacled septuagenarian with long quick fingers and a semi-permanent bun. When he hadn't heard her playing for a couple weeks, it had been easy to imagine she'd had a stroke or something and was trapped up there by herself. He'd become so concerned he'd knocked on her door a half dozen times and even called the landlord to find out if someone official needed to check on her.

Turned out, according to their landlord, Ms. Gregg was just on an extended vacation. Even knowing she was okay, it was surprisingly good to hear her again.

The Chopin segued smoothly into Moonlight Sonata and Will grinned to himself, stacking his hands behind his head.

He should bring her a welcome home gift. Maybe some muffins or Christmas cookies or something. His mother was always trying to fob her baking off on Will—as if he'd never developed the ability to feed himself in the decade since he moved out. Maybe next time she handed him baked goods, he'd take them up to little old Ms. Gregg. Seemed neighborly and he really owed her for all the hours he'd spent listening to her. Other folks paid big bucks for stuff like that and he got it for free.

When the Moonlight Sonata faded into something flowy and rocking that he didn't recognize, he rolled a glance at the clock and grimaced. After two already. He'd closed the bar last night, picking up an extra shift to compensate for the crappy weather they'd been having that had cut his usual ski lesson schedule in half. Today was his regular day off, but that didn't mean he could laze around all day. He was due at his parents' tonight for family dinner and caroling—which was always an adventure in a family as tone deaf as his.

He needed to do laundry, shower, and wash his car before heading over. If he didn't exude normalcy and radiate I've-got-my-shit-together vibes, he was going to get another round of We're Very Concerned About You from every member of the large and nosy Hamilton clan. As much as he loved them, he was sick of being the family project. Even if they were just trying to cheer him up.

The smooth, flowy piece ended and something bright and exuberant burst through the floorboards above.

Sure, he had terrible taste in women, which had led him to his current situation, living in a tomblike ground floor apartment, but at least the soundtrack was good.

Will grabbed his phone to Spotify the bright, flashy piece. *Frederick Kuhlau.* He scribbled the name on a receipt he found on the bedside table, deciding to check out the composer next time he went to the local library. It was small, as was pretty much everything in Tuller Springs, but had a fairly decent collection of classical CDs he was plowing his way through.

Suspending his musical education for the day, he rolled out of bed and wandered to the bathroom, flicking through text messages with his thumb as he walked. The family group chat had been active while he was sleeping. Somehow his sisters had gotten into an argument about which one of them got to bring a nice girl tonight to meet him. Will fired off a quick reply—informing all three of them that if he saw any non-family members tonight he had a feeling there would be a fire-fighting emergency that would call him away before they even said grace.

That nightmare handled, he checked his email, grimacing at the we'll-call-you-if-we-need-you brush off from the ski-patrol guys in response to his request for extra shifts and deleting a half-dozen ads that his spam filter had missed. He was still holding his phone when it rang and his oldest sister's face flashed on the screen— along with all three of her children and her husband who had all mashed their faces into the selfie.

He knew her too well to let the phone go to voicemail. She'd just keep calling. Stubborn didn't begin to describe Claire Hamilton Lancaster, but Will hadn't grown up with three older sisters without knowing how to get his way when he needed to.

"Non-negotiable, Claire," he said by way of greeting.

"You've gotta get back on the horse, Willie. Otherwise Bitch Face wins." At least she wasn't using the We're Very Concerned About You voice. Claire was more steamroller than tea and sympathy. Pity and poor-baby was more Julia's style.

"I'll remount, as you so elegantly put it, when I'm good and ready and when I do, I won't need my big sisters to set me up."

"I know, I know, you're a sexy stud muffin—"

"It is so gross to hear you say that."

"But you never know who is going to turn out to be your one and only. Don't look a gift hook-up in the mouth."

He strolled into the kitchen, the phone pressed to his ear and flicked on the coffee maker as *Oh Holy Night* began to play above him. "Do you realize that's the second time you've compared the girl you want to set me up with to a horse? Is that some kind of subliminal commentary on her appearance?"

"Don't be a jerk. I've found you some grade-A premium woman flesh and you can't even say *thank you, Claire. You're the best sister ever, Claire. My most favoritest sister ever and I shall love you most always.*"

"So you're saying this is really about beating Julia and Laney to the punch and making sure neither of them are the one to set me up with my dream girl."

There was a slight tell-tale pause. "Love isn't a competition, Willie," she said archly.

"Uh-huh. No dates. Just a quiet family dinner. At least as much as this family does quiet. Got it?"

"It's been six months."

And I was left at the altar when my fiancé ran away with my best man. I think I get a solid year on that one. The words burned on his tongue, but he didn't say them. They would only launch another lecture about holding onto things and releasing his anger and learning to love again.

No matter how many times he told his family he had released and forgiven and all that bullshit, and that he just didn't *want* another woman in his life right now, it never seemed to penetrate the haze of their concern. Every single one of them was married and revoltingly happy. Only Laney didn't have kids yet. His family was one giant, mocking picture of domestic bliss.

And here he was, tied up in a legal battle to get back the down payment he'd put up on the house he'd bought with Tria before The Wedding That Wasn't. Where she was currently living with his former best friend.

He was allowed to hang onto shit like that for six months.

"No one should be alone at Christmastime."

He groaned. "I'm never alone. No matter how many times I wish I could be an only child, if only for a day, my fairy godmother never grants my freaking wish."

"Willie..." Now the Very Concerned About You Voice was there. *Shit.*

"If I promise to start dating soon, will you all back off?" The constant pressure to prove to his family how happy and well-adjusted he was after his life had fallen apart wasn't exactly helping.

"I still wish you'd let me key Bitch Face's car. It isn't too late." Her voice lifted hopefully.

Will snorted. "I appreciate the thought. And if I ever decide vandalism is the way to go, I'll give you a call. Tell me again, how does that fit in with the whole forgiveness and letting-it-go thing?"

"Shut up. I'm your big sister. I don't have to ever forgive that bitch."

"Love you too."

"Uh huh. Let me know if you change your mind about the set up. She's super cute. Even Don said so."

"And then you punished your husband for agreeing with you that she's cute, didn't you?"

"He didn't have to say it so enthusiastically," she grumbled. "I'd like to see him pop out three kids and still look good in a cheerleader outfit. Though I can still work the pom-poms with the best of 'em." Her tone was cheerfully lecherous.

"Ew. Too much information, Claire." He would need maximum strength brain bleach to get rid of that mental image.

"Julia wants you to babysit on Saturday, but tell her you're already sitting for me, okay?"

"Have I agreed to take the kids for you?" he asked

skeptically.

"No, but you will because I'm your favorite sister."

"Is this about needing a day without the kids or pissing Julia off? Because you realize I can take your three and her two and put them all in a room together and they entertain each other."

"She asked me to join Weight Watchers with her."

Most men might not understand the affront with which the words were spoken, but Will had spent the entire thirty years of his life with three sisters. He cringed. "She might have just wanted moral support."

"She's a twig," Claire snapped. "She says she wants to lose her baby weight, which means she'll eat celery for a week and be perfect again and then I will have to kill her. And roast her and eat her because if I go on Weight Watchers again I will be hungry all the time and cannibalism will start to seem like a viable option."

Will bit back a laugh, not sure whether she was serious or not. "Unless it snows and I have to teach, I'll take your kids, but if Julia asks I'm gonna take hers too. I'm not getting in the middle of whatever Weight Watchers vendetta you guys have going."

Claire humphed. "You're so annoying when you won't take sides."

"Whenever you tell me I'm annoying, I always feel like I've done something right and virtuous."

"Be nice to me or I'll start sending women to your door, telling them that you're dying to take them out."

"Be nice to *me*. I don't have to babysit the monsters on Saturday."

"Yes, you do. Don promised me afternoon sex if we get all the presents wrapped. Do you know how long it's been since we've had sex on the kitchen table?"

"Jesus. TMI, Claire. I've eaten on that table."

"Oh relax. We wash it."

"I'm hanging up now."

"Hugs and kisses!" She made annoying smoochy noises into the phone until he disconnected the call.

As much as he might want to be frustrated with her meddling and tendency to over share about her sex life, he was grinning as he tossed the phone on the counter and poured himself a cup of the coffee that had been brewing while they talked.

That was the beauty and tragedy of family. They loved you and pushed you to be happy even when you just wanted to have a nice long wallow in the shit-show your life had become. Dinner was likely to be more of the same—only with more players. He'd be smothered by pity and well wishes all night. Maybe he could turn it into a drinking game. A slug of eggnog every time someone told him it was a crime to be alone on the holidays.

The music above had stopped and he flipped on the CD player to fill the silence with Dvorak.

Maybe he wouldn't take baked goods to Ms. Gregg after all. She probably had a cute little granddaughter she'd want to set him up with as soon as she realized there was a single male living below her. Much better to mind his own business and lick his wounds in peace and quiet. He had enough women in his life without adding one more. Even a septuagenarian music teacher.

CHAPTER FIVE

"Merry Christmas!" the Christmas tree on her landing shouted cheerfully. Then it pushed through the door and Caitlyn saw the petite form of her best friend buried in the branches.

"Well, if it isn't the Christmas elf."

Mimi glared through the pine needles. "One more crack about my height and I'm shoving this tree somewhere unpleasant." She grunted, tipping slightly to the side and Caitlyn leapt forward to steady her and the uneven pile of branches that vaguely resembled a tree. "Where do you want it?"

It wasn't the majestic twelve foot fir she'd always dreamed would look perfect in front of the windows, but the scraggly four foot pine would still be the most festive thing in her place. "Let's put it by the windows."

Together they carried their cargo, which was more awkward than heavy, over to the designated spot.

As soon as it was propped safely against the glass, Mimi tackle hugged her.

"Welcome back!" Mimi squealed. "I missed you like crazy. Did you have fun? Were the other girls totally catty? Is he even better looking in person? Why didn't you call me the second you got back?"

Mimi Kwan-Torres was five-feet of pure energy and enthusiasm. After years in sedate blacks as second chair viola at the Seattle Symphony, she'd embraced color with a vengeance since her retirement and taken to wearing eye-popping neon combinations. Today's lime green leggings, scarlet leg warmers and fluorescent blue *Naughty Is More Fun* sweater were no exception. Even her chin-length black hair was streaked with color—red and green, this week, doubtless in a nod to the season.

Caitlyn laughed, squeezing her friend tight and feeling lighter than she had in months. She ignored most of the questions, answering only the last one Mimi got out before she had to stop for breath. "I was jet-lagged to within an inch of my life. How did you know I was back?"

"Tuller Springs Gossip Hotwire. Monica over at the Lodge saw a fancy driver in a fancy black car unloading a bunch of bags in front of your place." Mimi bounced away from her. "It's so good to see you and you are going to tell me *everything*, but first things first. Do you have a Christmas tree stand?"

Caitlyn frowned, studying the Charley Brown tree. "I could probably come up with a bucket."

Mimi flapped a hand dismissively. "I brought one, just in case. It's in the car with the rest of the stuff."

"The rest?"

"I know you. You'll decide it isn't worth the trouble since it's just for you and I am *not* going to let my best friend have a grinchy Christmas when she just got back from being totally brave and throwing herself into the jaws of love. I know you don't have much stuff, but the kids are constantly making us Christmas decorations and I told Ty I'm donating the stuff we don't have room for anymore to a good cause. The Let's Drown Caitlyn in Christmas Cheer Charity."

Caitlyn tried to smile, but her throat closed and that

41

familiar pressure was back, leaning on her tear ducts.

Mimi was the reason she'd moved to Tuller Springs in the first place. And now she would be leaving her. Indiana or Los Angeles, they were both hundreds of miles away. Whenever she and Daniel had talked about their plans for the future, staying in Colorado hadn't even come up as an option. She'd been so caught up in the romance of Spain and Bermuda and Tahiti, she hadn't really thought about how much she would be giving up. Her students. Her little chalet with the mountain view that always made her feel warm and peaceful and safe. And Mimi. Mimi would be the hardest to give up.

"Hey. Don't get all sappy on me," Mimi demanded with mock severity. "We have decorating to do." But when she turned away, she took a surreptitious swipe at her own glittering eyes.

Caitlyn grinned through the wetness in her eyes. "Yes, ma'am."

Two hours later, they sat in the kitchen, surveying their work and eating gingerbread cookies Mimi had baked in Caitlyn's often neglected oven. The Christmas tree sat in Mimi's second best tree stand, listing slightly to the right, and glittering with white lights and round glass ornaments Mimi's children had declared too boring to be allowed space on their tree. A liberal sprinkling of tinsel helped cover up the gaps in the branches. Mimi had apologized profusely about the inferior tree quality, protesting that there wasn't much left this close to Christmas, but Caitlyn liked the lumpy, lopsided tree. It had character and she was tired of perfection.

The rest of the decorations were primarily of the construction paper variety provided by Mimi's kids, but sparkly red and white garland also wrapped around the loft banister. Garland Mimi insisted was ragged and hand-me-down even though Caitlyn had spotted her yanking the store tags off and stuffing them in her pocket.

The end result may not have been as posh and flawless as her mother's glittering Upper East Side show place was during the holidays, but it glowed with holiday warmth.

"You know, I think I'm actually looking forward to Christmas." Her last Christmas in Tuller Springs.

"Ty and I were talking. I know you usually come over in the afternoon and have Christmas dinner with us, but do you think this year you could stay over Christmas Eve too? You can play and sing carols with the kids and then help us do the Santa thing. Neither Ty nor I have any freaking idea how to put together Mia Grace's doll house and you're so good at that stuff." Mimi devoured a cookie in quick economical bites.

Caitlyn's throat tightened and she set down her own cookie, uneaten. "That's your family time."

"And you're family. Duh."

And just like that, Caitlyn was blubbering.

She'd never really had a normal family life. Her parents hadn't ever seemed to like one another much, even before they officially got divorced. Her father was flighty on the best of days, drifting around the world chasing whatever his latest passion was. Her mother was the prototype for a rigid and unforgiving socialite. When Caitlyn had demonstrated an unusual aptitude for piano at a young age, it had seemed for a while that the one thing they could agree on was her music. She practiced harder, for them, and by the time she was nine she was playing major concert venues.

But even her music couldn't keep them together. When her travel demands had escalated, they'd taken turns touring with her. On her thirteenth birthday, they gave up the pretense and told her they were divorcing. Her mother retained custody, her father drifted off, and for a few years Caitlyn had hated the piano. Hated the concerts and the unending display of it all. She'd only just begun to find her love of music again when she took a residency with the Seattle Symphony for the season she turned nineteen.

Mimi was second chair viola with Seattle at the time, already twenty-eight and dating the software engineer she would eventually marry. Caitlyn's mother had always told her not to get distracted mingling with the orchestra—if she needed to socialize there were plenty of other soloists who were on her level—but the first time she'd hung out with Mimi she'd laughed until her stomach hurt and they'd been friends ever since.

Shortly after Caitlyn left Seattle for her scheduled concerts in Vienna and Prague, Mimi married Ty Torres and moved with him back to his home town, Tuller Springs, but Mimi and Caitlyn had never lost touch. Mimi only played for the occasional wedding quartet and community orchestra these days, but when Caitlyn decided to give up touring and performing, it was Mimi's guest room she'd stayed in while she figured out what she wanted to do with the rest of her life. It was Mimi who'd gone with her to look at apartments and Mimi's husband Ty who had set up her website for lessons and debated with her around their kitchen table about how much a former world-renowned prodigy could charge to teach second graders their scales.

Mimi was more family than Caitlyn's flesh and blood. Mimi who hugged her as she sniveled over gingerbread before handing her a wadded handful of napkins. "Here. Pull yourself together, you sap." She snagged one of the napkins herself, dabbing at her eyes.

"I missed you." Caitlyn wiped away the worst of the damage. She'd never been a cute crier. Her face was probably swollen and blotchy, but Mimi wouldn't mind.

"Missed you too. Not hearing anything for months has been killing me." Mimi swiped up another cookie. "I felt awful when you left. Like I sort of bullied you into sending the audition tape in the first place and if you were miserable it would have been all my fault."

"You didn't bully. You not-so-subtly coerced, but you didn't bully."

Caitlyn would never have considered *Marrying Mister Perfect* if Mimi hadn't been so forceful about it. At the time she'd been fed up with e-Dating and complaining to Mimi about the whopping five single men in Tuller Springs to choose from. Mimi had been avidly watching the previous season of the show and had insisted that even if she didn't land Mister Perfect, any girl on that show would have men flocking to her from miles around.

Caitlyn had resisted at first—she'd just gotten herself *out* of the limelight—but after another particularly disastrous first date, she'd been willing to try anything and the infamous audition tape was born.

The irony was that the initial appeal of the show was that men would flock to her and she would never have to leave Tuller Springs, but now she would have to pack up and leave Tuller Springs to get that happily ever after. Without telling anyone in advance that she was planning to leave Tuller Springs. The whole thing was enough to give a girl a headache—and she couldn't even discuss it with her best friend without getting sued into the next decade.

"Was it awful?" Mimi asked. "Did you hate it?"

"I didn't hate it." She wanted to comfort Mimi that the show had worked out better for her than she'd ever imagined, but the damn nondisclosure agreement tied her tongue. All she could say was, "It wasn't always easy, but I'm glad I did it."

"Good." Mimi beamed. "And now you can sit back and watch the men come to you. It's gonna be a feeding frenzy." Her eyes lit as she popped another cookie. "Oh! Speaking of hotties. You remember Ty's friend from school? Don? Well, his wife's brother is a total catch—I met him at their summer BBQ and he's a doll. Not to mention hot enough to burn my retinas right out of my eyes. Anyway, he and his evil witch fiancé broke it off like six months ago, so he's had time to heal and he's ready to get back out there and I thought—with you just getting back to town that you guys would be perfect together—"

"Mimi, I can't," she interrupted before her friend could start picking out wedding colors. "I can't date as long as I'm still on the show."

"No, I know that, obviously, but I figure we should line this up for when you're good to go, because I am not exaggerating this guy's hotness and he is gonna go fast. The only reason he isn't bagged and tagged already is because his family has been giving him time to heal and providing like a buffer around him or something, but now that the ban is lifted, it's hunting season, baby, and some girl is gonna mount that on her wall."

"I'm not ready to bag and tag anyone. Let alone mount them."

Mimi's face scrunched with concern. "Oh honey. Did you really fall for Daniel? There are other fish in the sea. And the best way to get over someone is to get under someone new. That's my motto."

"You should get that embroidered on a pillow."

"Can you at least give me a ballpark of how many weeks we have to wait before I can start pimping you out?"

Caitlyn couldn't help it. She arched a brow. "What makes you so certain he didn't pick me?"

Mimi snorted and Caitlyn cringed, insulted, until she said, "If he did, he's smarter than I gave him credit for. Those guys never pick the best girls. They pick the ones who lead them around by their dicks. Obvious, sexy, forward girls who give them wet dreams and cock-tease their way all the way to the final ring."

A vision of Elena flashed in Caitlyn's mind. Daniel's runner up was indeed obviously sexy and not afraid of using her sex appeal to manipulate men. Caitlyn felt a little trickle of unease, before reminding herself that in the end Daniel had chosen *her*, not busty obvious Elena.

She shrugged. "I guess you'll just have to wait and see."

Mimi groaned. "I can't believe you're going to make me wait it out with the unwashed masses. Me! I'm your best friend in the whole wide world."

"With the biggest mouth."

"I resemble that remark." Mimi snickered, then sobered. "But really, you're okay? No regrets?"

"None."

She'd landed Prince Charming. What was there to regret?

CHAPTER SIX

Unfortunately, Prince Charming wasn't returning her calls.

He'd called once, on Christmas morning, but cell reception was notoriously crappy at Mimi's house and by the time Caitlyn realized she'd missed the call he'd been off to whatever important industry Christmas party he'd gushed about scoring an invite to in his latest text. The message was short and sweet – a breezy *Merry Christmas, baby. Miss you so much. Talk soon, okay? Things are crazy here. Love you.*

And then silence. For days.

She'd seen him on the Today Show and The View and The Chew and she couldn't check out at the grocery store without staring at four different pictures of him smiling back at her from the magazine rack. But he didn't call.

It was New Year's Eve. The night when everyone had someone to kiss at midnight and here she was again, alone in her pajamas at nine-thirty, sitting in her apartment with all the lights turned off as she waited for the annual torch-light parade of skiers and snow boarders down the mountain, followed by fireworks— promptly at ten p.m. so it didn't interfere with the Lodge's big New Year's Eve Gala that got swinging around eleven.

Caitlyn had been to the Lodge Gala before, but the last thing she wanted tonight was to watch a hundred other people kiss when the countdown ran them into a new year. Mimi had invited her over to ring in the new year with her kids waving sparklers in the backyard, but Caitlyn had used the weather as an excuse to cry off. It had started snowing on Christmas Day and hadn't let up for more than an hour or two since.

Christmas had been lovely—filled with warmth and family—and a constant reminder of all the reasons she'd gone on the show in the first place. So the kids squealing with joy on Christmas morning wouldn't always be someone else's. So the husband sneaking into the kitchen to snitch ham and steal a kiss from his wife would be hers for a change—not that she was likely to be baking a ham. Caitlyn would probably set the house on fire if she tried, but the thought was there.

She wanted domestic bliss, damn it. Every freaking Hallmark Channel movie on the planet had conditioned her to especially crave it over the holidays and she was supposed to be on her way. She was engaged to Mister Perfect.

But now Mister Perfect was spending more time talking to talk show hosts than her and all those idyllic moments from the last three months felt like a mirage. All week she'd been sneaking peeks at the Rock of Ages, tucked into her nightstand, as if that would make her engagement feel real again. If it ever had.

The first of the torches appeared at the top of the mountain, wending their way down. The snow had let up enough for them to hold the parade after all. Caitlyn burrowed into her couch, curled beneath her favorite throw, and tried to bask in the warmth of the season. If Daniel were here with her, she'd be leaning against his side, his arm tucking her tight to him. Maybe there would be holiday music playing softly over the stereo.

Her cell phone rang shrilly, shattering the lovely little holiday dream and Caitlyn scrambled to untangle herself from the throw to reach it before it shrieked again. It was the Marrying Mister Perfect phone. Only Miranda or Daniel would be calling.

Her heart leapt at the thought that it was him, then she kicked herself for being so pathetically desperate to hear his voice, then she kicked herself for being so cynical. She was allowed to be happy to hear from her fiancé.

Fiancé. It still didn't seem real.

She punched the button to connect the call. "Hello?"

"Baby! Happy New Year!" He shouted the words above a roar of background noise.

"Daniel? Where are you?"

He laughed. "You'll never believe it. The network invited me to their New Year's Eve—" The rest of the sentence was lost in a sudden surge of cheering.

"I can barely hear you."

"I know! It's a mad house. I think it's getting louder by the minute as we get closer to the ball dropping."

Her heart clutched hard as she put the pieces together. "You're in New York?"

"Right in the heart of everything, baby! We can see the crowds in Times Square. But it's nothing without you, baby. I wish you were here."

I wish you'd stop calling me baby. "I could have been," she said. "I have lots of excuses to be in New York. My mom lives there. We could have had a quiet New Year's Eve together—nowhere public, but at least we could have been together, if you'd let me know you were going to New York."

"Oh, baby, I didn't even think of it. Things have been so crazy. I don't even know my own schedule. The network has a girl whose entire job it is to tell me when and where I need to be places."

She wanted to forgive him. If only he hadn't sounded so self-important. So pleased that he merited his own scheduler. "I just miss you."

"And I miss you. More than anything. This won't last forever. Once the show starts airing, the promo push will die down after the first few weeks. Until the finale. And then we'll be together." The background noise receded, like he had walked away from the party, then dropped drastically, as if a door had shut. "I wanted to talk to you about that, actually. We need to give US Weekly and People an answer about whether we'll both do the cover feature the week after the finale airs. Obviously, we won't tell them your name just yet or that we'll be married, but they want confirmation that the winner will sit down for the interview with me. Magazines like to line that stuff up way in advance and we'd be the cover story, baby."

Her stomach roiled queasily. "I thought the publicity stuff was all you."

"It is for now. But when you win, it will be both of us. We're America's Couple, baby."

For the love of God, stop calling me baby. "But we will have just gotten married. I thought we'd be able to get away—"

"This would only be a short break before our honeymoon. Two weeks tops. Then we can get started on our lives. And trust me, baby, the money from the magazine spread will really help a young couple starting out in the world."

They'd never talked about money. She was only a

piano teacher now, but her parents had been very strict about putting her concert earnings in a trust for her. She'd never told Daniel about the trust. About the freedom it would give them so they wouldn't have to do publicity crap for money.

But he didn't sound like this was just about the money. He liked it. The attention. The fame.

All the things she'd walked away from.

Her stomach rumbled again. How well did she know him? Two months of carefully crafted dates. Was that really enough to build a marriage on?

"Daniel, I don't know…"

"Just think about it. Think about our dream house in Beverly Hills."

"I don't think my dream house is in Beverly Hills." Was he even listening to her? How wrong had she been about him?

"Sorry, right. I know. I just get so carried away. I want to give you everything, sweetheart. You're my Miss Perfect."

In person she might have been taken in by his tone, by his blue eyes sparkling with sincerity and sweet dimples, but now all she could do was sit in her darkened apartment and wonder if she was making the biggest mistake of her life. Was it too late to back out?

"I don't know, Daniel. Everything happened so fast. Do you think we're rushing it?"

"Hey," his voice lowered from its excited chirp, and for the first time she felt like she was talking to the man who had wooed her. "I know all this is madness, but all of it is about one thing. You and me. Through all the crazy distractions, it's always been you and me. Together. Right?"

"Right," she echoed weakly.

"Watch the show on Tuesday. Look at my face the first time I saw the girl of my dreams."

"Elena?"

He snorted. "Funny. I love you, baby."

"Love you too," she echoed, ignoring the growing certainty that she was lying with those words.

Or maybe he was right and it was just the chaos of the last few weeks. The publicity nonsense. She would watch the show. She would remind herself who he was and why she loved him.

They said their goodbyes and Caitlyn turned back to the window as Daniel rushed back to watch the ball drop with his important people. The torchlight parade was over. She'd missed it. Moments later, the first boom of the fireworks lit the night. Midnight in New York. A New Year. A new slate. Full of possibilities.

The year she would get married.

Her stomach roiled. She was going to have to stock up on Tums.

Will collected the last of the LED torches used in the New Year's Eve processional each year, shoving off hard and skating smoothly over the snow toward the storage locker where the rest of the ski patrol guys were already stowing the other torches and bragging about which of the out-of-towner snow bunnies they were going to be kissing at midnight at the Lodge Gala.

"That blonde was giving you the eye, Hamilton," Ray Schaal said as he took the torches from him so he wouldn't have to pop off his skis and trudge down the snow bank to the locker.

"She's just a flirt," he said, brushing the comment aside even though he had no idea which blonde they were talking about. He hadn't really been paying attention to who he was talking to as he handed out the torches at the top and collected them at the bottom.

Ray shrugged and joined the others, comparing the various attributes of the snow bunnies. There was never a shortage of girls to kiss at the Gala, but the idea of flirtation and forced laughter and barely disguised desperation to escape the loneliness for a little while just made him feel old.

Which wasn't far off the mark since most of the ski patrol guys were barely old enough to drink.

He was supposed to be past that stage of his life. Dating and playing romantic musical chairs. He thought he'd found his chair. He'd been ready to sit there for the rest of his life—and then his chair had knocked him on his ass and run away with his best friend.

Okay, not the best analogy. But whatever. He was too old for this shit.

He'd been busy since the snowfall had picked up last week. Busy enough to avoid most of his family's friendly interference in his love life. Thank God they'd gotten enough snow for the torchlight parade to go forward so he'd been able to say he was working tonight and avoid any well-intentioned New Year's Eve set ups.

The other ski patrol guys invited him to join them at the Gala as they secured the locker, but he waved them off, pushing off and gliding over the snow toward his place, the lights of the Lodge throwing his shadow across the snow in front of him.

The one advantage to his tomblike apartment was the ski-out deck and he slid onto it now, popping his skis off and brushing loose snow off before resting them against the wall. He leaned against the glass, flicking open the fastenings on his boots and pressing down the tongues until he could slide his feet out. Opening the deck door—which he really ought to lock one of these days, but it was Tuller Springs so he never thought to bother—he stepped from his boots directly onto the carpet inside in thermal socks. Knocking the snow off his boots, he dropped them next to the potbelly stove and tipped his head, automatically listening for the music from above.

But there was only silence and the apartment above had been completely dark when he skied in.

Even septuagenarian piano teachers had somewhere to be and someone to be with on New Year's Eve.

His cell phone vibrated against his chest—still on silent from when he was working and he fished it out of the inner chest pocket of his jacket. Probably Claire. Or Julia. They didn't know how to stop pushing.

But when he pulled out the phone, his breathing stopped as the numbers on the Caller-ID screen slammed into his brain like ice-picks.

He'd deleted her number, but he hadn't been able to delete the memory. He knew the damn thing by heart. Tria.

Six months of nothing and now she was calling him on New Year's Eve? What the fuck?

He stared at the phone, debating whether to answer it and tell her to go fuck herself or ignore it. He waited too long and it went to voicemail—the little missed call icon popping up cheerfully on the screen. As if that one call hadn't shattered him.

Fuck. Fuckety fuck fuck.

He waited, but no message appeared in his voicemail. Whatever she'd wanted, she'd wanted to speak to him personally. Maybe she hadn't wanted to leave a recording, proof that she'd called. Maybe she was tired of Andy already and looking for someone to cheat on him with.

The thought made his dinner lunge up toward his tonsils.

Maybe she wanted to beg forgiveness again. Or bitch at him about the lawsuit he'd filed to get the money he'd put into the house back.

She wasn't supposed to call him. The lawyers didn't want them talking to one another directly.

But Tria had never been very good at doing what she was supposed to. Case in point: The Wedding That Wasn't.

The piano upstairs began to pick out the tune of Auld Lang Syne.

Should old acquaintance be forgot…

If only.

CHAPTER SEVEN

By eight o'clock on Tuesday, Caitlyn had thrown up from nerves twice and switched to an all chewable Tums diet. Her mouth tasted like she'd been licking a chalkboard, but at least her stomach had stopped doing backflips.

Mimi and Ty had come over that morning to install a DVR—just in case reliving the horror once a week wasn't enough for her. Mimi had wanted to stay and watch with her, but the idea of Mimi watching her watch herself had sent her running for the Tums and thankfully Ty had managed to drag Mimi out.

It was bad enough knowing the entire town would be watching. There had been an article in the paper that morning. Sort of a local girl makes good thing. Very flattering.

Horrifying.

She wasn't an idiot. She'd known this was coming. She'd just indulged in selective amnesia to avoid thinking about it.

It had been easy while she was on the show. Whenever she started to fret about it Daniel or Miranda or one of the seemingly dozens of segment producers would be there to reassure her that everything was going to be fine, America was going to love her and all of this was going to be worth it when she and Daniel were married and living out their happily ever after.

But now she was alone, engaged to a man she could barely speak to and wasn't allowed to see, and keeping the biggest thing in her life a secret from everyone she cared about, while everyone in America was free to speculate about her love life.

Caitlyn reached for the Tums as the clock ticked over to eight and the red light fired on the DVR.

It was on.

She didn't have to watch. If she didn't look, maybe she could pretend it wasn't happening.

Stalling, she turned her back to the television, moving to the kitchen table to investigate the package that had arrived earlier today with an LA postmark. It said it was from Miranda, but if Daniel wanted to send her something, he couldn't very well use his own name. He'd sent her a text earlier—*the world stopped when I saw U, baby*—but that couldn't be all the contact his fiancé merited on a day like this.

When the box had been delivered, she'd handled it like it might explode, but now she grabbed some scissors and began hacking at the tape. Anything to avoid looking at that DVR light.

The packaging came loose and she peeled back the flaps of the box. Inside, an industrial sized bottle of her favorite liquor was nestled in something white and gauzy, along with a note. She plucked the note up, her heart picking up the pace at the thought of reading Daniel's words, his thoughtfulness. Hidden beneath the note was a squishy maroon stress ball in the shape of a heart.

But it was Miranda's name inside the note. Miranda's handwriting.

Relax. It's never as bad as it looks on screen. P.S. The

padding is from the props department. Everyone sends their love.

God. How terrible must she look if Miranda had to send her an economy bottle of marshmallow vodka to dull the pain?

She pulled out the bottle and the stress ball, investigating the loops of gauzy white material. It seemed to be one long strip, winding around on itself. She hauled it out of the box, hand over hand.

When she realized what she was holding, a strangled sound burst out of her mouth, half laugh, half sob.

A veil. They'd sent her a wedding veil. The kind that would drag the floor if she put it on her head.

She bit back the urge to laugh again—afraid if she started she wouldn't stop and hysteria was probably a bad way to start the night.

Vodka, however, sounded like an excellent way to start the night.

No harm in it. She wasn't going to be driving anywhere. How much trouble could she get into sitting in her own house, watching her own public train-wreck with a tall glass of marshmallow vodka on the rocks?

Caitlyn slapped the veil on her head and reached for the biggest glass she had.

"I've got thirty beautiful women just dying to meet you. Are you ready for this, Mister Perfect?"

Daniel chuckled and flashed his *aw shucks* smile— and Caitlyn slammed her finger down on the pause button, glowering at those pearly whites.

It might have been paranoia, or a side effect of the vodka she was slurping out of the giant plastic Rockies souvenir mug, but she'd become more and more convinced as she watched the scene over and over again that the perfect farm boy smile was a lie.

On her first viewing, she'd mostly been relieved that she only had a grand total of about three minutes of screen time. Her first meet with Daniel had been suitably cute—though she hadn't noticed any hearts or flowers exploding in either of their eyes.

The show had put each girl in a setting designed to demonstrate her particular talents—the LPGA golfer putting in a ball gown on the lawn, the bakery owner in the kitchen icing cookies—so of course Caitlyn had been at a piano. Thank God her fingers knew how to play through nerves. She'd dashed off a quick Bach Prelude...and then she'd had to face him.

She hadn't jabbered incoherently, which was good, since she hadn't been able to remember a single word of what she'd said. She didn't really remember the first time she saw him—just that she had been so nervous she'd been worried that her shaking knees would be visible through the flowing skirt of her gown. No grenades of true love exploding in her heart and reshaping her world. No symphonies in the air. Just nerves.

There was no evidence that the world stopped for him either. If it was love at first sight as he had professed, he was doing a good job of slow playing his hand as he told the cameras that she looked like an angel—too pure and sweet to touch.

Elena however was very touchable.

Caitlyn tried not to fixate on the way his tongue had practically fallen out of his mouth when he'd walked into the dance studio and seen the Latina beauty, or the guttural *whoa* that he'd practically groaned as she glided toward him oozing sex. She'd pulled him into her arms to teach him a basic tango step and the cameras had begun strategically filming from the waist up—*it's a family show, folks.*

Apparently there were angels and then there were sex goddesses. And Caitlyn fell squarely on the "cute" side of the spectrum. Damn it.

She watched the rest of the show, dreading seeing her own face again, but she had stayed clear of most of the first night drama, trying to fade into the background during the infamous challenges, and so there wasn't much footage of her. Other than the Elimination Ceremony, where Daniel offered her the fourth ring, she was invisible.

Thank God.

But even as she'd grown more and more relieved by her lack of notoriety, something else began to bother her. Tickling at the back of her mind, a little scratch of unease, fueled by marshmallow flavored clarity.

His smile.

His familiar *aw shucks* farm boy smile.

She'd restarted the show, watching back through it for the smile. And there it was. Beaming back at her. All teeth and folksy charm and sparkling eyes.

So why couldn't she escape the thought that it was a lie?

Did it look too smug? Too self-important?

The cell phone shrilled.

Caitlyn jumped, sloshing the smooth, sweet vodka of the heavens, and dove for the phone. "Daniel?"

"No. Miranda. Sorry."

Caitlyn slumped against the kitchen counter, miscalculated slightly and slid down the cabinets to plunk on the floor. She may have had slightly more to drink than she thought. "Miranda! Hey. Did Daniel's smile always look like that or did you edit it?"

A low chuckle hummed against her ear where she'd pressed the phone a little too tight. "I see you received the vodka."

"I did! And thank you. It's my favorite."

"I remember."

"Veil was a nice touch." She set the vodka against her leg, dipping a finger into it and lifting it to her lips to lick off the drops of sugary goodness.

"I'm glad you found it amusing. How are you coping?"

Caitlyn waved a hand in a so-so gesture, then realized Miranda couldn't see her. "He really likes Elena's boobs, doesn't he?"

She imagined she could hear Miranda's grimace. "We have him on camera saying flattering things about most of you ladies, but we're trying to create drama and Elena's overt sex appeal is going to be a major point of conflict for some of the girls in future weeks so it got a lot of screen time."

"Yeah, no, I get it. They're awesome boobs." She squinted back toward the television—the screen wasn't large, more a glorified computer monitor than the fifty inch mega-screen most people seemed to have these days. Normally she liked that it was small, easily ignored, but now she was irritated that she couldn't see his questionable smile clearly from the kitchen.

Miranda was speaking. Something about plastic surgery. Caitlyn made what she hoped was an appropriately interested noise in reply.

Miranda paused. "You should get some sleep. It won't look so bad in the morning."

Caitlyn hummed agreeably and thumbed the phone off after they said their goodbyes. No texts from Daniel.

No call. Nothing to reassure her that he liked her boobs too.

They were nice boobs, dang it. Not as big as Elena's, but at least Caitlyn wouldn't have back issues later in life from carting around cantaloupes on her chest.

She used the counter to lever herself back to her feet, nearly rolling her ankle before she found her balance on the little red high heeled sandals she'd decided completed her show watching ensemble. After collecting her Rockies cup of vodka, she made a remarkably steady crossing to the television.

Daniel was still smiling.

Maybe it was the lighting that made him look fake.

More light. Then she could see him better. Caitlyn turned, kicking aside the veil, and charted a course to the wall switch behind the potbelly stove.

She flipped the switch. Sparks crackled and sprayed, shooting out of the switch.

Oh shit. Caitlyn yelped and flung the liquid contents of her glass at the sparking switch.

For a moment nothing seemed to happen, then *whoosh.* Fire burst in her face, eating up the wall, heat slamming into her face like a slap. She screamed, leaping backward.

Or attempting to leap. Her heel caught on the train of her veil and she tumbled to the ground, landing hard on her butt. The Rockies cup plinked to the ground and rolled away from her hip. She tried to scramble backward, crab walking away from the flames as they traveled eagerly up the wall, but the veil tangled around her limbs, clinging and cloying.

"Shit, shit, shit." Her house was on fire and her brain couldn't seem to catch up. What was she supposed to do? She knew throwing water on grease fires was bad, but what were you supposed to do with electrical fires?

Obviously not throw 90-proof liquor on them, but she hadn't been thinking. Her hand had jerked out throwing the alcohol before she'd even registered what she was doing.

Daniel had poured wine over a brazier in Spain to smother the fire and it had worked like a charm. Maybe there was something about the percentage of alcohol?

The flames roared and crackled.

Shit. Her apartment was on fire and her brain was jabbering about alcohol content.

Think, Caitlyn. Call 911. Find a fire extinguisher. Save the piano.

Priorities.

A rain of thunder pounded against her door. "Ms. Gregg?" a deep voice bellowed through. "Are you all right?"

Oh thank God. Help.

But was she supposed to open the door? Adrenaline wasn't burning away the alcohol fast enough and she couldn't think. Something about oxygen feeding fires and not opening doors and windows?

The fire spit and sprayed, raining flaming embers of wall down onto the gauzy kindling of the veil. The tulle went up in flames.

A scream ripped out of Caitlyn's mouth.

The door exploded inward.

He was huge. Magnificent. A dark god storming down from Olympus. This was no angel, no savior. This was Mount Freaking Doom coming calling. The entire world went into slow motion. She could see each individual particle of ash floating in the air as he loomed there, framed by the doorway. Her jaw dropped, what remained of her mental functions abandoning her, leaving only one word echoing in the empty cavern of her mind.

Wow.

CHAPTER EIGHT

Will took in the situation with a single sweeping glance.

The fire seemed relatively contained—flames licking up a five square foot patch around a light switch on the exterior wall—but he knew how quickly that could change. Sprawled on the floor in front of the fire lay a tangle of long alabaster limbs and auburn hair, swathed in skimpy boy shorts, a clinging green tank top, red heels and what appeared to be twenty feet of wedding veil, twisted around her and burning in places.

He'd thought Ms. Gregg might have a granddaughter. He just hadn't expected her to be so gorgeous. Or so obviously out of her mind.

First things first. Get the crazy lady away from the fire.

Will dropped into crisis mode—calm and focused. He lunged into the room as she gaped at him. Something clear dripped down the base of the wall where she'd clearly tried to put out the flames without success. He was at her side in a blink. "Are you hurt?"

A wave of sticky-sweet alcohol scent fumes hit him and she blinked as if trying to bring him into focus. "You're too sexy to be an angel."

I'll take that as a no. He patted out the tiny fires on the veil and lifted her to her feet, her slim arms surprisingly muscular beneath his hands. "Where's your grandmother?"

She gazed blankly up at him. "What?"

He resisted the urge to shake her. Maybe Ms. Gregg was a great-aunt. "Ms. Gregg."

"Yes?"

Christ. "Is there anyone else here?" he said with excruciating patience, herding her quickly toward the door with a hand on one arm. "Anyone else we need to get out?"

"The piano." She said it with such vehemence it actually took him a moment to recall the piano was inanimate.

"Right." She was officially shitfaced to the point of incoherence. He'd search the place himself. Right after he got her out of here and contained the fire. It was small now, but it might not stay that way for long. "If I were you I'd be more worried about that Christmas tree catching."

Will shoved the girl toward the door, scooping an abandoned cell phone off the floor and tossing it at her. She caught it awkwardly, fumbling it against her chest. "Go outside," he demanded. "Call the Fire Department."

He ran back to the fire, shoving the Christmas tree, the sofa and anything else that might catch farther away from the blaze and grabbing a blanket to smother the flames. He batted down the flames, but no sooner had he extinguished them than they seemed to crawl out from inside the wall to reignite. Shit. The fire seemed to be centered around a switch. Electrical. It could be spreading through the walls to places he couldn't see. He needed to cut the power.

Another pair of hands with another blanket appeared beside him.

He shot an incredulous look at the crazy redhead in

the veil. She was lucky the damn thing hadn't caught again already. "What are you doing?"

"I can't leave the piano!" she shouted.

"Jesus." He did not have time to deal with a drunk girl flinging herself on the flames to save a freaking musical instrument.

He grabbed both blankets, bent and flipped her up onto his shoulder in a single, practiced move that was made somewhat less smooth by the yards of tulle that wrapped around both of them like a boa constrictor. She squealed, but thankfully didn't fight him, one of her hands gripping the back of his jeans for balance as he bolted out of the apartment and thundered down the stairs.

He was just glad he'd been clothed when he heard her scream. He tended to sleep naked and he didn't want to think about what she might be grabbing for leverage if he'd shown up in the buff.

He swore as his feet hit the driveway, snow instantly soaking into his socks and freezing his feet. The crazy redhead's smooth bare legs dangled in front of his eyes, red high heels hanging off her toes, but she was just going to have to wrap herself in that idiotic veil to keep warm.

Looking for someplace reasonably sheltered but away from the potential spread of the fire—which wouldn't be an issue if he could get back in there and stop the damn thing before it spread—Will jogged across the driveway to the carport, bouncing Miss Crazy as he went. His Jeep and Ms. Gregg's Subaru were parked close to the building, but beneath a tarp under the carport sat a massive sprawl of classic American machinery—his baby. A shiny red Thunderbird convertible. The top didn't go up anymore and one of these summers he was going to rebuild the engine, but right now it seemed like the perfect place to park his armful of trouble.

Will flipped Miss Crazy off his shoulder, tossing her onto the tarp where the backseat would be. She yelped as she sank down into it in a tangle of tulle, one of her little red heels flopping off. He jabbed a finger at her. "Stay."

A hard sprint back into the building. The breaker box was in the basement laundry room. He'd found it the day he moved in. Will bolted down the stairs, throwing open the laundry door, and cursed a blue streak. The entire side of the room where he remembered the breaker box was blocked with boxes. The owner was using the space for storage. By the time he got back to the breaker box, half the building could be gone.

"*Fuck*." Will ripped the fire extinguisher off the wall. At least the less-than-stellar landlord had kept the damn thing full. It was a solid weight in his arms as he took the stairs two at a time.

Back in the second floor apartment, the fire still hadn't moved beyond that one wall—though it was twice the size it had been. Black smoke rose to the ceiling.

Why the hell hadn't the smoke alarm gone off?

"Ms. Gregg?" he shouted, with no reply. If she was up in the loft, she was getting a lungful of smoke. He wanted to check to make sure she wasn't unconscious up there, but seconds might count when it came to saving her home and he'd just have to have faith that even the drunk veil lady would remember the presence of another person in the house.

Hopefully Miss Crazy was using that cell phone to call help.

There weren't many house fires in Tuller Springs. He'd been on the volunteer fire brigade for three years now and only three times had he been called on to save someone's home. Other than that it was mostly helping out with regional wildfires and responding to false alarms at the Lodge when some high-off-his-ass snowboarder yanked the alarm or caught his sheets on fire. And in all the fires he'd dealt with, he'd never been the senior man on the scene, never alone, always just keeping a calm head and following orders.

But this was different. This was all him.

He laid down a blanket of foam, liberally coating the wall and hoping like hell that the fire ran out before the canister did.

It felt like hours, but it must have been only a matter of seconds before the scent of the chemical foam replaced the scent of smoke and the last of the flames disappeared beneath the white.

"You did it."

Will spun around at the awed murmur. Miss Crazy stood on the landing outside the broken door, snow clinging to her feet in her little red heels, though she had gotten rid of the boa constrictor veil.

Of course she couldn't stay where he put her. "Jesus, lady, do you have a death wish or something?"

"You told me to call the fire department." She held up the cell phone. "I can't call on this phone. Besides, you put it out."

Shit. He must have tossed her a cell with a dead battery. This was why people needed freaking land lines. Since it looked like she wasn't going to wait outside like a good little civilian... "Come here. Make yourself useful."

She rushed forward so quickly she tripped over her

feet a bit. He caught her with one hand, shifting the fire extinguisher to the other. He frowned down at her huge black pupils, framed by thin lines of blue. "Have you been drinking?"

"*Oh* yes."

"Before the fire?"

"Mm-hmm. I've never seen it go whoosh like that before."

Great. Now he was going to need to get the arson investigator out here. But first things first.

He slapped the fire extinguisher into her hands. "Do you know how to use one of these?"

"Yes?"

He frowned. "Is that a question?"

"Well, I mean, I know in theory, but I've never actually done the spray spray thing."

Jesus. She was drunk off her ever-loving ass. He put her hands where they needed to be. "The visible flames are gone, but I think the fire was electrical and it might still be spreading in the walls. If you see sparks, aim at them and squeeze this. Got it? And if it looks bad, you get your ass out of the building, understand?"

She nodded, way too dazed for his comfort, but he wouldn't be relying on her for long.

Leaving Miss Crazy in charge of the fire extinguisher, he scrambled up the steps to the loft, quickly checking that there was no one up there unconscious from smoke inhalation. Empty. "Where's Ms. Gregg?" he called to Miss Crazy as he descended.

"I'm Ms. Gregg," she said, without relaxing her vigilance with the extinguisher.

Will's feet hit the floor at the base of the steps with a thud that sent realization shuddering up through his bones. Of course she was. If he hadn't been trying to save her crazy ass maybe he would have put the pieces together himself. He didn't know why he'd assumed his neighbor was a senior citizen when he moved in— maybe the lack of visitors other than her students, or the early-bird special hours she seemed to keep. He'd never even seen the woman, but it had never occurred to him for a second that she might be a hot little redhead in her twenties with more than a few screws loose.

Or maybe that was just the alcohol talking.

"Keep watching that wall," he told her. "And shout if anything happens."

"Where are you going?" she asked as he started for the door.

He kept one ear open as he jogged back down to the basement, but didn't hear a peep from the lovely Ms. Gregg. Hopefully that wasn't a sign that she'd passed out from alcohol poisoning. With that lovely thought as motivation to hurry, he fought his way through the boxes, finally managing to shove a path to the circuit-breaker box. He flipped all the switches, shutting off the electricity for the entire building. If a short at the light switch had caused the fire, he didn't want to risk running power anywhere until the entire house was checked out.

Ms. Gregg squealed when the house suddenly went dark and he cursed to himself. "Sorry!" He shouted up toward her place. "Should have warned you about that."

She should still be able to see a little, thanks to the lights illuminating the mountain for night skiing. On his way back up, he took a quick detour into his own apartment, grabbing a flashlight and his cell phone, already dialing emergency dispatch as he jogged back up the stairs to pretty little Ms. Gregg.

Her door was hanging strangely, listing to one side

and he realized he'd busted one of the hinges and cracked the wood when he kicked it in earlier.

Ms. Gregg was sitting cross-legged on the floor in the low light, the fire extinguisher resting in the circle of her legs as she stared at the ashy black patch on her wall.

He'd seen other people in the aftermath of fires. Stunned. Horrified.

She just looked puzzled. Like she couldn't quite figure out how the burned area had appeared on her wall.

Will quickly filled the dispatcher in on the situation and then tucked his phone into his back pocket when he knew the cavalry was on the way. The fire could spark up again. Technically they should wait outside, but it was cold and she wasn't exactly dressed for the elements.

He slowly approached the woman who had unknowingly serenaded him for months.

"Ms. Gregg?"

"I think you saved my life," she said softy, without looking away from the wall.

"It wasn't a big fire."

She looked at him then, all big blue eyes and pale, pale skin in the dim light from the mountain and the moonlight. He frowned. She might be going into shock.

He knelt down in front of her. "How are you feeling? Dizzy? Lightheaded?"

She blinked. "Who *are* you? Are you a real person? I was freaking out and then *wham*, there you were."

"I'm Will. I live downstairs. I heard a scream."

"I'm Caitlyn. I don't remember screaming, but it sounds like something I would do if my house suddenly decided to burn to the ground with me in it."

He gave a half-hearted laugh at her attempt at

humor.

"How did you know what to do?" she asked, staring at him so steadily he began to think she wasn't in shock after all.

"Tuller Springs is too small to have a standing fire department, but I volunteer along with some of the other citizens. We're trained to contain fires until the big boys from Aspen can get their asses out here."

"I'm lucky you were here," she whispered. "Thank you."

He settled down on the floor next to her. "No problem. I figure I owe you for all the free concerts."

It was hard to tell in the low light, but he thought she blushed. "You can hear me?"

"I'm developing quite a taste for Classical music."

Now he was sure she was blushing, her gaze flicked down. "I have a damper pedal. So it wouldn't be so loud. I can't use it when my students are here, but when it's just me—"

"No. I love hearing it."

Her eyes lifted. "Oh." Then her blush grew even more heated and she couldn't hold his gaze. "What happens now?"

"The rest of my guys are on their way to make sure the fire is really out. Then there'll be an investigator from Denver to tell us what started the fire and an electrician to make sure the house is safe. Do you have some place to stay tonight?"

"I have to leave? But my piano…"

"Is it insured?"

"Well, yes, but…"

"I'm sure you love it like family, but it's an instrument. No instrument is worth dying for. Do you have someone you can stay with tonight?"

"Yes." The word was whisper soft.

"Hey." He hooked one finger under her chin, tipping her face up so he could see those dark blue eyes again. "Hopefully we'll both get to come home soon and you can serenade me some more, but better safe than sorry, right?"

She wet her lips, staring at his eyes and giving a minute nod. Then her gaze slid, heavy and slow, down to linger on his mouth.

And suddenly he couldn't help himself from looking at hers. The curve of it. The lush, rosy temptation.

His breath grew shallow. And damn if hers wasn't coming short as well.

He hadn't really looked at a woman in so long. Hadn't been interested. Hadn't *wanted*. Not like this. Attraction hit him like a mule kick to the gut. Suddenly her pale, soot-stained skin looked pearlescent in the lights from the mountain. Her eyes were huge and vulnerable—but not weak, just hopeful, like everything she had ever wanted was piled into each look and it all hung on him. She looked at him like he was a god or a genie—or the angel she'd called him when he first appeared—someone who had the power to make all her dreams come true if he just said yes.

And damn if he didn't want to say yes to her. He didn't know how a man would ever be able to tell this woman no. Not when she was looking at him like that.

His free hand lifted of its own volition to tuck a stray auburn curl behind her ear, the little brush of her skin against his finger impossibly soft. And still she watched him. He couldn't tear his eyes away. She listed forward, just an inch, her eyelids going to half-mast.

"Caitlyn…" He breathed her name like a caress, soft and inviting, but it broke the spell.

She flinched, blinking rapidly, jerking back. "I'm sorry. I don't know what I—" She shook her head, hard.

"No." He came to his feet in one movement, occupying himself with the flashlight. "No, it was me." He yanked his cell phone out of his pocket, extending it down to her. "You should call your friend. It's late."

"Right." She took the phone, blushing, looking down, whispering again, "Right."

The wail of the approaching siren sounded like salvation on multiple levels.

CHAPTER NINE

Caitlyn groaned at the throbbing in her skull, then coughed as the groan shredded against the rawness in her throat, then whimpered as the volume of the coughing made the jackhammer in her head pick up the pace.

Hangover with a side of inferno.

And deathly embarrassment.

She hauled the comforter up to her eyebrows, wondering how long she could pretend the last twenty-four hours hadn't happened. Though if she was erasing history, maybe she should go further back. About six months should do it.

No more Mister Perfect. No more public humiliation or setting her apartment on fire and making an idiot of herself in front of insanely hot fireman neighbors.

She lowered the comforter enough to peek at the clock on the bedside table. Ten sixteen. She had no idea when she'd finally gotten to sleep the night before, after the rest of the fire-fighters showed up and Mimi arrived to pick her up. She'd left her apartment in their hands, Will promising to lock the building's exterior door, since hers no longer sat right on its hinges after he'd kicked it in to get to her.

She wasn't worried about her stuff. It was Tuller Springs, after all, where crime was pretty much limited to the occasional act of vandalism or reckless endangerment by thrill-seeking snowboarders and no one was more than two degrees of separation away from anyone else.

Which didn't explain how she'd never met Will.

She'd had no idea her downstairs neighbor was so hot. Tall and rippling with muscle, with dark brown hair a little on the long and shaggy side and the most soulful brown eyes she'd ever seen in her life, fringed by lush black lashes that any girl would kill for.

He must be taken. It was the only reason Mimi or one of her other friends wouldn't have tried to set them up with one another. Not surprising. That body, those eyes, a core of heroism—guys like that were never single.

But there'd been a moment last night when she'd been so certain he was about to kiss her.

Probably her imagination. She'd never been very good at reading signals. Homeschooling and world concert tours hadn't exactly done her any favors when it came to social interactions with the opposite sex. She'd been so relieved when everything was so natural and easy with Daniel.

Daniel.

Her stomach rolled nauseously.

And kept on rolling.

Caitlyn scrambled out of bed and bolted for the bathroom, making it there just in time to empty her stomach in a wrenching heave. She flushed and groaned, sagging to the floor beside the toilet in case her stomach decided it wasn't done rejecting the vodka. "Never again," she promised the sink.

"That's what they all say."

Caitlyn looked up, grimacing as the bathroom light hit her squarely in the eyes. It was tempting to tell Mimi to get lost and let her wallow in peace, but then the objects in Mimi's hands registered – a jumbo bottle of aspirin and a glass of water.

"Bless you."

Mimi handed over the goods and folded herself down onto the bathroom floor beside Caitlyn, in the narrow space between her feet and the vanity. Today her yoga pants were hot pink, the streak in her hair was electric blue, and layered tank tops of yellow and purple completed the color assault. "I believe this is what is known in the business as a cry for help."

"What business is that?" Caitlyn rinsed with the water, downed the aspirin and let her head thunk against the wall—it was entirely too heavy for her neck right now.

"I think getting drunk and setting your own house on fire is a cry for help in pretty much every business ever invented," Mimi said dryly.

"I didn't set my house on fire. It was a tiny little electrical issue."

"Of course it was. But to ease my mind, you won't be watching any more episodes by yourself. *Capisce*?"

"Yes, Don Mimi." She should get up. The last thing she needed was for Mimi's two kids to see Auntie Caitlyn in a hangover sprawl on the bathroom floor. "How long do we have before Trent and Mia Grace come investigating?"

"I had Ty drop them off at Monica's for a play date. Figured you could use the peace and quiet. I need to pick them up at noon, but until then I'm all yours."

Caitlyn cringed. She knew Mimi valued kid-free time like manna from heaven and jealously guarded her play dates. "Sorry you had to use one for me."

"Shut up," Mimi said mildly, and when Caitlyn

looked over there was a suspicious shine in Mimi's eyes. "I wanted some girl time. And I'm worried about you. Since when do you drink alone? You barely have a glass of wine with dinner and suddenly you're binge drinking like a rock star and burning down houses?"

"I didn't try to burn my house down, Mimi. It really was electrical. And minor. The firefighter guys said it would have happened even if I'd been stone cold sober."

"I'm a bad friend. Friends don't let friends get drunk and watch their hearts get broken on national television alone. I should have been there."

Caitlyn swallowed hard. She wanted so badly to tell Mimi everything. That it wasn't a broken heart that was making her feel sick every time she thought of the show. That she was engaged to a man she was terrified she didn't love—and that she was becoming more and more sure she didn't even know who he really was beneath all the layers of reality-TV hype that had been piled on him. That she'd actually agreed to *marry* him on the reunion show and every time she thought of walking down the aisle with America watching she had to reach for her Tums. That she wanted nothing more than to run and hide until the show was all over—but she was terrified this was going to be her only chance at the life she wanted and the universe wouldn't give her another if she wasted it.

"You aren't a bad friend," she whispered. If anyone in that bathroom was, it was her. With all her damn secrets.

It wasn't that she didn't trust Mimi. She did. She trusted her not to tell on purpose—but she knew her friend well enough to know sometimes things just popped out of her mouth when they weren't supposed to. She'd get so caught up in a story she wouldn't even remember that part of it wasn't supposed to be told.

Five million dollars. The nondisclosure promised to sue her for five million if she let the truth slip. So she sat on the bathroom floor and hated herself for the lie of omission, but kept her mouth shut.

"Do you want to talk about it?" Mimi asked hesitantly. "About watching the show last night?"

Caitlyn grimaced. What she wanted was to pretend it wasn't happening. *Cowardice, thy name is me.* All she could think about was Daniel's smile—which she'd never thought was smarmy and smug before last night. She'd freaking *loved* his dimples. Maybe that was the alcohol talking. Or her own doubts. Maybe she just needed to hear his voice on the phone and she'd forget all her fears.

Damn. She'd left the MMP cell phone at her apartment.

Though that was probably for the best. She hated that she'd become this girl—this needy creature who was desperate for a call from her fiancé. She didn't want to be that girl. Maybe she should drop the phone down the garbage disposal.

"You looked gorgeous in that silver dress," Mimi said hesitantly, when Caitlyn had been silent for too long. "He wasn't lying when he said you looked like an angel."

Angelic. Caitlyn cringed. She'd been so focused on making a good impression, she couldn't even remember what she'd thought of her first glimpse of him.

Not like last night. The moment Will burst into her life felt like it was branded into her memory, never to be erased. It was probably the adrenaline from the fire that made him seem larger than life in her memory. A dark god come to save her. The adrenaline and the alcohol.

He was probably just another guy. Normal. Average. Forgettable.

But she hadn't been scared as soon as he appeared. And then, when he'd thrown her over his shoulder like she weighed nothing...

"Are you okay?" Mimi asked. "Your face is turning all red."

Damn redhead complexion. She'd never been able to hide her feelings. "Do you remember the first time you met Ty? Like the very first second?"

"Not really. He was a friend of a friend and we were all just sort of hanging out. I remember he said something funny, but I don't think I even knew his name until my friend said he wanted to take me out. Not like the movies. Why?"

Caitlyn shook her head. "It's weird. The show makes such a big deal of first impressions and tries to add romantic impact to all these moments, but I can't remember a thing from meeting him. I must have thought he was handsome, because..." She waved a hand in a *well, obviously* gesture. "But I was so swallowed up in nerves, I probably wouldn't have noticed even if my heart *had* skipped a beat and the world stood still."

Mimi frowned. "So you were really into him? I saw your hair a few times in the preview footage for coming weeks and thought you might have gone pretty far since at least one of the locales looked tropical, but I wasn't sure your heart was in it. But it was?"

Again, the truth burned on her tongue. The Rock of Ages was tucked in the bottom of the overnight bag she'd brought. She could just put it on and wag her hand in front of Mimi and she wouldn't even have to say anything.

And then get sued for five million dollars when Mimi accidentally blabbed.

"He seemed really nice." She carefully selected her words, trying for truth without giving anything away. "He always knew the right thing to say and I thought I might have really strong feelings for him—even when I left—but now when I watch it back, I don't know what to think."

"I sometimes wish I could watch pieces of my life over again without the perception filter of whatever I was feeling at the time," Mimi said. "Maybe this'll be, like, the best break-up therapy ever. Just no more watching by yourself."

"I repeat: the fire was not my fault."

"Hey, no need to get testy. I believe you. But just in case we should probably head over to your place and make sure the arson investigator isn't going to press charges."

She'd been feeling much better—the aspirin had kicked in and her brain was no longer trying to escape her skull through brute force—but at the mention of arson charges, her stomach did another backflip and probably would have hurled its contents toward her throat if there had been anything left to hurl.

She needed a T-Shirt.

I went on a reality TV show and all I got was this lousy prison sentence for arson.

And a fiancé she wasn't sure she wanted anymore.

Some years needed a reset button. And this one had just started.

CHAPTER TEN

From the outside, the chalet looked perfectly normal. The fire hadn't made it all the way through the exterior wall, so when they pulled up in Mimi's Mini Cooper, Caitlyn had a moment of idiotic hope that maybe the entirety of last night had been an alcohol fueled hallucination.

But inside, reality intruded. The door to her apartment was lying on its side on the landing with a note taped to it. Caitlyn plucked up the note and trailed Mimi into the apartment, nearly knocking her friend over when Mimi stopped suddenly, gaping at the damage.

"You said it was a little fire."

"It was."

But that little fire had blackened a ten square foot patch of the wall behind the potbelly stove, leaving the drywall hanging off the charred studs in ashy fragments. The white foam from the fire extinguisher had not miraculously evaporated, though someone had used a dingy grey beach towel to mop up the worst of it, the towel itself now spread on the floor near where she had fallen the night before. There was a smoky scent in the air, but it wasn't nearly as strong as she'd expected it to be.

All in all, it wasn't so bad. Better than she'd hoped

for, actually.

But Mimi hadn't come inside last night when she'd picked her up. She hadn't known what to expect. Her friend took in the damage, pivoted, and wrapped her arms around Caitlyn, squeezing tight. "You suck. But for some reason I like you, so don't get hurt, okay?" she muttered against her shoulder.

"Likewise," Caitlyn said, squeezing back and gazing at the charred patch of wall over Mimi's shoulder.

Thanks to the windows, the room was still bright, even without power, but it was eerily silent without the subtle hums of the appliances in the kitchen.

"You want lunch? Everything we don't eat today is going to go bad if the electricity stays off for long."

Mimi nodded, shoving away and swiping at her eyes before squaring her shoulders to tackle the task at hand. "I'll make us a feast. Then we'll clean up."

While Mimi went to investigate feast options, Caitlyn unfolded the note, tamping down the little shiver of excitement at the thought of who it was from.

She should *not* be excited about reading words Will had written. He was taken and she was engaged.

But that didn't stop her from smiling when she saw his oddly formal salutation, *Dear Ms. Gregg.*

She should not be charmed. But lately she wasn't doing so well at obeying the shoulds.

I spoke with the arson investigator and the electrical short was definitely the culprit. I also spoke with the landlord and as soon as the investigator's official report is in, he'll file the insurance claim and we can get started on the repairs. I have a brother-in-law who is a contractor, if you'd like me to get him out here to put in a bid for the wall. I know he'll give a fair price. I'll repair your door since that one was on me. The electrician said he would be by at two o'clock to check out the rest of the wiring in the house so we can find out if it's safe to turn the power back on. I have a class to teach, but I should be back by two to meet him, if you can't be here then. Take care.

P.S. Your smoke detector battery was dead. I've replaced it.

Somehow Caitlyn resisted the urge to press the paper to her chest like a Victorian maiden. She'd begun grinning at "culprit" and by the time he mentioned the smoke detector, her knees were downright wobbly. He'd thought of everything, taken care of everything. Not only had he saved her life—he'd saved her half a dozen awkward or time consuming conversations.

She'd been dreading contacting the landlord and letting him know she'd burned a hole in his wall. Done.

She hadn't had the first idea who to contact about repairs or checking the wiring. Done and done.

He was her one man fix-it team. She'd never be able to repay him.

And damn if the way he swept in and took care of her wasn't sexy as hell.

Would Daniel have stepped up in such a manly way?

Almost as soon as the thought crossed her mind came the guilt chaser. The niggling sense that she was betraying Daniel by doubting he would be as magnificent as Will had been. It wasn't fair of her to compare them. Her fiancé was hundreds of miles away, oblivious to any troubles she might be facing. He deserved better than to be judged and found lacking in absentia.

Will was taken and so was she—by a man who always did the right thing and would probably have been her knight in shining armor himself, given the chance—so she mentally smacked the stars from her eyes, folded the note and tucked it into her pocket, striding over to the kitchen area to see what Mimi had found in her rapidly warming fridge.

After a quick hodge-podge lunch and a dozen reassurances that she would be fine on her own, she shooed Mimi off to pick up her kids. As soon as the door closed behind her friend, Caitlyn made a beeline for the loft and the MMP cell phone she vaguely remembered dropping on her bed while she was packing her overnight bag.

Ever since she realized she'd left it behind, she'd been haunted by visions of the phone ringing while the firefighters or the fire investigators were in her apartment and one of the guys answering it—just to be neighborly, just to tell the caller that she wasn't available and take a message—but if it was Daniel and he gave away his identity before he realized who he was talking to…

Hello, Five Million Dollar Lawsuit.

It had been agony, waiting for Mimi to leave, but if it had happened, the damage was already done. She rapidly scrolled through the call log. One missed call from Daniel. No message. And a text from Miranda. What looked like the ingredients to a hangover cure.

No sign of anything that would put her in debt to the network for the rest of her life.

And no indication that anyone in the Marrying Mister Perfect family knew she'd had a minor incendiary incident last night. A ten pound weight seemed to float off her chest.

Until she felt that weight lifting, she hadn't realized how certain she'd been that they would know somehow. For months they had known every little movement of her life. The idea that something so dramatic could happen and it would be no one's business but her own… it was beyond liberating.

But the wild, heady sense of freedom didn't last.

She would have to tell them. It was one call Will couldn't make for her. Better she let Miranda know what had happened and let the PR people spin it than to have it come out on TMZ. Though maybe it wouldn't. She was just one of many Suitorettes right now, no reason she should be stalked like a celebrity.

"Ms. Gregg?"

The voice floated up to the loft from her open doorway and Caitlyn felt a giddy rush that she told herself was just a result of the timely distraction. She stepped to the loft railing, pressing her stomach against it. "You can call me Caitlyn, you know. After carrying me out of a burning building over your shoulder, I think we can dispense with formality."

Will looked up at her first word, a slow smile spreading over his face. "Hey."

Caitlyn's brain short circuited as her hormones threw a party. *Yep, not a hallucination,* they declared. *He's just as hot as we remembered.* Messy brown hair, luscious black lashes, and the eyes a girl could fall into for days.

"Hi."

Oh, brilliant, Caitlyn. Dazzle him with your witty repartee.

"I, uh…" She wet her lips, trying to restart her brain. "Thank you. For everything. You've been amazing."

His grin widened. "I never argue when a pretty girl tells me I'm amazing."

A blush burned her cheeks. She pushed away from the railing and scrambled down the stairs from the loft with more speed than grace. "I can't thank you enough—"

He waved a hand, cutting her off. "Anyone would have done the same."

Would they? she wanted to ask, but he was already turning away, strolling toward the charred wall and assessing the damage.

"We were lucky. Looks like the damage is pretty contained. Easy to fix." His hand sketched through the air over the blackened holes. "Replace the electrical and reframe. Hang some drywall and you're good to go. Probably won't even need to refinish the floors. Fairly low cost, two, three days of solid work for a good crew, and you're set."

"So you're a carpenter in addition to being a fire fighter?" As if the one wasn't hot enough on its own.

He looked away from the wall, his grin easy and self-assured, but somehow modest at the same time. "I'm just a volunteer with the fire department. And work on the mountain isn't always steady, so I help my brother-in-law out with brute force labor when I could use some extra cash. I've learned some, hanging around those guys, but I'm no expert. We'll get him out here to give you a proper bid. And either way, I'll fix your door frame and rehang your door tomorrow morning—if that works for you. I don't usually teach on Thursdays."

He nodded toward the windows as he said teach and it took Caitlyn a moment to realize he meant ski school. *So add sexy ski bum to the tally of hotness.* If it was physical, it seemed like he was good at it.

She refused to dwell on that thought.

"Tomorrow morning would be great."

"Great. The good news is it's Tuller Springs and you don't really need to worry about security. We'll keep the outer door locked so none of the tourists get lost and wander in, but since it's just the two units, you don't have to worry about anyone invading your privacy tonight." He held up his hands like she'd told him to stick 'em up, dark eyes gleaming wickedly. "I promise to keep my distance."

What if I don't want you to?

Caitlyn bit back the urge to say the flirty words. What the hell was wrong with her? She was *engaged*. And she'd never been a flirt to begin with. It was like being possessed by the world's trashiest demon.

"How soon can your brother-in-law get out here to look at the rest of the damage?"

"That's one call I didn't get to yet," he said. "Hold on and I'll see if I can get him out here."

He pulled out his phone and wandered over to the giant windows for a little privacy as he made his call. She watched him move, noting the way his jeans hugged his ass in a nearly indecent way. They were damp about halfway up the calf to the knees and she realized his dark hair glistened with a hint of moisture too. He'd been teaching. Skiing with those snug blue jeans tucked into his boots. Would his ski jacket come down far enough to hide his ass or would his students see every flex as he led them down the mountain. She'd seen the women who came to the mountain—taut and Botoxed in their winter couture. Will was probably a *very* popular instructor.

Which was none of her dang business.

He wasn't her knight in shining armor. He wasn't her anything. Just a neighbor. Being neighborly.

Caitlyn forced herself to turn away. She crossed to the kitchen area and plucked a still mostly cool bottle of water out of the fridge. Maybe she could get the contractor to add in a water filtration system while he was at it. And a breakfast bar. And maybe expand the bathroom from its current microscopic proportions.

She grimaced. "I'm an idiot," she informed the

fridge, in case there was any doubt. She was planning upgrades and improvements to an apartment she was leaving in a matter of months. She just couldn't seem to get it through her brain that her life really was about to change that drastically.

Los Angeles. She was going to be living in Los Angeles. With her *husband*.

"You're in luck."

She whirled around at the voice behind her, hoping he hadn't heard her talking to the refrigerator.

Will strolled over from the windows with his easy—*sexy,* her hormones commented helpfully—gait, pocketing his phone as he came. "No one wants construction done over the holidays and Dale's next job doesn't start until the kids head back to school next week, so he's free this afternoon and he can come by to give you a bid right away. I played the brother-in-law card and he said he may even be able to squeeze you in around other projects so you don't have to wait for a break in his schedule. Since it looks like a pretty straightforward repair—no fancy parts that need ordering—he *could* probably start as early as tomorrow, but I doubt our fabulous landlord Les is going to have any idea what kind of insurance settlement he's getting for a few weeks at least, so you'll probably have to wait until then to start work."

"What if I paid for the work? Could we get it done by next week? Before my students start up lessons again on Monday?"

He frowned. "We could probably get most of it done, yeah, but you don't want to do that. Let the insurance guys work it out with Les."

"He can pay me back when he gets the settlement. It's worth it to me not to have the damage and then the construction distracting my students off and on for the next several weeks. And besides, it's kind of my fault anyway."

"Hey." He came around the café table and propped his hip beside hers on the counter. "It wasn't your fault. Shorts like that happens sometimes. Especially in houses where the wiring hasn't been looked at in thirty-five years."

Her heart thudded so loudly she was surprised he couldn't hear it. So close. He was tall, but not so massive that he towered over her. Just large enough to be a firm, masculine presence. Broad and warm and stable in a world that kept trying to shift out from under her. She felt her face heating and couldn't meet his eyes.

"I'd been drinking."

"Yeah, I figured that part out," he said dryly.

The heat in her face kicked up another few degrees. "I threw a glass full of vodka on the fire." She didn't know why she said that—the arson investigator had already decided she wasn't to blame and she had to go and practically *ask* to be sent to prison. But as soon as she confessed, the tightness in her chest eased and more words rushed out in desperate explanation. "I didn't mean to. It was a reflex. I went to turn the light on and it sparked and I panicked. The cup just—" She mimed a flinging gesture. "And then *fwhoosh*." Her hands sketched the explosion of flames in front of her face.

"That explains the vodka at the bottom of the wall," he said. "We thought you'd just dropped it when you fell."

"What?"

She looked up to find him watching her, a strange tightness across his features, like he was trying very hard to keep a straight face. "I'm pretty sure you missed."

"What?"

"You threw the vodka at the foot of the wall. You missed the fire by a good two feet."

"But it went *fwhoosh*."

"Yeah, the fire started in the wires behind the wall. The *fwhoosh* was when the drywall caught. So it really wasn't your fault. I'm not surprised your memory of it wasn't the clearest though. You'd definitely tied a few on. When I asked you if there was anyone else in the apartment, you told me to save the piano."

Her blush was going to be permanent at this rate. "I'm sorry."

"No, it was kind of cute. In retrospect. At the time I thought you were a crazy person."

"That isn't me," she swore. "I don't drink like that. Ask anyone."

"I believe you. But I have to ask. What was with the veil?"

There was something in his eyes, something that was so ready to be understanding—as if he expected her to have a good reason for putting on a massive wedding veil and going on a bender in her own apartment. And she did have one. She could tell him the veil was a joke—which it was. She could tell him she was self-medicating her way though her first reality television experience—which was true, too. She just couldn't tell him the biggest part—that she was engaged and freaking out about it.

The half-truths would paint a very compelling picture, but the second she drew breath to tell him about *Marrying Mister Perfect*, the words caught in her throat. She'd been nervous about going on the show before, excited and afraid of making a fool of herself, but she hadn't been embarrassed. Now the idea of telling this gorgeous man that she needed reality television to make someone want her was beyond mortifying. *Yes, I am that pathetic.*

She didn't want his incipient understanding to morph into a pitying oh-you're-one-of-those-desperate-Suitorettes. Though, was that really worse than being caught playing Miss Havisham in her living room?

"Gag gift," she managed to mutter.

His eyebrows lifted and he leaned in, murmuring conspiratorially, "I have a feeling there's more to the story than that."

Oh my. When he looked at her like that, every self-preservation impulse she had gave up and left the building. She could tell him anything, his eyes promised. Or she could just lean in a little more and stop the conversation a different way. The tangle of want that never seemed far away when he was in the room was tight around her now. It would be so easy...

"Will?" The shout carried through the open doorway.

"Saved by the electrician," Will said for her ears only. Then, louder, "Up here, Rico."

Caitlyn let herself breathe again when Will's depthless eyes finally turned away from her. *Saved, indeed.*

CHAPTER ELEVEN

Miranda dialed the number for the unregistered cell from heart, tension coiling around her. She hadn't heard from Caitlyn in over two days, not since Tuesday night, and now one of her minions—as she really ought to stop thinking of the production interns—had just handed her a report with a very disconcerting story highlighted.

"Hello?"

Caitlyn's voice came over the line, muffled, as though she was trying to avoid being overheard, but definitely her. She was fine. *Thank God.*

"Would you care to tell me why I'm looking at a report that says you burned down your house on Tuesday night after the show?"

Her tone may have been a touch more biting than usual, but she hated being blindsided. Especially by disasters. Miranda reached for her stress ball, squeezing it and breathing through the tension unknotting from her shoulders.

"That is a wildly exaggerated version of the story," Caitlyn protested. "There was a slight electrical fire at my place on Tuesday, yes, and I meant to call you about it, but I've been very busy getting repairs taken care of so it doesn't disrupt my teaching schedule and I just forgot. Sorry." A momentary pause. "How did you find out anyway?"

"I have interns scouring the net for any mention of any of you girls. Apparently a report was filed this morning about the fire."

"Aren't things like that sealed?"

"I don't know and I have interns who are trained not to ask whether or not they are allowed to get the information. They just get it." She dropped the stress ball and flipped idly through the report—no other mentions of Caitlyn. "Does Daniel know?"

"We haven't had a chance to talk and I didn't think it was the kind of thing you left on a message."

"No, probably not."

She could hear the disenchantment in Caitlyn's voice. Crap. Daniel was screwing it up already and they hadn't even gotten to the part of the show where he started making out with other girls. He was so busy running around being Mister Perfect that he seemed to have forgotten he needed to make Caitlyn feel like *she* was perfect or there wouldn't be a happily ever after. Dumbass. Men were so unbelievably useless.

"I know it's been hard so far, with him so busy with the publicity, but that will be dying down this week. Now that the initial push is over, we won't have to trot him out again until the final weeks. You guys should get a chance to reconnect."

Caitlyn hesitated and her words, when they came, were hesitant and soft. "Miranda, if I were having second thoughts…"

Oh shit. This was so much worse than she'd thought it was. "Jitters are perfectly normal, hon. Especially at this phase when you feel disconnected from him. I know your relationship came on fast and then you didn't have time to settle into it before he was whisked away, but don't make any hasty decisions until you see him again.

Give him a chance to remind you why you love him. Focus on that mid-season getaway. Okay?"

"Yeah. Okay."

They said their goodbyes and Miranda disconnected the call, not wasting a second before texting Daniel. *Call your fiancé.*

She somehow resisted the urge to add "dumbass" to the end.

The first marriage on a reunion show in *Marrying Mister Perfect* history. It could still happen. The social media reaction would be epic. And it would be a good thing. A mark in Miranda's karmic plus column.

Provided Daniel didn't screw it up.

Her desk phone bleeped, her assistant Todd's voice following. "Bennett Lang on line one for you."

Her heart thudded hard. Shit. What did he want? Two months of nothing and now… what? They hadn't exactly parted on good terms, but calling her office line when he could just text her cell… what did that mean? Was this how he meant to apologize? If it wasn't, did she even want to hear what he had to say?

Miranda depressed the button, keeping her voice ruthlessly calm. "Take a message, please."

She waited, her thoughts racing around her brain like a mice in a maze. She got nothing done for the next ten minutes, but forced herself to wait that long before gathering up her tablet and heading to the editing bay, stopping at her assistant's desk right outside her office and asking with studied casualness, "Was there a message?"

"He didn't leave one." Todd looked up, eyes gleaming. "That's a name I haven't heard around here in a while. You two getting back together?"

Miranda frowned repressively at her gossip-hungry

assistant—even though she knew it would do nothing to quell his curiosity. "I don't know what you think you know, but our relationship was always strictly professional." *If you don't count the hot monkey sex we had for a few months before he decided I was morally beneath him and needed to be fixed.* "He was probably calling about some cross promotion for the shows. If it were personal he wouldn't be calling the office line, would he?"

"If you say so."

But Todd's expression showed he wasn't buying what she was selling. Not that she blamed him. MMP and ADS were on different networks. Cross-promo was highly unlikely.

"Do you want me to put him through next time, since the great Bennett Lang is apparently above messages?"

"No. Keep screening his calls. Eventually I'm sure he'll deign to leave one."

Todd's brows arched and his lips curved cattily. "Yes, ma'am."

"I'll be in the editing bays."

Trying to make a show that is entertaining enough to satisfy the ravening hordes without destroying the relationship of our happy couple. Lucky me.

CHAPTER TWELVE

Daniel called so soon after she got off the phone with Miranda Caitlyn was certain the producer had told him he had to—which pretty much ruined any romance attached to the act. Caitlyn grabbed the phone and snuck back out onto the dingy landing, letting the newly hung door fall shut behind her and block out the sounds of the three man crew, including Will, working on the wall.

The electrician had given them the all clear to turn the power back on—and it turned out he was the same guy Will's brother-in-law used for electrical work, so he'd come back this morning to redo all the wiring in the wall that had fried, and any other areas that looked suspect. Will's brother-in-law had given her a ridiculously low bid and agreed to begin work immediately, but give her a few weeks to work things out with the landlord before demanding payment—all part of the friends and family package, he declared, doing a terrible job of hiding the speculative glances he kept flicking between her and Will.

Glances which had her wondering if Will might be single after all. Not that it made any difference. She was engaged. And her fiancé was calling.

"Baby! It's so good to hear your voice. I've been missing you so much."

She wasn't sure which was more disconcerting. The

fact that she didn't actually believe the man she was going to marry missed her, or the fact that for the last several days, she hadn't missed him. "Daniel, this isn't really a good time. I'm having some work done on my place."

A completely empty excuse. The guys were more than capable of proceeding without her input—in fact, if she tried to help, she would probably only be in the way. Though she had certainly been enjoying "supervising"—which had consisted mostly of watching Will swing a hammer and trying to develop mind control so she could convince him to take off his shirt. The man looked good with a hammer.

"Why?" Daniel asked. "Baby, just sell it as is."

"I rent. And could you please stop calling me baby?"

It was only after the words were out that she realized she'd never spoken so sharply to him before. He'd always seen her with her "company manners" as her mother called them. But sometime in the last week, her desperate desire to hear from him, to be reassured that she hadn't imagined everything they'd shared, had turned a corner and now she didn't even want to hear his voice.

A long pause stretched as he digested what she'd said.

"Sweetheart," he said finally—rotating through endearment lottery. "I wish I could say your name aloud, but someone could overhear me and we can't risk that."

And just like that, she felt like a heel. He had to be understanding and logical, didn't he? She sank down to sit on the steps. "No, you're right. I'm sorry."

"Are you all right? I'm sorry I've been so terrible about keeping in touch. I know this is a hard time for us.

Every day I wish I could be with you. You're my everything. And I'm sorry I've been so caught up in work that I've neglected you. Will you forgive me?"

The urge was strong to hold her grudge. To tell him that shilling for a reality TV show wasn't *work*. But she was doing it again—not giving him the benefit of the doubt. Running away and sabotaging their relationship, just like she always did.

"Of course. I'm sorry too. I'm just cranky." She plucked at the ratty carpet beside her hip. "The workmen are because there was a little electrical fire at my place."

"Oh my God. Sweetheart, why didn't you call me? Are you all right?"

"I'm fine," she murmured. Though she might start hating *sweetheart* as much as *baby*. "It was scary, but a neighbor helped me and now we're getting things put back together."

"You know, maybe this is a good thing."

"I'm sorry?" She couldn't have heard that right.

"It could be good exposure for you."

"A house fire is good exposure?"

"If the networks pick up the story. Or even if they don't, it's the perfect excuse to get out of there. You could move to LA. We won't be able to be seen in public together, but you can get started on your new life. Make contacts with music people in the area. This could be a great opportunity, bab—ah, sweetheart."

"I don't want to move."

His voice grew more persuasive, slathering on the charm. "It would only be a couple months early. And we might even be able to work out a system for a secret rendezvous or two."

She'd always let him guide the conversation when

they were talking about their future, but now that she was home, it felt different. "I don't think I want to move, Daniel. I love it here. This is my home."

"Hey, it's my home too. Home is where the heart is, right? And my heart is there."

It was sweet. Romantic. The kind of line that would have worked a few weeks ago. Hell, maybe even a few days ago. But now it just felt like a cheap ploy to get what he wanted without having to take her wishes into account. Like he could throw *but I love you so much* into any argument he wanted to win.

"I just don't know if I want to move to LA."

"Hey, it's okay. We have lots of time before we start our new life together."

"No, I meant…" *Ever.* But he was talking again.

"Don't worry, baby. I mean sweetheart. Sorry. It's going to work out. All you need is love, right?"

And what if I'm not sure I ever loved you in the first place? "Daniel…"

But he'd always seemed to have a sixth sense whenever she was about to say something he wasn't going to like. Something she hadn't really thought about until she saw that first show and saw him dodge other girls and their drama. He spoke quickly now, before he could hear her doubts—which would make them real.

"I'll let you get back to supervising your workers. Gotta keep a close eye on 'em. Make sure they do it right. Love you. So much, ba—sweetheart."

She couldn't say it back. The words had never rung with truth, but now they felt like an outright lie. She ought to say something, but with Will and the guys in her apartment this didn't seem like the time to get into it with him. So she let him evade.

"Goodbye, Daniel."

Will knew the moment Caitlyn reentered the apartment, and it had nothing to do with the soft click of the newly hung door. The air seemed crisper, charged with a certain kind of tension when she was in the room. Light brighter. Sounds louder. All of it waking him up.

And earning more than a few speculative glances from Dale—who would undoubtedly be reporting back to Julia, who would spread the word to his entire family. But maybe that wasn't such a bad thing. They were hardly subtle when they decided to match-make, but he wouldn't mind being set up with Caitlyn. He hadn't been interested in a woman in a long time, hadn't been looking, but something about Caitlyn opened his eyes.

Though he kept getting mixed messages from her on whether or not she returned his interest.

For the last two days it had been a constant back and forth. He'd catch her watching him, undeniable heat in her eyes, but then she'd blush and avoid his gaze. They'd be working side by side, easy and comfortable, laughing and flirting—and then she would seem to realize what she was doing all of a sudden and she'd stammer awkwardly, retreating again.

Hot and cold. Playful deep blue eyes and bashful rosy cheeks. Back and forth.

But maybe the mystery of her was why he couldn't seem to look away.

He looked away from his work as soon as the task allowed, in time to see her tucking a cell phone into the pocket of her jeans. She seemed different. Subdued.

"Everything okay?" he asked softly when she was closer.

She nodded absently. Then she seemed to shake

herself. "Wow, you guys are making amazing progress."

Dale looked up from his side of the drywall patch they were hanging. "My guys are the best," he bragged with a grin. "We should be out of your hair by tomorrow afternoon at the latest. Just finish work now."

Dale led her away to talk about the final details of the project and Will watched her go, feeling that tug of awareness go with her.

"If you ram that hammer into your thumb, I'm just going to laugh," Ben, one of Dale's regular guys, drawled beside him. "No sympathy."

"Shut up," Will grumbled, turning back to the job at hand. But he was grinning as he said it. Yeah, he was smitten—but it was so nice to feel something *different* after six months of anger, he couldn't be embarrassed by it. What was the harm in a little crush?

CHAPTER THIRTEEN

The night skiing lights on the mountain were flickering on in the twilight dimness as Caitlyn watched Will slowly packing up his tools. Dale and Ben had already gathered up their things and headed out for the night, slapping Will on the back as they went and nodding with courteous *ma'am*s for her. Will didn't have any more stuff than the others, but he took his time with each and every tool, lingering.

She didn't mind. She'd love nothing more than to find some excuse for him to stay.

She had a good idea what she would do when he left. Her stupid guilt over the conversation with Daniel would return and she'd call him back. If he took her call, in her current mood, she'd probably end up agreeing to move to Los Angeles after all—or breaking things off entirely.

Will would be the perfect distraction, but he'd already helped her remove all the dust covers from the furniture and she didn't have any more tasks for him.

He probably had plans anyway. A girlfriend waiting for him. A sexy dinner date waiting.

He stood finally, picking up his tool bag. "Well, I guess I should—"

"Do you want some pizza?" she almost shouted, then blushed at the volume. "It's just, I have all that leftover pizza from lunch and I certainly can't eat all that by myself." She forced a laugh. "I should probably be supervised if I'm gonna use the oven, too."

He frowned. "You've gotta stop making cracks like that. The fire wasn't your fault."

"No, I know. It was a joke. Ha." Her face flamed. She'd blushed more in the last three days than she had in the entire eight weeks she'd been on *Marrying Mister Perfect*. She wasn't sure what that meant.

"Was it? You know what I think? I think you want to be perfect all the time and you make jokes at your own expense when you think you've messed up—which you *didn't*—and you would take on the guilt of the world if it let you, making everything that happens in your life your fault, whether you have any say over it or not. Am I wrong?"

Her jaw dropped. A smart-ass remark rose to her tongue. *Who knew Sigmund Freud moonlighted as a ski instructing fire fighter?* But she swallowed it. Because he wasn't wrong. And he'd somehow figured out in three days what Daniel hadn't been able to learn in two months. And as terrifying as it was to be *known* like that… it was also unspeakably hot.

"So… no pizza?"

He laughed. "I'd love some pizza. If you still want me to stay."

And never leave. Caitlyn blinked, startled by the clarity of that little voice in her head. She squashed it. She was engaged. They were just friends sharing some pizza after a hard day's work. That was all this was. "I could use the company."

He grinned cockily. "I've been told I'm excellent company." He dropped his tools next to the door before joining her in the kitchen. "Napkins?"

She pointed him to the right cabinet and turned the dial to pre-heat the oven—and suddenly everything was easy and natural. No stiff, formal manners needed. Not even plates. Just laughing as they shifted the freshly reheated pizza from hand to hand to keep from burning their fingers through the napkins.

Cold beer would have been perfect—especially since Caitlyn had never had a beer in her life—but they made do with the liter of flat soda left over from lunch. Turns out she didn't need alcohol to feel that giddy, fizzy feeling around Will.

And then Will went looking for red pepper flakes and found the vodka.

He held up the half-full bottle, eyebrows arching. "Is this the infamous marshmallow vodka I keep hearing about?"

"Hey, don't knock it 'til you try it." She sat at the café table, the nearly empty pizza box in front of her, bonelessly relaxed.

He took off the cap, sniffing gingerly. "You just drink it straight?"

"It's good on the rocks, but you can mix it with soda or cranberry juice too."

He returned to his chair and splashed some into his coke. "You only live once, right?" He sipped carefully and pulled a face.

Caitlyn smothered a giggle.

"It's like drinking sugar."

"Pretty much."

"I am far too manly to drink anything so sugary." He tipped the bottle, pouring another liberal draught into his cup. Caitlyn's giggle escaped. He tilted the bottle questioningly over her cup.

"No, thank you. I'm still in recovery."

He grinned, setting down the bottle in the narrow space not taken by the pizza box. "Tuesday night was something else."

Not to mention the previous two months.

It was on the tip of her tongue to tell him about the free-flowing bar that was the *Marrying Mister Perfect* experience. They wanted their Suitorettes loose and entertaining—which meant alcohol was never hard to come by. Caitlyn hadn't been much of a drinker before she went on the show, but a cocktail to take the edge off before filming had become part of her daily ritual. And now it was a habit she wanted to get out of.

In a way, it was tempting to tell Will all the things she wouldn't normally admit about the show. She trusted him—probably far more than she should—but she also loved that he knew nothing about the show. He didn't see a reality TV girl when he looked at her. He just saw Caitlyn. It was unbelievably freeing talking to someone who had no idea where she'd been for the last two months. He was a different world. A little pocket of calm that felt a thousand times more real that her recent reality.

What would he think of Daniel?

"Do you believe in love at first sight?"

She slapped a hand over her mouth. She couldn't believe she'd asked that. And she wasn't even drinking.

Will laughed, ignoring her shock, eyes crinkling. "Absolutely. The first time I saw you, you were lying on the floor in a puddle of tulle and marshmallow vodka. How could I resist?"

Her face flamed. Why couldn't she seem to keep her verbal filters on when she talked to him? She was usually so reserved. She didn't over-share with strangers—but he didn't feel like a stranger. Maybe all the rules evaporated when someone saved your life. "I didn't mean *me*. I just meant in theory. The idea. I mean obviously you and I didn't..." Though her first sight of him had definitely been memorable. *The dark god...* "We don't... it's not like—"

"Caitlyn," he interrupted gently when she would have babbled herself deeper into the hole she couldn't seem to stop digging. "I was teasing you."

She wrinkled her nose, disgruntled. "How do you even know what tulle is?"

He lifted his marshmallow vodka filled cup in a mocking toast. "Three older sisters."

"Oh wow. I can't imagine that. I'm an only child."

"I can picture that. With envy." He sipped his drink. "So what about you? Do *you* believe in love at first sight?"

"*No.*" She hadn't thought about her answer. It just jumped out her mouth, hard and firm. "We trick ourselves into believing in this magical, mystical connection. Our brains play these games, trying to mash what we want and what we see together even if they don't quite fit. You've got the square peg and the round hole, but sometimes we want so badly for them to fit that we don't notice how wrong they are."

"Let me guess. Bad break up? That was him on the phone earlier, wasn't it? Seemed great at first and then when the shine wore off... I've been there."

There was such understanding in his eyes, which for once weren't melty and soft, but brittle and defensive. He did get it. It was like he understood her life better than she did—until she was with him and it all came spilling out. But she couldn't tell him the truth. Not about Daniel and her doubts. Not about the show.

God, he was too intuitive by half. She didn't know if

it was growing up surrounded by girls or just something about *him*, but he got her in a way that was scary. And appealing.

Too appealing for a woman who was still promised to someone else. Even if she was having doubts. She wasn't free yet.

"I should let you go." But the whisper was weak, her voice betraying her, the lilt of it begging him to stay.

He nodded. And his gaze fell to her lips.

CHAPTER FOURTEEN

Suddenly the hot and cold vibes he'd been getting from her all week made sense. Bad break-up. He'd been there. Hell, if he was honest with himself, he was still there. And he'd had six months to get used to his new baggage. He had a feeling Caitlyn's relationship drama was much more recent.

He hadn't noticed any men coming and going from her apartment since he moved in, but she'd been gone for the last two months. With the guy from the phone call? He recalled the tightness on her face when she read the caller ID, her distraction when she came back after talking to him. Whoever he was.

An old lover? Maybe one who was unavailable. Had she discovered he was married? Maybe he'd run off with the maid of honor.

Not that it mattered. His imagination could take him on all the joyrides it wanted. It didn't change the fact that the woman in front of him was working her way through heartache and didn't need him complicating her life. No matter how tempting her lips were.

He forced his gaze away from her mouth, scrambling for a light, safe topic of conversation. He jerked his chin toward the wall. "A few coats of paint and you won't even know anything happened."

"I can't believe how quickly you put everything back

to rights. I'll never be able to repay you."

"It was good timing. Dale was glad to have the work—you're helping him pay off his Santa Claus bills."

"And I'm sure he's undercharging me, but it's you I really owe. You have to let me buy you dinner."

He arched a brow at the pizza that had been lunch for the whole crew and dinner for the two of them.

"A real dinner," she insisted.

"Caitlyn Gregg, are you asking me out on a date?"

A blush instantly painted her cheeks. "No, of course not. It's a thank you meal. Between friends. Just friends."

She was so cute when she was flustered he almost wanted to let her keep babbling, but he took pity on her. "A friendly dinner sounds nice," he said, smooth and calm, holding her gaze.

If anything, her blush deepened. "Good." Her voice was surprisingly husky. She looked away, breaking the connection. "This weekend?"

He grimaced. "I can't this weekend."

"No, of course you have plans," she instantly began chattering and he cut her off before she could really get going.

"I traded shifts with another of the ski instructors. I'm gonna be doubled up all weekend covering his schedule and doing ski patrol for night skiing."

And he had no intention of telling Caitlyn he'd switched up his schedule, getting Ray to cover his Friday classes so he could be here with her, giving his brother-in-law an extra pair of hands so all the work would get done before Caitlyn's students were scheduled to come back. It was a small thing to him, but would make a big difference to her, so the decision had been easy, but he had a feeling she'd get all tangled up in misplaced guilt if she knew. She was already trying to guilt feed him.

"Tuesday," she blurted. "How about Tuesday?"

He grimaced. "I have a family thing. Every week my sisters ritualistically dissect my life and tell me what I need to be happy. Usually it's the love of a good woman, so if I told them it was a date they'd probably let me play hookie—"

"Wednesday."

Okay then. Apparently the word date was off limits even for jokes. "Wednesday sounds great. I'll be looking forward to it."

"I…" She hesitated. "Me too."

Caitlyn sat staring at the door long after Will had gone back downstairs, citing an early morning as he made his escape. She had a date. Though it wasn't a date because of course it couldn't be a date.

But it felt like a date.

Butterflies in her stomach. Anticipation. Counting the days, the hours.

She might as well admit it. She had a freaking enormous crush on her neighbor. Which was fine. He was decidedly crushworthy. As long as she didn't do anything about it.

Like go on a date with him.

Oh, Chopin's Pinky Finger, she was so screwed.

She went to the Steinway, lifting the dust cover off the keys, though she left it draped over the body of the grand. She slid back the key cover and let her fingers whisper over the keys, letting her mood seek out the perfect piece. Mozart erupted into the air—bright and sparkling, dizzy and effervescent, bursting with possibilities and hopes. Her fingers danced and as always happened when she played, she let herself feel it—whatever it was she couldn't let herself feel any other hour of the day, it came out at the keys.

Caitlyn played, and smiled.

Will tipped his face up, listening to the flurry of notes dancing through the ceiling, and he couldn't help but grin.

He remembered the first song he'd ever heard her play, that first night when he'd moved in. He'd been broken, newly jilted, forced out of the home he'd thought he would raise his children in. He'd wanted to block the rest of the world out. And then he'd heard it. A slow, aching ballad reaching through the ceiling and wrapping around his heart. He'd sat in the dark and listened to the music for hours. Sad and sweet, poignant and piercing in its loneliness.

He'd heard her play hundreds of times, always seeming to resonate so perfectly with his emotions, but now it wasn't his own emotion he heard in the music. It was Caitlyn. Everything she held inside pouring out. And tonight that was happiness. And hope.

She could say it wasn't a date all she wanted. He could hear the difference.

Will sat in the dark, listened, and smiled.

CHAPTER FIFTEEN

"Would you care to tell me why I had to hear you're dating someone from Julia? You know I hate it when she gets the good gossip before I do."

Will leaned against the ski patrol shack at the top of the chairlift, cell phone pressed to his ear as he scanned the mountain for problems and listened to his oldest sister air her grievances. "I'm not dating anyone," he told Claire.

"Julia said Dale said the pheromones were stifling."

Dale needs to keep his mouth shut. Though he had a feeling Dale had said nothing of the sort. "Julia needs to stop reading so many romance novels."

"Bite your tongue. You never would have gotten laid in high school if we hadn't forced you to read romance novels to understand the female psyche."

"And I'm forever grateful." He even had a few choice romances on his bookshelf now. "I only meant Julia was getting carried away with accusations of pheromone saturation."

"She does buy into the sappy, angsty stuff a little too much," Claire admitted. "I pretty much only read them for the sex."

"Another sentence I could have lived my entire life without my sister saying to me."

"I'll stop telling you about my sex life if you tell me

about the girl."

"The family that blackmails one another…"

"If you need tips on cunnilingus, Don can—"

Will choked. "Jesus, Claire, *stop*, for the love of God. I'll tell you whatever you want. Just stop."

He could practically hear his sister bouncing with glee. "Is she pretty?"

"She's gorgeous, but we're not dating."

"You can't say gorgeous and not dating in the same sentence. It doesn't work that way."

"There are lots of gorgeous women I'm not dating. Scarlett Johansson. Emma Stone."

"Oh my God! Does she look like Scarlett Johansson?"

Will rolled his eyes, safe in the knowledge that Claire couldn't see him and smack him upside the head for it. "More like Emma Stone actually, but more, I don't know, delicate."

"Dale said she was a redhead."

"She is."

"And a piano teacher."

"Do you really need me to tell you about her? Or did you get all you needed from Dale already?"

"You're sure you're not dating?"

"We're not dating. But we are having dinner next week."

Claire squealed at an ear-splitting decibel. "Will! Oh my God! I'm so proud of you!"

"It isn't a date, Claire. I like her, but neither of us is in a place right now to want that."

"That's what people say right before Cupid cold-cocks them!"

"Cupid isn't going to—" About fifty yards down the hill, a snowboarder took a facer that looked like it rattled his bones and didn't immediately pop up. "Shit. Claire,

I've gotta go. It's not a date." He folded the phone and clicked into his skis, grabbing the back-board just in case and skiing down to where the boarder still lay motionless. His friends had stopped below him and were making slow, hopping progress back up the hill to the crash site.

Will had work to do. Arguing about his love life would have to wait until Tuesday when all his sisters could gang up on him.

"This is so cool! I'm watching *Marrying Mister Perfect* with an actual Suitorette! Do you have any idea how exciting this is for me?"

Caitlyn grinned at Mimi's enthusiasm. "Believe it or not, it isn't half bad for me either."

She hadn't been sick with nerves at all in the last few days—which may have been a function of the fact that she was getting used to the show, or relaxing knowing she would have Mimi's support when she watched it... or it could have been because she was more nervous about her secret not-date on Wednesday than her very public one on Tuesday. She was almost glad Will had his own plans for tonight and she hadn't been able to use him as *Marrying Mister Perfect* avoidance. For the first time she felt brave and strong sitting down to watch.

Which lasted until the end of the opening credits. Then her stomach began to roil and she started regretting the Chinese take-out feast she and Mimi had ordered in.

They huddled around her tiny television, Caitlyn on the couch and Mimi curled in the matching chair, eating chow mein directly out of the carton and punctuating her comments with her chopsticks. Ty had been told to call if one of the children needed to be rushed to the ER, but barring that Mimi was taking a Girls' Night In and he was on his own.

Caitlyn's nerves came back the second Elena was selected for the first date. She was about to watch her fiancé romance the woman he'd *almost* asked to marry him.

Mimi snorted. "Of course he picks Boobs McHottiepants as the first individual date. Tell me the truth, is she a total bitch?"

Thank God for friends and distractions. Caitlyn let the images on the screen wash over her, not really penetrating. "Actually, she isn't that bad. Most people forget it when they look at her, but she's hella smart. She wants to be an actress or a dancer or something and I'm pretty sure she came on the show for the exposure—"

"Like Craig from last season."

"Yeah, but she was more subtle about it. When she realized she was going to be portrayed as the show's villainess, I think she started playing it up more, but she was never actually mean to anyone. Just sort of snarky and smug—like she knew she was the hottest piece of ass in the house. Which she totally was, so what are you gonna do? And she could be really nice. I'm sure they won't show those parts. But she could."

"So you guys are friends?"

"I wouldn't say that. It's more like we're both survivors of the same natural disaster."

Mimi blinked. "Ouch."

"No. I didn't mean it like that. Daniel wasn't a natural disaster. It's the show. It's this insane experience that distorts your reality for months and it feels like only the people inside that echo chamber with you really understand what you went through, so there's this bond. Does that make sense? There's no television, no books, no cell phones, no computers—you're completely cut off from the world. If war broke out while we were in there, we would have had to wait until the producers decided it was the right time to tell us so they could film the moment."

"Jesus." Mimi looked back to the television with a dubious expression.

"Yeah. The women with children got to call home, but only on designated phones at designated times when they could be recorded telling their babies how much they missed them and how hard it was to be apart."

"That's messed up."

"Yes it is."

Mimi eyed the women on the screen. The current scene involved all the Suitorettes sitting around the pool at their mansion, talking about how great Daniel was. "Did you make any friends? Samantha seems pretty great."

"She is. And intimidatingly together. She's so... *perfect.* I was so certain she was going to go all the way—"

Caitlyn swallowed the words, her face turning red as she realized what she'd almost revealed. Stupid nondisclosure. Luckily Mimi was only giving her half her attention, the other half on the screen and didn't seem to have noticed the slip.

Mimi frowned. "Where are you? Did you forget to pack your bathing suit or something?"

Caitlyn turned her attention to the screen. The time at the mansion was a bit of a blur—not helped by the alcohol that had always been on hand—but she hadn't spent much time by the pool so it wasn't surprising she wasn't in the shot. "I was probably hiding in the music room. They had a piano and I spent most of my time there. You know how shy I can be and it was such a strange situation. Like living in a sorority house where everyone is chasing the same guy—they sabotage one another and gang up on one another, but then air kiss and gossip and everything is forgiven. Some of the girls do seem to really form friendships—I think mostly because you have nothing to do but talk and work out and lay by the pool and write in your journal. I think I would have lost my mind if I hadn't been able to sneak off and play. I would close the doors to the music room and stay in there for hours. They probably won't show that on the show."

The scene changed and abruptly, Daniel and Elena were being strapped together, chest to chest, for the show's inevitable bungee jump-into-love segment. Daniel was flushed, Elena was practically purring.

She did not want to watch this.

Caitlyn looked anywhere but at the screen, searching for anything else to talk about. "I got along really well with Sidney."

"The hot blonde wedding planner? Oh my gosh, I *love* her."

"Yeah, she's fantastic. And she wasn't into the competition aspect of the show as much as some of the other girls. Sidney was the one I could relax with, you know? The only one who made me feel like I wasn't alone. I just wish she'd stayed longer."

"Oh, no! Sidney goes home soon? She was one of my first night favorites."

Caitlyn winced. "You can't tell anyone I told you that. I could get sued for like a bazillion dollars for leaking results."

"Lips sealed. Scouts honor."

Caitlyn was going to have to watch what she said more carefully. When she'd signed the nondisclosure agreements, she'd thought it would be easy—just avoid talking about sensitive details. Easy. But now, after filming the show and living through it, it felt like there was a giant gaping hole in her life that she couldn't talk to anyone about. Even calling Sidney was against the rules because she wasn't allowed to know any of the results beyond her own departure.

What would Mimi think when she found out that Sidney went home of her own volition, taking herself out of the competition? She'd said she just wasn't feeling it with Daniel and wasn't going to stay any longer for a guy who wasn't her prince charming.

Caitlyn had respected the choice, especially when Sidney explained that she and Daniel never *laughed* together. That there was never any *fun* with the two of them.

On screen, Daniel and Elena laughed into the cameras, breathless and bright eyed after their screaming plunge and dangling upside down first kiss— a *Marrying Mister Perfect* tradition.

Had Caitlyn laughed with Daniel? She couldn't remember a single time. Things between them were romantic to the extreme, but always intense, never light. Always soulful gazes, never winks and grins.

Will's grinning face flashed in her thoughts.

"You know." Mimi waved a chopstick at the screen. "I really wanted Daniel to be chosen as the next Mister Perfect when I saw Marcy's season, but now I'm afraid he's going to be one of those guys who seems totally nice the first time around, but by the second season has turned into a total douche."

Caitlyn winced. Mimi had no idea she was calling Caitlyn's fiancé a douche. She thought she was comforting Caitlyn after a bad break up by ragging on the guy who had broken her heart. Offering *you're-better-off-without-him* support.

Caitlyn didn't know if that made it better or worse. *The road to hell was paved with good intentions.*

"We should start a drinking game. With soda," Mimi amended quickly when Caitlyn shot her a look. "Take a sip every time he gets that smug, douche-bag, I-deserve-gorgeous-women-fighting-over-me-because-I-am-the-catch-of-the-universe smile on his face."

Caitlyn sank deeper into the couch. If she defended Daniel, would she give away the secret? "Great idea."

What would Mimi think of Daniel the first time they met? Would it be all forgive and forget or would she still think he was a reality TV douche-bag?

"The wall looks good."

Caitlyn looked up. Mimi was twisted around with her back to the television, taking advantage of the commercial break to inspect the good-as-new wall that had been a gaping charred hole less than a week ago.

"Yeah, Will and his brother-in-law did an amazing job. I can't believe how quickly they put my life back together again." Now if only there was such an easy patch for her love life.

"Will?" Mimi turned slowly back to face Caitlyn, eyes wide, brows arched speculatively.

"My downstairs neighbor. The one who pulled me out of the fire. His brother-in-law is a contractor and they took care of everything."

"Wait, Will Hamilton?"

Had he told her his last name? She couldn't remember. Had she really walked past his mailbox for however many months without registering the name? "Maybe?"

"Tall, darkish hair, built, freakishly sexy eyes?"

"That sounds like him."

"Oh my God!" Mimi squealed, nearly upending the carton of chow mein she'd propped against her hip. "This is totally fate."

"Fate?" Caitlyn echoed skeptically.

"Will Hamilton is Ty's friend Don's wife's brother!" At her blank look, Mimi flapped a chopstick at her. "The one I wanted to set you up with! With the bitch ex-fiancé!"

He's single. "Oh."

"Yeah, *oh*. God, Cait, you have to jump on that man like he's a landmine who might explode at any moment. You've seen him. You know that kind of hotness isn't going to be on the market for long."

But I'm not on the market.

She'd already found her happily ever after. Was she betraying Daniel by even entertaining fantasies about another man? Because she hadn't been able to stop thinking about Will and what might happen on their date-that-was-definitely-not-a-date if things had been different and they'd both been free. But it turned out Will *was* free. Did he think the date really was a date? Did he want it to be?

Did *she?*

"I can't date while the show is airing," Caitlyn murmured when Mimi gazed at her expectantly. "It's in the contract."

"Well then at least lick him to claim him for later."

She blinked, jolted out of her musings by the words. "Excuse me?"

Mimi waved a chopstick. "It's something the kids do

so no one else will eat their treats when they're trying to save them. Like the last piece of pizza in the fridge. One kid licks it in front of the other and then the other kid is so scared of the cooties that they stay away from the treat. You just need to lick Will for later."

"Because that doesn't sound creepy at all."

"Hey, all's fair in love and war."

"I'm not sure the cooties principle translates."

"Shush, it's back." Mimi flapped at her to be silent, glued to the screen.

Caitlyn turned back to watch her personal natural disaster.

CHAPTER SIXTEEN

"Will! Get in here. You have to see this!"

Claire's shout echoed through the house from the media room, reaching him all the way in the kitchen where he was hiding with his brothers-in-law. After dinner, his parents had taken their grandchildren to the basement with plans to build a Guinness World Record worthy fort, his sisters had retreated to the media room to watch some reality show Laney was addicted to, and the men of the middle generation had claimed dishes duty so they could stealthily raid the beer fridge as they cleaned.

The cleaning was all done, but there were still beers to be had and football to be discussed and Will had no intention of throwing himself into the estrogen pit of the media room if he could avoid it. Especially since he had miraculously evaded being grilled about his love life during dinner and he wanted to continue his streak.

"No, thanks, Claire," he shouted back. "I'm good."

Second later she appeared in the doorway. "Seriously, you have to see this. It's the girl! Don's friend Ty's wife's friend. She's on *Marrying Mister Perfect!*"

"There's a show called *Marrying Mister Perfect?*" He didn't bother to hide his horror.

"It's premium grade reality schlock. But you have to see her! She's adorable."

"I somehow doubt anyone who would voluntarily go on a reality television show can be described as human, let alone adorable."

Claire pivoted, glowering at her husband for reinforcements. "Don."

Claire was five-six in three-inch heels, with a round sweet face that didn't look like it disguised a brain to rival Mussolini's. Her husband was a towering bear of a man who could have been a celebrity impersonator for Vin Diesel without much effort. And he still held up his hands in defeat the second she looked at him. "The girl's cute," he offered.

As if that settled it, Claire latched onto Will's arm and began dragging him toward the media room. He was twice her size, but she had a grip like a wolverine.

"What made you think I would want to date some reality TV starlet?"

Claire rolled her eyes and kept dragging. "I didn't *know* she was on the show. No one did. It was this giant secret."

"But you still want to set me up with her. Even though she's probably a soulless fame whore."

"Wow, way to be judgmental, champ. And no, I don't want to set you up *now*, not when you have your fire girl. But she might be a good fall back plan, for later."

His fire girl. He liked the sound of that. There was certainly a fire inside Caitlyn, embers burning low, and he was looking forward to fanning those flames.

"I got him," Claire announced as she hauled him into the media room, finally releasing the wolverine grip and flopping onto one of the giant plush recliners fanned out in front of the mega-screen—his parents had gone all out when they remodeled the house, turning Laney's old bedroom into a home theatre.

He saw a bevy of bikini-clad beauties cavorting around the pool—like something out of his teenage fantasies—all of them gazing up at the man in the three piece suit as if he was about to deliver the Eleventh Commandment.

"And the winner of the next individual date is…" The camera scrolled wildly over the eager faces.

"It'll be Amanda," Laney announced confidently.

Claire and Julia immediately chimed in, arguing for their own picks, the three of them so loud they all missed hearing the name called.

Then the camera zoomed in tight on a shocked face. A very *familiar* shocked face.

"*Caitlyn?*"

Three pairs of eyes swung to lock on him.

"You watch the show?" Laney asked.

"You know her?" Julia demanded in the same moment.

Will couldn't quite process what he was seeing, his eyes still locked on the screen. "That's my upstairs neighbor."

"*That's* fire girl?" Julia said.

"You're dating the *Marrying Mister Perfect* girl?" Laney yelped.

"I get credit for this," Claire crowed. "I was going to introduce them through Don."

"You don't get credit," Julia argued. "You *didn't* introduce them. If anyone gets credit, I do, because Dale was there when they were all flirty-flirty for the repairs."

"No one gets credit," Laney declared. "They met on their own."

"We aren't dating," Will protested, but the words were weak. Caitlyn had been gone for months *because she was on a reality television show.* "What is this show?"

"It's a dating show. Like the Bachelor. Or all those VH1 ones—Flavah of Love, Rock of Love. A bunch of girls—or guys in the alternating seasons—go on national television, competing to date the dude who has been picked as Mister Perfect. Who is sometimes flippin' awesome—like Doctor Jack, be still my heart—and sometimes kind of a dick—like that Randall from four seasons ago. Ugh. Jury's still out on this guy, though he seems pretty cool so far. And I will confess when he literally swept Marcy off her feet last season I about swooned."

The guy. Her bad break-up. It had been on national television. Damn. That would be enough to make anyone gun shy.

But why would she put herself through that? Why would she voluntarily go on the show? Yes, he'd been instantly infatuated with her, but now he was realizing he didn't know the first thing about her. He hadn't thought she was the kind of girl who would go on reality television. Why hadn't she said something?

This was why she'd been drinking last Tuesday. And the veil. *Marrying Mister Perfect.* The gag gift made sense now.

Had she really hoped to marry that guy? A complete stranger she met on national television? Or had she had some other motivation for going on the show?

Who *was* she?

"Will?"

His sisters seemed to have finally noticed he wasn't responding to them.

"I have to go." He had a lot to think about. "And we aren't dating." At this point, he wasn't sure they ever would be.

"I can't believe you didn't tell me you got an individual date on the *second episode*," Mimi exclaimed for approximately the seven hundredth time since the host had announced Caitlyn would be accompanying Daniel on the romantic opera-and-fine-dining date, referred to among the Suitorettes as the *Pretty Woman*.

"They only picked me because I have a musical background and am less likely to say something on camera to offend the entire opera community."

"Yeah, but *Tosca*? Your all time favorite opera ever in the history of man? What are the odds?"

The odds were pretty good because she'd filled out extensive questionnaires telling the producers what her favorite and least favorite *everything* was. "It was pretty amazing."

The Puccini had swept her away, as it always did, and for the first time—but not the last—she'd forgotten she was on camera. She'd just been on a date with an insanely handsome man who seemed as happy as she was to be at the opera with her—though she'd gotten the sense he loved the spectacle of it more than the musical majesty. Still, it had been pretty close to perfect and she'd been transported.

When he'd whisked her away during the curtain call to a candlelight dinner on a rooftop overlooking the city, she hadn't even minded missing the bows. Not when he was gazing into her eyes with his blue eyes sparkling. Dazzled, charmed, she couldn't help wonder if he might really be her Mister Perfect. If she could possibly have gotten that lucky.

Then he'd kissed her.

"Is he a good kisser?" Mimi demanded, pausing and

rewinding the kiss several times. It had been brief, but lovely. A dignified show of interest and intent. Perfect.

"Yes," she said softly. She could feel Mimi watching her, but she just looked at the screen. Daniel leaning in, keeping that magical eye contact until she felt drugged by it. He certainly knew how to work a romantic moment. That had never been in doubt.

She'd been swept away that night. He'd made her forget the cameras, so caught up in him. But had she also forgotten herself? Had she been playing a role too? Miss Perfect to his Mister? Had she wanted the happy ending so badly that she'd forced it when it wasn't there?

She watched for the warning signs, looking for the seeds of doubt that would sprout into the reservations she now felt about spending the rest of her life with him—but all she saw was charm and charisma and smiles and the perfect, light lingering kiss. It looked a lot like love.

She'd gone home that night and admitted to the cameras in the confessional that she might have just had her last first kiss. From the way the producers had sighed, she *knew* that line would make it into the show.

She waited, knowing it was coming, and when she spoke, eyes shining, smile beaming, Mimi moaned, pressing a hand over her heart. "Oh, *Caitlyn*."

She shrugged, not meeting Mimi's eyes, afraid her friend would see too much. Seeming to sense her mood, Mimi hit pause and lightened the tone. "Well, you certainly make good television. You're going to be America's favorite for weeks. Unless you go all psycho stalker on him next week. Tell me the truth, did you try to sneak over the wall between the mansions? There's always at least one girl who tries to scale the thing."

Caitlyn giggled, relieved at the change in subject. "I

can neither confirm nor deny any attempts to scale the wall this season."

"I bet it was Michele. She's got those crazy eyes. It's always the Micheles."

"She's a sweet girl. Just a little... intense."

"Bunny-boiling intense, you mean. Be honest. She gives herself a prison style tattoo of his name on her ass, doesn't she?"

Caitlyn giggled helplessly—a little hysterical after the emotional stress of watching the show. "You'll just have to watch and see."

Mimi grinned and pushed play. They watched the rest of the show—the frantic desperation of the final cocktail party and then the Elimination Ceremony—with Mimi editorializing wildly.

Caitlyn didn't miss the fact that Mimi kept her comments thoroughly ridiculous and avoided saying anything about Daniel at all. But if her friend suspected there might still be feelings between Caitlyn and Daniel, she kept those suspicions to herself.

Watch and see. Caitlyn would do the same. Watch and see if it was love or illusion.

And now the whole world knew she'd been infatuated with him. Mimi wasn't the only one who watched the show. She wouldn't be able to escape the speculative looks in town.

At least Will didn't know. She wouldn't have to worry about the way he would look at her tomorrow on their non-date.

It wasn't a date. She was taken.

For now.

CHAPTER SEVENTEEN

Will was late. Only two minutes, but why couldn't he just get here already? She already felt strange about the non-date. She didn't need the waiting to amplify her uncertainties.

She'd had a good talk with Daniel today. Their relationship felt like it was on firm footing for the first time since before the proposal. Which didn't help her emotional state at the moment.

She'd dressed simply, taking care to project an unmistakable Just Friends image. Snug dark jeans, low heeled black ankle boots, a loose-fitting cowl-necked royal blue sweater, and combs to keep her hair out of her face. Nothing fancy. Just the barest swipe of make-up.

She owed Will. She was just paying back a friend for everything he'd done for her. So what if that friend was ridiculously attractive and made her feel like her insides were carbonated? It was perfectly innocent.

She hadn't told Daniel about the dinner. Or about meeting Will. They'd talked for nearly an hour, about everything and nothing, catching up, reconnecting, but whenever the conversation had veered toward the fire or the repairs or anything having to do with Will, she would find herself tripping over her tongue to change the subject. Until the end of the call when she had very purposely said she had to leave to get ready for dinner *with a friend,* as if to prove to herself that she could tell Daniel because there was nothing to hide.

But now Will was late—six minutes and counting—giving her time to question herself.

It felt like a lie, not mentioning Will to Daniel. But if she told Daniel about her feelings for Will—supposing she even knew what those feelings were—what was the benefit to him? Was it selfish to want to confess to him? Especially when there was nothing concrete to confess. So she was excited about the dinner, excited about seeing Will again. It was just because he was a nice guy and outside of the reality TV bubble. She could ignore that entire stressful chapter of her life with him and that was unspeakably relaxing. That must be why she felt this fizzy pop of anticipation in her veins. It wasn't crazy chemistry making her rationalize things...

The knock was firm and brisk.

Caitlyn nearly sagged with relief. He was here. Finally.

She rushed to the door and yanked it open. "Will."

He didn't return her smile of greeting and his eyes held none of their usual amused warmth as they studied her. His hair was still damp—either from the snow or a shower—and he wore a pair of jeans that had seen better days and a faded grey Henley. A winter jacket hung over one arm. Clearly he'd gotten the casual dress Just Friends memo.

He jerked his chin, looking as tense and awkward as she felt. "Caitlyn."

She plucked her purse and coat off the piano bench. "Ready to go?"

He leaned one shoulder against the doorjamb, looking like he was settling in for a while. A slight frown creased his brow. "I saw you on television last night."

And just like that, her bubble burst. That lovely cloud of ignorance that had kept him from looking at her like she was a reality show freak. Gone. "Damn," she whispered.

His eyebrows arched. "Don't you want people to know you're a big TV star?"

She rolled her eyes. "I'm not a TV star. And no, I don't particularly like it when people know. So far when people find out, they all either want something from me—usually gossip about what's happening next on the show or what Josh Pendleton is really like—or they look at me like I'm a freak for going on a reality TV show. Kind of like you're looking at me right now."

He winced and rubbed a hand down his face. "Sorry. It just caught me off guard. I was with my sisters when I saw it. You should have heard the three of them crowing about how I was dating 'Miss Perfect'."

"*What*?" Panic made the word a shout. "We aren't dating! You can't tell people that. I could get sued! I'm not allowed to have public relationships. Not while I'm on the show. Breach of contract! If they say something— if they even post it on Facebook—oh my God. You have to fix this!"

"Hey, relax. I told them we were just friends."

"And you're positive they believed you?"

Will though that one over for a second and grimaced. "I'll call them."

Caitlyn wrapped her arms around her waist, pacing as she listened to Will call each of his sisters in turn. She couldn't hear the other side of the conversations, but she could tell by his multiple repetitions of "I swear we're *just friends*," that they weren't exactly buying it.

He groaned as he put his cell phone back in his

pocket. "They're all convinced we're going to get married and have a dozen fat babies, but I got them all to vow secrecy. That's the best I can do." He rocked his shoulder back against the doorjamb. "Maybe we shouldn't go to dinner."

"I understand if you don't want to be seen with me, but I do want to find some way to repay you."

His expression darkened. "Caitlyn, you don't owe me anything."

"Not even a burger at the Lodge pub?" She told herself she was pushing because she didn't want to be in his debt. It had nothing to do with that itch beneath her skin to spend more time with him. "You know how good those burgers are. Don't be hasty turning down an offer that good."

"I guess I could do a burger." His usual grin slowly returned, though at a quarter its usual strength.

"Great."

But it didn't feel great.

They slipped on their coats in silence. As they departed the chalet and tramped side by side through the snow past chair lifts and ski school buildings to the far side of the resort where the Lodge sat, the conversation was non-existent and the air between them charged with a stilted awkwardness. Caitlyn pulled a knit hat and matching gloves out of her coat pockets and pulled them on to battle the chill in the air—the chill that seemed like it was coming from him. It was only a fifteen minute walk, but by the time they were half way it felt like they'd been going for hours.

If the night kept on like this, she didn't know how she was going to choke down a burger. Even one of the famous Lodge Burgers.

Maybe if they talked about it, it wouldn't be so

weird. "How much did you see?" she asked, eyes on the ground to find steady footing in the snow. Had he seen the kiss? Her talking about her last first kiss? God, how embarrassing.

"Just a few seconds. Your face on screen mostly. They were announcing you'd won something."

"A date," she murmured.

"Right," he agreed. "I suppose that's what you win on shows like that."

That or a fiancé.

They reached the Lodge then. It looked like an outrageously large log cabin, squatting over a small man made skating pond. It was the resort's main building, housing restaurants, equipment rental, and a wing of hotel rooms for out-of-towners. When it was built, the owners had intended it to be only the first building of a massive, sprawling resort, but the valley Tuller Springs was tucked into was too remote and it had never caught on as a destination city for skiers the way Aspen, Vail, and Telluride had.

The Lodge had changed ownership several times over the years, each new owner struggling to make a profit where others had barely been able to break even. The ski resort survived largely as a haven for Colorado skiers who wanted to avoid the crowds at the major resorts. In the years Caitlyn had lived here, she'd never seen it busy.

But the pub always did a good business. A favorite among locals and out-of-towners alike.

They circled the main entrance of the Lodge and descended the exterior stairs just beyond it, down into the basement pub, where everything was rich wood paneling and soft Celtic music.

Tammy, the pub's weekday hostess and occasional

back-up waitress, grinned when she saw them approach the hostess stand. She had short brown curls liberally salted with grey and a round, matronly figure, but that didn't stop her from batting her eyes at Will, even though he must be half her age.

"Well if it isn't Will Hamilton and Caitlyn Gregg," she called cheerfully. "I didn't know you knew each other."

"Turns out we're neighbors," Will said smoothly, before Caitlyn could stammer out something incoherent and incriminating.

"Just the two of you?" Tammy asked, one eyebrow sliding up with the question, as they shucked their winter gear.

Will laughed. "Don't get any ideas, Tammy. We're just here for the burgers."

Tammy grinned. "Can't blame a girl for dreaming. Come on." She led them back to a booth in the back. "Saw you on that show, Caitlyn," she said as she handed over the menus.

Oh Lord, not another one. "Oh yeah?"

"Tell me, is that Daniel really as hot in person as he is on TV?"

"Hotter."

Will shot her a look, but the truth was the truth. Daniel's looks had certainly not been a problem.

Tammy sighed and fanned herself. "Be still my heart. You kids enjoy."

Will waited until Tammy had disappeared back to the hostess stand before turning his gaze to Caitlyn. "So is that why you went on the show? Because that guy is *so hot*?"

He hadn't bothered to look at his menu and Caitlyn slid hers aside without opening it as well. She knew it by heart anyway. "We didn't know who the next Mister Perfect would be when we auditioned. They don't reveal that until the show has already begun taping. Not since a few years ago when they had a PR issue and had to change guys at the last minute."

"PR issue?"

"The astronaut they picked was a little more of a thrill seeker than they reckoned for. He got caught trying to take his Speedster over two hundred on a public highway. So they switched to the Dreamy Doc, Jack Something-or-Other."

"Let me guess, you watch religiously and you were heartbroken when the astronaut was bumped which is why you call him Doctor Something-or-Other."

"Actually, I just don't remember his name," she said sharply. "I'd only seen one season of the show before I went on it—and I only watched that one to prepare. But the other Suitorettes liked to gossip and I got most of the details from them."

"Suitorettes? Seriously? That's what they call you?"

Caitlyn reached for the coat she'd dropped on the seat beside her. "Look, I'll pay for your burger, but if you're going to be a jerk all night, I think I'll take mine to go."

His expression was arrested for a moment, then the chill slowly thawed, melting into a grimace. "Sorry. I'll behave. I just can't imagine what would make someone want to make a spectacle of themselves like that."

"You could just ask me."

The waitress appeared then to take their order and flirt shamelessly with Will—even though she was happily married with two kids who took piano from Caitlyn. Caitlyn ordered the Lodge Burger and a Coke, for here, giving Will the benefit of the doubt. Will asked for the same—though his came with a wink and an extra sashay from Melissa as she headed off to put in their order and collect their drinks.

"You're awfully popular," Caitlyn said, more amused than jealous, especially when Will blushed.

"Pity flirtation. All the ladies here really stepped up their game after my break up last summer."

She eyed his muscular shoulders, stretching the seams of his soft grey Henley. "Somehow I doubt pity is the main reason most women flirt with you."

"You don't exactly look like the sort of girl who is lacking for masculine company either. So why did you do it?"

"Do what?" He wasn't asking her why she'd flirted with him, was he?

"You said I could just ask. So I'm asking. Why did you go on the show?"

Right. The show. Now it was Caitlyn who blushed, but there was no sense evading the question. He could just watch the show to learn the truth. "Honestly? I wanted the happily ever after."

His eyebrows arched, a reaction she was coming to expect whenever he was skeptical. "Hey, I get that. I want a family too, but there are easier ways to get it."

"Oh really?" she challenged. "When you're a hot male ski instructor who meets a dozen sexy little ski nymphs every day, maybe. But some of us are homebody piano teachers in a town with exactly five single men and every guy we spend time with is either married to a friend or the married father of a student."

"Ski nymphs?"

She ignored the interjection, and the wry—*sexy*—twist of his lips, plunging on. "So yeah, maybe it was desperate and stupid to go on the show. But when you want something, sometimes you have to be stupid."

Though maybe agreeing to marry a man you barely know is taking that stupidity a bit far.

Caitlyn pushed on, ignoring the little voice in her head. "I love my life, but I was starting to hate my empty apartment. I had to do something. Even if it was ridiculous and even if I fell flat on my face. I had to take a chance on love."

Will blinked, his face—which had been clinging to an unusual hardness all night—finally softening that last notch. "I'm sorry," he murmured. "I get the empty apartment thing. I think you're a lot braver than I am, and I should have given you credit for that. Pax?"

She nodded, as Melissa returned with their drinks. "Pax."

CHAPTER EIGHTEEN

The tension, that awful stilted tension, evaporated then, and soon Caitlyn found herself grinning, leaning forward over the table, laughing and telling him things she'd never have dreamed she'd blurt out on a first non-date.

He was a great listener—when he wasn't silently judging her, so thank God that had stopped—and everything she'd told Daniel on the show was public record anyway. For the first time, being exposed like that felt sort of freeing. Like the normal restrictions she placed on herself had been lifted.

By the time their burgers arrived, Caitlyn was sharing stories about the show, her musical career, even her deeply dysfunctional childhood—and Will seemed genuinely interested.

"Are you glad you did it?" he asked, sinking his teeth into his own burger as she shook ketchup onto the corner of her plate.

"The show?" She stalled for time by swiping a fry through the ketchup and popping it into her mouth, chewing slowly. Was she glad? She *was* glad. Before. For those few little slivers of time in there when everything had been perfect and she'd thought her happy ending was assured. But looking back she was starting to realize that by the time the exotic two day dates had rolled around, she'd begun to have doubts. Now she wasn't so sure. And without that certainty... "I don't know. Ask me in a few weeks."

"Mysterious," he murmured.

She hummed around a bite of burger and for a moment they fell silent, eating. This time the silence was comfortable, but she didn't let it stretch too long.

"I learned a little something about your history too," she admitted.

"Oh?"

"My friend Mimi wanted to set me up with you as soon as I got back. She said you were engaged last summer before I auditioned to be on the show, but you aren't any more?"

"Jilted." Will set down his burger, reaching for his soda. "Not quite at the altar, but close enough that we had to return a lot of gifts."

"Ouch. Sorry. I guess I just assumed it was you who..." She couldn't imagine a woman deciding she didn't want to wake up next to Will Hamilton every morning.

"You though I was the dumper, not the dumpee." His face moved the right muscles for a smile, but it didn't look right. There was too much suppressed emotion beneath it. So much pent up inside. "I guess it was naïve of me to think if you promise to spend the rest of your life with someone, then you're expected to keep that promise."

Wow. He really was not over that. Not that she had any right to tell him when he should have emotionally processed something, but *wow*.

And here she was, the girl who had impetuously agreed to marry a man she barely knew and now was wavering on whether or not she could keep that promise.

He splashed ketchup over his fries. "I guess you understand about people like that, don't you? The vowbreakers."

"I do?" She swallowed past a knot of guilt. Was she breaking a vow to Daniel?

"Sorry, I shouldn't have... I just thought, from what you said about your mom—"

"Oh! Oh, yeah, there wasn't a vow she didn't break. To my dad or to me. I guess I just hadn't thought of it that way."

Was it the same? She certainly hadn't had a Brady Bunch upbringing, but she'd fantasized about one and Daniel had seemed like her hope to get it. If she broke her word to him, was she just like her mom? Lying and not caring whose feeling got stepped on as long as she got what she wanted?

Her mother had been the last person Caitlyn had wanted to grow up into, so she'd run as far from her mother and all her mother wanted as possible. Tuller Springs had been a far cry from the Upper West Side, and about as close to paradise as she could have imagined. The only thing that could have made it perfect was a partner to share it with.

Daniel. Except he didn't seem to want the Tuller Springs life. But relationships were about compromise, weren't they? They would find a way to build a life that was the culmination of both their dreams.

Will's face was set again. Stiff. His eyes shadowed. Caitlyn regretted bringing up his ex, but she had a feeling if she apologized that would only make things worse.

She dragged a French fry through her ketchup. "What made you want to teach skiing?"

The darkness in his expression eased. "What made you want to teach piano?"

"I wanted to stop performing and it was pretty much my only marketable skill."

He blinked, seeming startled by her honesty and she shot him an arch *I showed you mine* look. He half-grinned. "Would you believe skiing is my only marketable skill?"

"This from the man who also fights fires and repairs houses and… I'm sorry, how many other jobs do you have? I can't keep up."

His grin spread until it started to look genuine. "Okay, fine. You want the real story? I warn you, it's pretty boring."

"Bore me," she dared him.

"I was a slacker in college, skipping classes to hit the slopes whenever the powder was fresh. I graduated— barely—with a degree in sociology and zero marketable skills. I came back home for a few months to get my shit together, crashed at my parents' house and picked up a job as a chair lift operator so I could ski for free. The resort wanted all their instructors to have basic first aid training and the best paid guys on the mountain were on ski patrol, so when they offered to promote anyone who took the EMT training, I signed up. After that it was only an extra couple classes to get the certification I needed to volunteer at the fire department and once I had that training I was more valuable as a river guide—since I could revive any idiot who fell into the river and drowned. I never really thought about a career or picked a path, I just fell into what I was good at and patched it together. Then suddenly I'm twenty-eight, still working on the mountain, and I realize I've got a pretty sweet deal going. My 401-K is for shit, so of course my sisters nag me about doing something real with my life, but to make more money doing what I'm doing now, I'd have to leave Tuller Springs, and I don't want that. So I keep on doing what I'm doing."

"Wow. I can't imagine not having a plan. I feel like every day of my life has been scheduled since birth—either by me or someone else. And here you are, playing it by ear and patching it together."

"Don't act too impressed. I'm just a ski bum who's never played Carnegie Hall."

"There's more to life than Carnegie Hall." Something it had taken her far too long to figure out.

The weather had shifted while they were in the pub. The wind was biting and the footing more treacherous as they made their way back to the row of chalets that included their building. Caitlyn hooked her arm through his for balance and Will kept her tucked tight to his side, as much for the feel of her as to use his bulk to buffer her from the wind. The top of her white knit cap came just above his shoulder and he could feel the soft warmth of her pressed against his arm as she leaned in.

The night hadn't gone at all how he'd thought it would on Friday when she'd asked him to dinner. Nor how he'd envisioned after his shock last night after realizing she was a reality TV diva.

But she wasn't a diva and after he'd gotten over his prejudices, he realized a lot of things made a lot more sense.

"The show explains the hot and cold routine."

She looked up at him, cheeks rosy and eyes bright from the chill. "Hot and cold?"

"Mixed signals," he clarified. "One second I think you might be into me a little and then…"

"Oh." He had a feeling the rosy cheeks weren't just from the cold as her gaze skittered away from his. "That might have just been me being completely inept at social cues. I don't think I would know how to send a clear signal if I tried."

"So if I kissed you right now…"

Her head jerked up so fast she would have clocked him if he'd been leaning in to try to get some sugar. "I couldn't! I really can't date." Her face was definitely flaming now. "The show. It's against the rules."

"Did you really buy into the show?" he heard himself asking. "Were you really into that guy?"

Her gaze skittered away again. "It's easy to get caught up in it," she murmured. "Last night, the date I won, it was heavenly. One of the most romantic experiences of my life."

"But is it really romantic if it's all fabricated? I feel like real romance is about an honest connection and I don't know how anything can be honest when the trappings are so obviously fake."

"The settings are carefully controlled by the producers, but the people involved are real. The emotions are real. Amplified, maybe, because of the circumstances, but real. When Daniel kissed me last night, I really did think he could be the one. That it might be the last first kiss I ever had."

Will found himself staring at Caitlyn's lips. A little pang struck him at the idea of another guy kissing those lips and he knew he was in trouble. Maybe it was the fact that he couldn't kiss her, but he suddenly wanted to more than anything in the world. He wanted to prove to her that she hadn't had her last first kiss yet, because she hadn't had *his*.

He didn't realize he was leaning toward her until she

pulled away.

"I can't," she said again, disentangling her arm from his. They were at the entrance to the chalet now. As soon as they were inside, she would head upstairs and he would stay down and their Just Friends date would be over. "I do like you, Will," she said softly. "But there isn't room in my life right now for anything more than a friend. Even if I wanted more, it's just… complicated."

There was a hitch in her voice, a hesitation that spoke of something she wasn't saying.

He'd been there for too long to hold it against her. He slid his key into the lock and opened the door, holding it for her.

Caitlyn slid past him. She paused on the first step, the shadows of the foyer obscuring her face. "Friends?"

"Absolutely."

A flash of teeth in the dark, a little spark of a smile, and then she turned away, climbing the stairs.

"Thank you for dinner, Caitlyn," he called up after her, leaning a shoulder against the door to his apartment.

She paused with her key in the lock. "Thank you for everything, Will."

Then she was gone.

He watched the door close behind her like a lovesick idiot before unlocking his own. He stripped out of his jacket, replaying the evening in his mind. He wanted more than friends, and now that he could read the code of her hot and cold, he was pretty sure she wanted the same. She'd never said no. She'd only said she couldn't *now*. He could be patient. He could be her friend. He could woo her slowly and when her obligation to the show was over, he'd be there with open arms as soon as she was free.

He hadn't realized how closed off he'd been until something happened to make him want to throw himself open again.

Or someone happened.

Above him, the sounds of the piano crept through the ceiling. The tune wasn't one he recognized. Dreamy and romantic, the song wove around him like a magic spell, dripping with sweet, soulful longing.

He'd made her feel that.

Unless it was the other guy. The famous one.

Will kicked aside the thought. He refused to make himself crazy. If she was still pining for the other guy, he'd be able to tell, wouldn't he? But that wasn't what he saw when he looked in her eyes. He saw hesitant hope and the promise for a future. He would just have to hang onto that look until she was free to say the words.

CHAPTER NINETEEN

"Quick, turn on TMZ!" Mimi yelped as soon as Caitlyn answered the phone.

Caitlyn's stomach bottomed out. It had been a blissfully quiet three days since the second episode aired. She'd almost felt normal. *What now?* "Oh God, is it Daniel?"

"Hurry, Caitlyn!" Mimi squealed.

Caitlyn obediently flipped on the television. "What channel?"

"Four. You're missing it!"

She turned to channel four and her breath whooshed out when she saw the image there. "Oh my God."

"It's us!" Mimi squealed delightedly.

It was indeed them. In the still photo that dominated the screen, she and Mimi were walking down the main street of Tuller Springs, carrying shopping bags and to go cups from the Java Hut. Mimi's hair was still red and green. Christmas shopping, she realized distantly as the rest of her brain jabbered hysterically. The photo had been taken weeks ago. And she'd had no idea. Someone had stood on the far side of the street, or sat in a car, and shot pictures of her while she was completely oblivious.

The picture vanished and another story popped up to take its place.

"What were they saying?" She hadn't been able to

process any of the words, too busy taking in the horror of her first paparazzi experience. She'd never been that kind of famous when she was a musician.

"They found out about the fire. They were joking about turning pyro because you were forced to date Daniel and stuff. Usual TMZ snark."

"But that photo had nothing to do with the fire."

"I know, but it was *us*," Mimi squeaked. "I was on TMZ! Admittedly, it was as 'and friend', but who's complaining? Oh! Do you think it's on the website too?"

"Oh God."

"Caitlyn? You okay?"

"I didn't even know he was there. He was taking pictures of us and I had no clue." He could have walked up to her and asked and she would have smiled and given him his shot. She'd had media training. She knew what to do. Mimi would have loved it. But no. He had to take it from across the street like a freaking peeping Tom. "Did you know we were being photographed?"

"Well, no. But that's the price for fame, eh?"

"I never wanted to be famous. I didn't think reality TV people were really that big a deal—I mean yes, people know who the Kardashians are, but who cares who the third runner up on last year's *Survivor* was?"

"Honey," Mimi said, her shrill enthusiasm somewhat tamed, "in a year no one will remember who was on this year's *Marrying Mister Perfect*, but this is your fifteen minutes. Try to enjoy it. Or at least accept it."

"You sound like…" *Daniel.* She almost said it aloud.

Everyone was telling her to suck it up and accept the attention—even if she couldn't quite embrace it. Maybe she should start listening. A shot on TMZ wasn't going to hurt her—not that kind of shot anyway. Was she overreacting? To all of it?

She'd had this idea, ever since the finale of the show, that Daniel was more concerned with his fame as Mister Perfect than he was with actually settling down with her, but had she been blowing things out of proportion? Had she heard him accepting and embracing the fifteen minutes of fame that came with the territory and just assumed he'd gone over to the dark side? She had fought so hard to get out of the limelight, was she hypersensitive to any signs that she might be pulled back in?

"Mimi, I have to go. Thanks for letting me know."

She hung up and immediately fished out the MMP phone, punching Daniel's number. He answered on the second ring.

"Sweetheart!"

"Hey. How's Los Angeles?"

"Loud. And lonely. I miss you."

"I miss you too." As she said the words, she realized she did miss him, in a way. She missed the way she used to feel connected to him. If she could only get that back. "I just got my first taste of what you've been going through."

"Oh?"

"I'm on TMZ."

He chuckled. "I know. I got a Google Alert about it."

"You have a Google Alert for me?"

"For myself. They mentioned both of our names in the article."

"Does it bother you?" she asked. "People following you around, taking your picture when you don't know they're there?"

"Goes with the territory. They're following you to try to get spoilers for the show and all they got was a shot of you shopping. As TMZ photos go, it's incredibly tame. They must not have had anything from the actual fire."

Caitlyn winced as she thought of what they might have seen. Her thrown over Will's shoulder or running through the snow wearing a freaking twenty foot wedding veil. Thank God no paparazzo had been on duty that night.

"It's not a very juicy story," Daniel mused. "Won't even last a news cycle. They're only running it because you're popular after this week's episode. Now, if they had a better image to go with it…"

Irritation flickered. "You almost sound like you wish it were a juicier picture."

"It's good publicity for the show, which is good for us."

Caitlyn went very still. How many people had known about the fire? How many who would tip off TMZ? "Daniel," she said very slowly, "did you tell them about the fire?"

"Sweetheart, relax. It's just a little article. You need to get used to this. The scrutiny is only going to get more intense over the next few weeks."

"You didn't answer my question."

"Does it matter?"

Mozart's Ghost. He'd really done it. Her fiancé had ratted her out to TMZ. Arranged for her to be mocked on national television.

She hung up the phone. No goodbye. No waiting for more explanations. No straining to hear through the lies.

She didn't think she'd ever hung up on someone before. It was rude. Terribly rude. But she couldn't bring herself to care. A few minutes later the MMP phone rang again. Miranda this time. But Caitlyn ignored it. She didn't want to talk. Didn't want to think.

Stalking to the piano, she went straight for Wagner.

Some days just called for pounding, thunderous

music. Shutting off her brain, she let the music roar.

Will's first hint that something was wrong was the Wagner making his ceiling fan vibrate. His second hint came five minutes later when Claire called to tell him Caitlyn was on TMZ.

Thirty minutes later, he knocked on her door, pounding hard to be heard over the frenzy of Rachmaninov. The music didn't even pause. He pounded again. This time the silence was instant and jarring.

She swung open the door, fast and sharp, cheeks flushed, poised for a fight.

Will lifted the box of brownie bites he'd sprinted to the store to pick up like a shield. "I come bearing chocolate." He jiggled the other grocery bag. "And ice cream. And whipped cream and everything else I could think of that would drive any sane person into a sugar coma." He jerked his chin toward the DVD case tucked under his arm. "And Bond, James Bond."

She frowned. "What's all that for?"

"My sisters are firm believers in chocolate therapy. And Sean Connery." When she still stared at him blankly, he shrugged. "Claire saw you on TMZ. I figured you might need some moral support. We're friends right?"

She tipped her head to the side, still blocking him in the doorway. "You don't think I should be happy about the exposure?"

"Happy about a creepy dude following you around with a telephoto lens? I'd be worried about you if you were."

She swung the door wider. "You can come in. Bring

the brownies."

"I know you can't tell me whether or not you're engaged to Mister Famous—"

"Mister Perfect, if you please."

Will snorted. "Whatever. But I figure if I deduce the truth on my own, no one can blame you."

"A brilliant plan." Caitlyn lay sprawled on the couch, Will beside her on a mound of pillows on the floor. They'd given up on passing the brownie bites back and forth between them, Will simply chucking them up at her regularly as they sporadically watched Sean Connery battle Dr. No, since they'd already established that they'd both seen the movie enough times to quote it from memory. "And how do you plan to deduce this truth?"

"Elementary, my dear Caitlyn. *Who* is Mister Famous—"

"Daniel," she supplied pertly.

"Very well. Who is *Daniel's* favorite Bond? No woman would agree to marry a man without knowing whether he prefers Connery or Craig."

"There might be a slight flaw in your logic."

"Nonsense. My logic is unassailable." A brownie bite sailed toward her face.

She caught it, snickering, and muffled her laughter with the chocolatey goodness. They had already discussed the relative merits of the various Brits, agreeing that Connery—Will's favorite—was undeniably the most suave, but Craig's muscle-bound shoulders won Caitlyn's vote.

The TMZ photo was almost forgotten. Almost. One little picture, a tiny little story... it was amazing how much her frustration over it had lessened as soon as Will agreed that she had a right to feel violated rather than delighted by being stalked by paparazzi.

Of course, the chocolate hadn't hurt.

Another brownie bite arched toward her and she lurched up to catch it in her mouth, laughing when it bounced off her nose and rolled onto her stomach. "Your aim is improving."

"I've stopped aiming. I'm just randomly chucking them at you now."

"I thought athletes were supposed to have good hand eye coordination?"

"Are you questioning whether I'm good with my hands?" The words were dark, sinful, sending warmth shooting straight down to her erogenous zones.

Oh my. "Will. Behave."

He muttered something that sounded like, "This *is* me behaving," but she couldn't quite hear him over the villain speech coming from the television.

The thought that he might want to misbehave with her made warmth spread liquid-smooth through her limbs. She'd never just hung out and watched movies with someone she had a crush on before. Was this a normal pre-dating step? Her only relationships before Daniel had been with other musicians—some of whom were just looking to score with the big name, some of whom seemed to genuinely like her but never seemed to know how to look beyond her music and see that there was more, and then there had been Tai—a brilliant cellist she'd had a crush on for years and then when they'd met he'd just sort of taken her adoration as his due for as long as she wanted to give it to him, barely seeming to notice when she left.

No, she was hardly a dating expert. Especially out in

the real world.

She rolled onto her side, peering down over the lip of the couch at him. "Have you had a lot of girlfriends?"

His gaze slid off the screen and up to her. This was probably how he looked in bed—dark hair rumpled from the pillow beneath it, dark eyes gleaming with a sensual, slumberous light. "What's a lot?"

"I don't know. What's a normal number?"

"What's *normal*?" he countered. "Everyone's love life is a special snowflake in its own right."

She frowned at his evasions. Exactly how high was his number that he wouldn't tell her? "Do *you* think you've had a lot of girlfriends?"

"I've had exactly one less than the perfect number." His dark eyes met hers.

"Oh." Okay. Good answer. Her heart thudded so hard she fancied she could feel it in her fingertips.

She scrambled for a safe topic of conversation. Like mushrooms. Or the Amish. Anything. But Will spoke before she could change the subject, his eyes heavy-lidded and intent. "You told me about your last first kiss… when was your first one?"

It wasn't exactly safe, but it was safer than talking about who she wanted her *next* kiss to be.

"I was seventeen," she admitted, blushing. "My mother thought dating was a distraction, but when I was playing in Paris there was this Czech violinist only a couple years older than me. Very dashing. We barely spoke ten words of the same language, but it was Paris and I was desperate for romance so I let him kiss me at the top of the Eiffel Tower. I wanted so badly for it to be magical, but it was just sort of… wetter than I expected."

Will groaned sympathetically.

"And you?" she asked. "When did you get your first

kiss?"

"I was twelve. Middle school dance. Doing the classic slow dance sway." He pantomimed rocking back and forth. "My sisters had coached me since I was about eight on what girls wanted and when I hit middle school I started listening. I'm pretty sure *Lady in Red* was playing and I'm almost positive it was wetter than she expected. I had no freaking idea what to do with any of my body parts. But I felt like the man and she was my girlfriend for two whole weeks after that—complete with hand-holding in the hallways. Until my friends convinced me I was whipped and needed to dump her. And then one of those same friends swooped in and consoled her and *they* started dating. Massive betrayal. My seventh grade heart was shattered. Though, come to think of it, I think those two are married right now so on a karmic level I call that a win."

Caitlyn pressed a hand over her mouth to stifle her laughter. She felt so light when she was with him. Like she might float away. Had Daniel ever made her feel like that? Would she ever be able to stop comparing them?

"Hey. What happened?" Will asked, propping himself up on an elbow. "You got serious all of a sudden."

She couldn't tell him she was wishing she'd met him before the man she'd agreed to marry. God, *marriage.* What had she been thinking?

"It's nothing. Just the TMZ stuff again."

"Want me to distract you?"

"Yes, plea—" The word broke into a yelp as he moved, startlingly fast, catching her ankle where it dangled over the edge of the couch and giving it a measured tug. Firm enough to send her sliding off the lip of the couch.

Landing right on top of him.

"*Will.*" His name was meant to be a scold, but came out more of a breathy gasp. All that muscle. All that hard, contained strength spread out beneath her. God, he felt *incredible*. The sound of her own thoughts was being drowned out by her hormones screaming the Ode to Joy.

"Distracted?" he rumbled sexily, his chest vibrating where it pressed against hers.

"From what?"

His smile was dark and deliciously promising.

She was in so much trouble.

CHAPTER TWENTY

She blinked down at him from a distance of inches, those big blue eyes consuming his focus. She was lighter than he remembered as she lay stretched out on top of him, her strong, slim arms trapped between them and her long, slender fingers flexing on his pectorals as if she wasn't quite sure what to do with them—or maybe she was just enjoying the feel. She certainly wasn't fighting to get away.

If anything, she was leaning into him. All big dazed eyes and lush inviting lips.

"We aren't in public," he murmured. He knew she couldn't publicly date, but it was just the two of them tonight. No one had to know. Was it really anyone else's business but their own?

She said his name again, but this time instead of a breathy invitation, it was a low reprimand.

"I'm sorry," she whispered, and pushed away, nearly giving him an appendectomy with her elbow as she awkwardly disentangled herself.

He put a hand on her hip to help and she released another breathy little whisper of a gasp. He let her go and she scrambled back on the couch, all but vibrating with tension, and he realized he wasn't going to get that lazy, easy companionship back. At least not tonight.

The credits were rolling on Sean Connery anyway.

"I should go. I've got five kindergartners at eight thirty tomorrow morning. They'll run roughshod over me if I don't get some sleep."

"Right, of course," Caitlyn said, still not meeting his eyes as he came to his feet.

"Play me a lullaby?"

That got her attention. "What?"

"I love listening to you play. I only brought you brownies to butter you up so you'd take requests."

A flicker of a smile teased her lips. "I knew you had ulterior motives."

"It's all about the *Pathetique*."

"The *Pathetique*?"

"The Beethoven sonata?" He hummed a few bars.

"No. I know which one it is. I play it all the time."

"I know. It's my favorite. Play it for me?" She hesitated and he shrugged off the request, not wanting to push her tonight. "Some other time. G'night, Caitlyn."

"G'night, Will."

"Do you have any idea how many times in the last week I've almost kissed Will?"

Mimi squealed with unabashed delight. Caitlyn had only waited until she heard Will's door shut downstairs before diving for the phone, needing a dose of sanity. Though maybe she should have called someone else. Mimi didn't sound terribly sane.

"Why haven't you? Go for it, girl!"

"I can't go for it. I can't have relationships, remember? Reality television? Bajillion dollar lawsuits?"

And that didn't even touch on the fact of Daniel. Her fiancé. She was *engaged*. Even if she didn't feel engaged. Even if she was starting to wonder if she even liked

Daniel, *he* didn't know that and he deserved her fidelity for as long as they were together. Even if they couldn't physically be together.

God, what a mess.

"So have a stealth relationship," Mimi encouraged. "No one has to know."

"Yes," Caitlyn said dryly. "Because I'm so good at secrets and deception. That sounds like a *brilliant* idea."

"I'm detecting a note of sarcasm."

"Well spotted," she said, mimicking a British conductor she and Mimi had played for.

"Fine, don't be secret lovers—though *come on*, how often do you have a chance to enjoy the delicious hidden lover scenario without actually betraying anyone?"

But I would be betraying someone. Caitlyn sank down on the piano bench, thunking her forehead down on the key-cover.

"If you can't enjoy him now, think of it as foreplay," Mimi said. "All that sexual tension, building up, oooh, mama. By the time you can actually jump him, the two of you will be so primed you'll go off like rockets."

She was already primed.

Caitlyn groaned. "I need to stop this. Right now. I'm leading him on."

And the hell of it was, she wasn't even sure whether she was referring to Daniel or Will when she said that.

"He's a big boy. He understands the situation. It's not leading him on if it's his call to stick around. And, Caitlyn, I know you have relationship issues the size of the Titanic, but, baby, you are *worth the wait*. So even if you can't ride him like a naughty cowgirl just yet, don't sabotage things by shoving him away. You wanted the guy, the family, and the picture perfect home life, right? And it's my job as your friend to smack some sense into you when you try to screw up your chance at that. Hang onto Will. He's a good egg. He'll wait until the show is done."

Yes, but will he understand when he watches me accept another man's proposal?

"I've gotta go, Mimi."

"Don't be stupid!" Mimi said in lieu of goodbye.

Caitlyn turned off the phone and set it on top of the piano, sliding back the key cover. She let her fingers roam, too confused to even try to figure out what piece would suit her mood. She tried not to read anything into it when she realized her hands had just naturally begun to move through the opening chords of the *Pathetique*. Just one of the mysteries of the universe.

The flowers arrived on Monday morning. Two dozen gigantic ruby red roses. The sender was listed as Miranda, but the card was all gushing apology. Daniel.

Caitlyn put them in water and hid them up out of sight in the loft, where they would raise fewer questions from her students. She always shut the ringers off her phones while she taught, and by the end of the day's lessons, she had over a dozen missed calls on the MMP phone. Only two from Daniel. The rest from a number she didn't recognize. Four new voicemail messages. She was about to listen to them when the phone lit up—still on silent mode, but alerting her to a new call.

Miranda.

"Hey, boss lady."

Miranda didn't bother with a greeting. "I hear you've been dodging the wedding planner's calls all day."

"I've been teaching all day. And you told me not to take calls on this phone from anyone other than you and

Daniel."

"Oh. Right. My mistake. I gave the wedding planner your number. Please take her calls so she stops harassing me about cake flavors. I don't even like cake."

"I thought everyone liked cake."

Miranda ignored the comment. "You're okay? Everything's good?"

I'm thinking of calling off the wedding, which would alleviate the questions about cake. "I got the roses."

She could almost hear Miranda's frown. "Someone sent you roses?"

"I thought you knew. The sender used your office address."

Miranda groaned. "Please tell me Daniel didn't send you roses from my address. That idiot. I'm going to have to kick the shit out of him."

"I take it these were not sanctioned roses."

"Of course not. Now I'm going to have to send diversion roses to several of the other girls just so it doesn't look suspicious. That dumbass. Tell him to stop trying to be so disgustingly romantic. That's my job."

Caitlyn snorted. "He was begging forgiveness, actually."

"A little early for that, isn't it? The episode doesn't air until tomorrow night."

Caitlyn snapped to attention. "What's on tomorrow's episode?"

"Oh." Miranda groaned. "I am really off my game today. Look, sweetie, just remember what I said. It's never as bad as it looks."

"What does it look like?"

"Flirtation, mostly. He was a little bit of a kissing slut, but that's part of the show and you knew that going in."

"Oh." She tried to feel jealous, but mostly just felt tired. So her fiancé was going to make out with the world tomorrow. How delightful.

"What was he apologizing for?"

"He leaked the fire story to TMZ."

Miranda cursed. "I really am going to have to kick his ass."

"I thought you'd appreciate the publicity."

"We have a team of people who very carefully handle releasing stories like that. Daniel knows better than to run around leaking material to any old gossip rag. Or at least he should. His job is to be perfect. Our job is to control his image and the image of the show and all the girls on it. Including you. Don't talk to the press without talking to me first, Caitlyn."

"I wasn't planning on it."

"Good girl. I'll tear Daniel a new one. You just keep on being lovely. And maybe consider not watching tomorrow night."

"I'll take it under advisement."

Miranda stared down at her phone after she hung up with Caitlyn, wondering when, exactly, she'd become so shitty at her job. Mister Perfect was leaking stories. His fiancé sounded like she was inches away from calling off the wedding. The wedding planner was driving Miranda up the wall with constant questions about how strict the budget for the Wedding of the Year really was. And she couldn't seem to focus.

And it was only week three.

Tomorrow's episode would be explosive. It was supposed to be. They were still in the scandalous and scintillating part of the show when cat fights and teary breakdowns kept the audience's attention while America slowly but surely fell in love with the favorites. The romantic portion of the show came later. The first few weeks were all cheap entertainment.

She usually loved this part. Miranda was an expert at giving the crazy girls their fifteen minutes of fame while showing the sweet and lovely sides of the girls who would make it to the end.

The problem was Daniel. If she wasn't careful the audience was going to start rooting against him, and as soon as they did, Miranda had a feeling Caitlyn would too.

So much for happy endings.

"Miranda, Bennett Lang for you."

"Take a message," she snapped.

"Um..." Todd, usually so self-assured, hesitated over the intercom. "He's *here*."

Her heart rate tripled from one beat to the next.

Shit. If he was there, he'd just heard her crack assistant tell her he was there. Which mean she couldn't hide underneath her desk and pretend she was out.

Maybe he's here to apologize.

"And demons are ice-skating in Hell," she muttered to herself. Then depressed the intercom. "Send him in."

She stood, smoothing her pencil skirt, wishing stupidly that she'd worn a pant suit, as if that would somehow be better armor against him. She didn't want to look feminine. Not when he made her feel so damn girly.

The great Bennett Lang walked into the room like he owned it, but then when you'd been King of Reality Television for as long as he had, you pretty much entered every room that way. Tall, handsome, and lean—with the body of a marathon runner, which he was. His full head of dark hair was showing more and more silver these days, but it worked for him. He looked like he could have been a newscaster, with that same sort of distinguished gravitas.

She'd been awed by him from the second she met him, back when she was green and eager.

Now she just wanted to kick him. Preferably in the balls.

"Miranda, you're looking well."

She glowered at him as the door clicked shut behind him. "Really? That's what you're going to open with? Pleasantries? Then by all means." She waved him to the chair opposite her desk and sank back into her own. "You look to be in good health also. Did you run a satisfactory time in the New York Marathon?"

He frowned, seating himself in the chair she'd indicated and adjusting his cuffs, carefully ignoring her sarcasm. "You won't take my calls."

"You won't leave a message."

"Still angry, I see."

"Still patronizing, I see."

"Miranda."

She fisted her hands in her lap, where he couldn't see them. "Don't scold me, Bennett. You don't get to come to my office and scold me."

He cursed under his breath. "This isn't how I envisioned this meeting."

"Funny, this is pretty much exactly how I figured it would go down."

She'd been head over heels for him, declared her freaking *love* for him and he was still trying to mold her into what he wanted her to be—like he was still her mentor rather than her lover. That wasn't what she wanted from him. Not anymore. But wanting him to actually engage his heart was an unwinnable war. There was probably a picture of thrice-divorced Bennett Lang next to "Emotionally Unavailable" in the dictionary.

"This is ridiculous." Bennett stood abruptly, rounding her desk.

"What are you doing?" She ignored the way her heart leapt as she jumped to her feet and retreated—hating to give up ground, but needing the distance.

"I miss you." He continued to stalk her.

"Deal with it." She continued to retreat.

"I'm trying to."

"Good. I know a good therapist if you—"

"I have a job for you."

Her feet stopped moving as all of her lust coalesced into anger. God damn it. This again. The man *could not learn*. "I *have* a job, dickhead."

"A better job."

"Screw you."

He was close enough for her to snarl the words in his face. Then he was closer still, his hands hard, gripping the back of her skull, the small of her back, hauling her forward, holding her in place, his mouth slamming down on hers with unmistakable possession and a need that had been denied too long.

She bit him.

He jerked back, lifting one hand to his bleeding lower lip, even as his other stayed tight around her waist. "*Fuck*, Miranda."

"No, thank you," she said sweetly, twisting out of his grip. "That ride is closed."

He raked a hand through his silvering hair, his usual debonair calm deteriorating as she strode back to her desk. "At least tell me what I did."

"What you *did*?" She drew up short, tempted to

throw everything not nailed to her desk at him—which was everything on her desk. She'd start with the sharp things. "What do you think you did? I adored you." She would *not* say the L word again. "And you seemed to feel the same way, though God forbid you actually *say* how you feel, and for about two seconds I actually convinced myself that you saw me as an equal, but then you made it very clear what you really thought of me. What was it you called me? A parasite?"

"You knew what I meant," he growled. "The kind of television you produce—"

"You aren't my mentor anymore. And you sure as hell aren't my father. You don't get to tell me what to do."

His face pulled into a grimace of distaste. "I never wanted to be your daddy."

"You could have fooled me," she snapped. "You miss me? Fine. I miss you too, but I'm not going to be your pet or your adoring disciple. I'm not wired that way. I'll be your equal and a woman you respect or I won't be in your life at all. Now get out. I have a job to do. A job I am fucking good at."

"Miranda. I'm serious about the job—"

"I'll call security if you make me. Then maybe I'll call TMZ. What do you think of the headline *American Dance Star's Executive Producer Bodily Ejected from Marrying Mister Perfect Offices*? Catchy enough?"

"Fine," he growled. "I'm leaving. Call me when you come to your senses."

When Hell freezes solid, buddy.

Bennett left Miranda's office swearing a blue streak, for once not caring if he looked unprofessional as he stalked past her stunned assistant and the rest of her staff.

She was his equal. She was better than he deserved. But she was also too good for the work she insisted on doing. Pandering to the lowest common denominator of entertainment. It was cheap and degrading and she was capable of so much more. Why couldn't she see that he just wanted the best for her?

He slammed the already-illuminated button to the elevator, all but growling to himself. An intern had been there before him and now scuttled frantically toward the stairs. Fine. He wasn't fit for company right now anyway.

Two months. Two hellish months she'd been holding this grudge.

He'd thought he would give her until the end of the shooting season to get over it. They were both frantically busy during the fall anyway. He'd forced himself not to contact her again until the first of the year, telling himself over and over again that she would have calmed down by then.

He should have known. Miranda was the only person he'd ever met who was more stubborn than he was. They were too damn similar.

And he'd never wanted anyone as badly as he wanted her.

"God*damn* it."

"Mr. Lang, sir?"

He whipped around, all but snarling until he saw it was Miranda's assistant. Had she changed her mind?

"You forgot your..." The assistant held up his laptop bag and Bennett barely stopped himself from growling.

"Thank you." He took the bag as the elevator dinged and then stepped inside.

She thought he didn't respect her. Hell, couldn't she see that it was *because* he respected her that he couldn't give ground on this? Shows like hers were destroying modern culture. Miranda could do *anything*. She could run a network someday if she wanted to, but what she wanted to do was exploit the emotional damage of talentless reality television *personalities*. He refused to call them stars.

And he refused to lose her over this.

It was an excuse to push him away because she was scared. She'd been pushing him away from day one, but she'd admitted that she missed him, as good as telling him she still cared.

Bennett Lang didn't give up. And he wasn't going to start with the love of his freaking life.

CHAPTER TWENTY-ONE

"Oh, Daniel. Oh... oh yes... oh Daniel."

The slurping and moaning sounds continued on the television as the cameras took on a soft focus to avoid FCC violations. Mimi and Caitlyn just stared.

"I... uh..." Mimi coughed. "Oh crap. Is that her top floating there?"

"Yes," Caitlyn gritted out.

"God, this is so uncomfortable," Mimi muttered, flicking a neon purple thatch of hair out of her eyes. "I feel like I'm watching private investigator peeping Tom footage of a guy cheating on his girlfriend."

You aren't far off the mark.

Another moan—this one definitely masculine—sounded from the slightly fuzzed out screen and Caitlyn's stomach turned.

"Did you know...?" Mimi choked off the question.

"That Daniel got to third base with Elena in the Jacuzzi on their second date? Not a clue." And the bastard really should have warned her. Miranda had warned her, sort of, but she still hadn't been prepared for *this*.

It had started as a group date—the girls jello wrestling on a beach in string bikinis with all of their assets bouncing around—and then Elena had been declared the winner through some very fishy scoring,

171

and received the very intimate personal time with Daniel that they were now watching.

The camera swung away from the moaning couple, zooming in and focusing tight on the hot pink postage stamp of a bikini floating amid the bubbles. The music amped up and there was a slow fade to black, followed by the cheerful strains of a diaper commercial.

Oddly fitting. Straight from procreation to the ultimate result.

Mimi groaned with relief. "Thank God. That was painful. You okay?"

"I'm…" Caitlyn scanned her emotions, trying to figure out what she felt about what she'd just seen. "Fine."

It wasn't even a lie.

There was a low simmer of anger in her blood, but it wasn't about the startling level of physicality he'd already achieved with Elena.

It was about what Daniel had said about *Caitlyn* during the one time she'd made an appearance on screen so far this episode. This had been the one week Caitlyn hadn't received a date, twiddling her thumbs at the Suitorette Mansion all week. She'd known that going into tonight's episode. She just hadn't known *why*.

The two solo dates had been given to Sidney, who'd come home unimpressed, but hadn't left for another week, and Amanda, who'd let a little too much of her crazy show, talking about how they were soulmates within five minutes of meeting, and earned herself a ticket home.

And then there'd been the jello wrestling.

Daniel hadn't wanted Caitlyn on the date because she was a *lady* and he didn't want her to *demean* herself. Of course he'd had no problem watching eight other girls demean the hell out of themselves for the shot at more time alone with him.

Caitlyn hadn't wanted to put on a bikini and tackle another slippery Suitorette, but as she'd listened to Daniel go on and on about how she was a precious treasure and he didn't want her to sully herself, she'd started thinking about the other dates he'd taken her on—and those she'd heard about from the other girls that he'd excluded her from.

He never asked her to do anything embarrassing or awkward, but he also never took her for anything fun or adventurous. Strolling hand-in-hand through a cute town square? Yes. Zip lining through the Costa Rican rainforest? Hell, no. Dressing up for an elegant picnic on a floating platform in a lagoon? You bet. Swimming with sharks? Never.

He'd all but admitted on national television that he thought she was made of porcelain. And maybe she wasn't as tough and strong as some of the other girls, but she wanted a chance to prove she could take a risk too.

It was like Daniel had built her a pedestal on week one and then just kept raising it higher and higher, never once asking her if she wanted to be up there, if she wanted to be treated like a treasure, or if maybe she wouldn't rather be seen as a woman—one who could get a little dirty and still be a lady.

Daniel would never throw brownie bites at her. He would only hand feed her caviar as they were sitting rigidly upright at a gorgeous antique table.

Coarse, sexual behavior was for Elena.

"Do you think he's attracted to me?"

Mimi's head snapped around, classic deer-in-headlights. "What?"

Sure, he kissed her over the weeks and it was lovely and romantic, but it was never *hot*. He never looked at her like he would die if he couldn't get into her pants that very instant. Even on the overnight date, right before the finale, Caitlyn had told him she wasn't ready to sleep with him and he'd instantly acquiesced, swearing that he wouldn't respect her so much if she had said anything else.

But she didn't know what had happened on his overnight with Elena. She had a feeling it hadn't been chaste, if the Jacuzzi was an indication.

The one night they'd spent together when Caitlyn had his ring on her finger they had finally gone the distance, but it had been... sort of anticlimactic.

He'd been so *respectful*. Not that sex couldn't be worshipful *and* satisfying, but there was nothing raw or hungry about it. She'd never had raw and hungry in her less-than-impressive history of sexual experiences and she wanted it. She wanted to be the woman who inspired it. She wanted a man who looked at her with barely suppressed heat.

The way Will looks at me.

"Caitlyn?" Mimi prompted, but luckily the show came back on at that moment, forestalling her explanation. Elena was arriving back at the Suitorette Mansion—*without* her bikini top underneath her sundress—and proceeding to gloat to every Suitorette who had stayed up waiting for her.

Caitlyn sighed, letting her attention drift away from the screen.

She remembered the tension of the next few days and weeks. All of the girls ganging up on Elena, calling her trashy and manipulative behind her back. And sometimes to her face. Whining to Daniel that she wasn't there for the right reasons. Throwing themselves at him to prove that Elena wasn't the only one with sexual wiles.

It hadn't been fun the first time and Caitlyn didn't particularly want to relive it. Thank God for the piano. If she hadn't been able to escape and play, she would have gone crazy listening to the cattiness in the house.

That cattiness was probably what Will had thought of when he'd learned she went on *Marrying Mister Perfect*. No wonder he'd reacted the way he had.

"Awww…" Mimi sighed and Caitlyn focused back in on the screen. It was the night of the Elimination Ceremony and two dozen red roses had been delivered to the Suitorette Mansion while they were all getting dressed. Roses for Caitlyn.

She'd forgotten about that. The roses. The card— *Thinking of you even when we're apart. Your Daniel.*

She'd melted at the time, smiling like she had a secret and pressing the card against her heart. It had seemed so romantic, so thoughtful.

Now she thought of the roses wilting where she'd hidden them up in the loft. Same old Daniel, using the same old playbook. *Screw up? Send flowers! Instant fix!*

Come to think of it, she seemed to remember him showering Marcy with roses during the previous season as well.

They watched the Elimination Ceremony and the preview for the following week, then Caitlyn subtly ushered Mimi out the door as quickly as possible. She wasn't surprised when Daniel didn't pick up the phone. He was a master at avoiding things he didn't want to face. The message she left was simple.

"Daniel. We need to talk."

Now to see how long it took him to man up and face

the music. The clock was ticking.

CHAPTER TWENTY-TWO

Will's cell began to vibrate as he was kicking the snow off his boots on his deck on Thursday night. It was his day off, but the powder had been too good to resist. It was one of those crisp clear blue-sky days where the vistas were so beautiful they hurt your eyes and every breath of air reminded you how good it was to be alive. The only thing that would make his ski-high better would be if he could see Caitlyn. Maybe grab some dinner, coax her into a little fooling around, get her to play something sexy on the piano…

And as soon as he'd thought it, his phone began to buzz.

He used his teeth to pull off his gloves, yanked at his jacket zipper and fished out the phone in a rush to get to it before it could go to voicemail. He didn't bother to check caller ID, grinning as he lifted the phone to his ear.

"Hello?"

There was a pause, as if he'd caught her off guard and she had to mentally regroup after planning to leave a message. Then a hesitant. "Will. It's good to hear your voice."

His blood froze. Not Caitlyn. *Shit.* "Tria. I can't say the same."

"I suppose I deserve that," she murmured, soft and wounded. She'd always been good at playing the victim.

Even when she was the one waving the knife and stabbing him in the back. "We saw you on TMZ. She's really cute, Will. Your new girl. We're so happy for you. We've been hoping you'd find someone. Move on."

It took him a while to process what she was saying. He kept getting caught up in the *we*. She'd been doing that from the day she'd broken off the engagement. *We're* sorry, Will. *We* never meant to hurt you. *Andy and I* care about you very much. It was like they'd stopped having opinions of their own. A united front against him. *We* are breaking your heart.

Wait, TMZ? What the hell?

"It's Caitlyn, right? That's her name? We'd love to meet her. Maybe we could all get together—"

"She isn't my girlfriend. She's just a neighbor."

Tria was silent for a moment, as if stung by the sharpness of his denial. Always the victim. "Oh… I'm sorry to hear that. She has a really sweet face."

"What do you want, Tria?"

A slow gathering breath. "We want to put this behind us. Andy and I never meant to hurt you. And we certainly never intended to screw you out of the down payment on the house, but with the economy the way it is, you know how hard things have been for Andy financially, and we just couldn't scrape together the capital to buy you out last summer. If you'd just talk to us, I'm sure we can work something out and forget the legal nonsense. We're trying to secure a loan. We just don't want to lose our home, Will."

"It isn't your house, Tria."

"I thought you didn't want it. When you moved out…"

"I moved out because I couldn't stand to look at it knowing what you'd done. That doesn't make it yours."

Andy had always been awful with money. He'd never be able to afford to keep her the way she wanted to be kept anyway. Best they discover that now. Will had used half his savings and borrowed from his parents to get together enough money to buy the damn thing for her. Because he'd thought they would be filling all five of those bedrooms with their kids. Growing old there.

Tria sighed, so damn wounded. "Will, I'm trying to make things right. What do you want me to do?"

"I want you to stop calling me. If you have something to say to me, tell my lawyer."

"Will, please. Be reasonable. We don't want—"

We, again. "Goodbye, Tria."

He must have stood on the deck for five minutes, holding his phone in one hand while his brain simmered incoherently. Then the other shoe dropped.

"Goddamn TMZ."

Her recently re-hung door shuddered under a rain of blows. Will's voice came through the wood, hard and urgent. "Caitlyn, open up."

Her hair still wet from the shower, dripping down the back of the T-shirt and work-out shorts she'd put on after, she rushed to the door. Was there another fire? She hadn't heard that sharp, demanding tone from him since the night they met.

She threw back the lock, yanked open the door, and there he was. The dark god. Anger stood out sharp on his face, making his cheekbones seem even more starkly chiseled and his dark eyes almost devilishly black.

"We're on TMZ."

"Oh Jesus." She swayed back, opening the door wider, and he stalked past her into the apartment.

Panic flared. What could they have seen? What if there had been a photographer lurking around the other night? Shooting through her windows. Her lying on top of Will—not kissing, but just that would be enough.

Hello, Breach of Contract. Goodbye, Life Savings.

"What do they...?"

He extended the smart phone she hadn't noticed in his hand. "See for yourself."

The first picture took a moment to register because it was so far from what she was expecting. Two blurry bodies, wrapped around one another in a hot tub—Elena and Daniel. It was a still from Tuesday's episode—an interlude which Daniel had yet to explain, though he'd left messages when he knew she would be teaching, telling her it had been edited to look worse than it was. She scrolled past the picture, and the two following which showed Daniel wearing a starlet like a human blanket at what was captioned as a "popular LA nightspot." Only then did she see the photo that had Will pacing angrily across her living room.

The pictures were much more innocent than she'd feared. The photographer had caught them the night of their non-date, walking back to the chalet through the snow. She was holding his arm, tucked against his side, but there was nothing intimate or scandalous about the shot. Her face was turned away from him, toward the camera, smiling shyly, and he was looking down at the top of her head, a slight smile quirking his own lips. They definitely looked friendly and it *could* have been intimate—which was exactly what TMZ was implying. Especially in combination with the next shot, which showed him holding the door to the chalet as they went inside.

They'd just gone home to their separate apartments,

nothing could be more innocent, but it *looked* incriminating and that was all that mattered to the gossip rag.

"It's not that bad," she said, watching Will prowl the room. "It looks like they don't even have your name."

"Is that supposed to make me feel better?"

She held his smart phone out to him and he snatched it out of her hand on his next prowling pass. "I can talk to the show's PR people, see about issuing a statement that we're just friends."

He shook his head, more in anger than denial. "I didn't sign up for this."

"I know. I'm sorry. I should have expected something like this after the pictures with Mimi popped up. It was too much to hope that the photographer would have left town."

He was still stalking, barely looking at her. "I never wanted to be mixed up with a celebrity."

"I'm not a celebrity. This'll blow over."

"Maybe if we'd met at a different time, things could have been different."

She suddenly got the sense they were having very different conversations. "Will, what are you saying?"

"I don't need this right now. I'm sorry, Caitlyn."

He was breaking up with her. Except they weren't dating. A spike of something drove into her heart—panic, denial. She didn't want to lose him. She was more frightened of the thought of never seeing him again than she'd ever been of losing Daniel. She couldn't be with him, not in any real way, but to lose him...

"Will, *wait.*"

"I'm sorry," he said again, the words sharp and final. Like the sound of the door shutting behind him.

So much for perfect.

CHAPTER TWENTY-THREE

Of course Daniel called first thing Friday morning. He had the photos of her with Will to use as ammo now if she started a fight about Elena and the Jacuzzi. But if he thought that balanced the scales, he had critically misjudged her.

She'd had a sleepless night thinking about Will, Daniel, Elena and what she really wanted out of life. Daniel might be a master of side-stepping confrontation, but she was having this out.

When she saw his number on the display, she didn't even bother with a greeting.

"Do you have that TMZ photographer on speed dial?" she snapped after swiping her thumb to accept the call.

"Sweetheart, I don't know what you're implying, but I had nothing to do with this most recent story." His voice was scolding, with a note of indulgence. "Do you want to tell me about those photos?"

She wanted to snap *I don't have to explain myself to you.* But he was still her fiancé. For at least another two minutes. And she didn't want him thinking she'd cheated on him. He didn't deserve that.

"He's just a friend. My downstairs neighbor. Nothing happened." *Not that I didn't want it to.* "We were walking back from grabbing a burger at the pub and I took his arm to steady myself on the ice. It was completely innocent." *Even if I wanted to be much less innocent.* "Can you say the same about Elena and the Jacuzzi?"

"I know that looked bad," Daniel said sheepishly. "But you know how the show is. Everyone telling you to go with it and she's so aggressive. I put a stop to it almost immediately, but of course they don't show that part. I had no idea it was going to look so graphic. I'm sorry you had to see that, sweetheart."

Sorry you had to see it. Not sorry I did it. Not I love you and I would do it differently if I had it to do over. Just *sorry you caught me.* She'd heard too much of those sorts of lying apologies out of her mother's mouth not to recognize one.

"Daniel, I don't want you to think this is about Elena. It's a lot more than that—"

"My thoughts exactly. There's a story about us being played out in the press and we need to get in front of it. They're portraying our relationship as toxic and saying you're hooking up with that guy to retaliate against me for what happened with Elena on Tuesday. Of course, it isn't true, I believe you, baby, but it's catching on and we need to get on the same page and approach this with a solid counter story—"

"I don't think I want to get married."

"*Caitlyn.*"

And there it was. He *was* capable of saying her name.

"And I'm positive I don't want to get married on the reunion episode. I'm not saying we can't ever have a future together, but I think I need to not be thinking about getting married while the show is airing. Afterwards, when we can have a normal discussion that doesn't include the press, we can talk about it, decide what's right for us, but right now, when I can't even see you, I think the best thing—"

"Whoa, whoa, whoa. Baby. I know this week has been rough, but let's not be hasty. I don't want to fight. Let's both take some time to think about this and we'll talk about it again in a few days. Remember Barbados? Remember how great it was? That's next week. Watch the episode. You'll remember why we fell in love in the first place. Okay? Just give us a chance."

"Daniel—"

"I love you, baby. I love you so much. Give us a chance. That's all I'm asking." The connection went dead.

Caitlyn somehow managed not to throw the phone across the room. She dropped it in the trash can instead.

Twenty minutes punishing the piano with bone-jarring Wagner didn't help her mood.

She put on her professional face when her first student of the day arrived, but her smile felt more and more forced as the day progressed and more and more parents who usually dropped their kids off and picked them up without coming inside felt the need to pop in just to *see how she was handling things* and find out *how she was holding up*.

By the time her last student of the day left at six-fifteen, she was ready to scream.

So of course her house phone blared as soon as she turned on the ringer and the caller-ID listed a New York number. "Of course," she growled, "the one thing that could make this day complete."

She stabbed the button to connect the call. "Hello, Mother."

"Who is that scruffy man with you on Access Hollywood? Are you screwing things up with that lovely Daniel?"

Caitlyn grimaced. She really should have known things with Daniel were too good to be true when her mother *liked* him. "What makes you think he isn't screwing things up with me? Did you miss the video of Daniel sucking face with Elena?"

"You're the one who wanted to go on a show like that. It's what they do."

Caitlyn gritted her teeth. "Were you calling for a reason? Or just to make me feel worse about myself?"

"Caitlyn. The things you say." Her mother sniffed indignantly. "I just thought you would want to know that I spoke with our contacts at the Los Angeles Philharmonic and they're very receptive to the idea of hosting you as a resident artist as you make your comeback."

"Mother. We've been over this. I'm not making a comeback. I hate performing."

"Darling. No one is as good at something as you are without enjoying it. Daniel told me how amazing you were when you performed for him at Carnegie. Just imagine every chair filled for you."

The pieces fell into place. The Los Angeles Philharmonic. His not-so-veiled attempts to get her to move out to LA early. "Have you been talking to Daniel about this alleged comeback?"

A slight, telling pause. "We both want what's best for you."

"And what I want is to be allowed to decide what is best for myself. Like an adult. I don't like performing." She was drowning in déjà vu. How many times had she and her mother had this argument in the last few years?

"Your music is a gift to the world."

"My music is for me and my students now. And I'm done discussing it. If this is all you called to talk about,

I'm going to hang up now." She actually loved this woman, though sometimes it was hard to remember that.

"This stubbornness is very unattractive, Caitlyn."

"Goodbye, Mother."

She disconnected the call, turned the ringer back off, and turned off both her personal and *Marrying Mister Perfect* cell phones. She sat on the couch, not bothering to turn on the lights as the sun set, hugging herself and watching as the night skiing lights came on up the mountain.

The show had been a mistake. She could wallow in that or she could fix it. But how? What could she do to undo the mess her life had become? She was sort of engaged to a man who kept hanging up on her when she tried to break off their engagement. Her mother was planning her comeback tour with her unwanted fiancé. The one man she *did* want was probably up on that mountain now, mad at her because she'd splashed his face—and now his name, since the reporters had uncovered it—all over the national gossip shows. Her life had become a sideshow and all she could do was hold onto her sanity by a thread as her love life was writ large across television screens all across America for another month and a half.

She slumped on the couch, the previous night's lack of sleep catching up with her, until finally the dizzy spirals of her thoughts sank into a restless sleep, plagued by nightmares of Carnegie Hall, filled with hundreds and hundreds of Daniels, all applauding wildly and telling her she was happy and it would all be okay, as she played until her fingers broke against the keys, bent and mangled.

She woke with a jolt, holding her hands up in horror

until the dream cleared enough for her to recognize the nightmare for what it was.

Sunlight streamed through the windows, painting her apartment in morning, and a low knocking came from her door. Caitlyn stumbled to her feet, smoothing her slept-in clothes and made her way to the door. The peep hole showed Will and her heart leapt wildly before she firmly informed it that he was pissed at her and had been a total jerk about the TMZ thing.

She rubbed the sleep out of her eyes and cracked open the door, squinting up at him dubiously.

"I'm a dickhead." His expression was abjectly repentant. "I'm sorry I freaked about the TMZ thing. I tried calling, but your voicemail box is full."

She let the door open a little more. "I'm sorry you got caught up in the show drama."

He shrugged. "You're worth it."

And just like that her heart rolled over in her chest. *Still off-limits, dummy*, she told it. She may or may not still be engaged to Daniel, but she was still absolutely forbidden from having relationships for another six weeks.

"Have people been staring at you as much as they've been staring at me?" he asked.

"I've been hiding," she admitted. "Is it bad?"

"You'd be amazed how many people want selfies with me now. I think half of them didn't even recognize me, they just saw other people wanting pictures and jumped on the bandwagon. I'm the most popular guy on the mountain."

She groaned. "I'm so sorry—"

"I know. Look, yesterday was nuts so I traded some shifts to clear my schedule today. Give it some time to die down. I was thinking of ditching my phone and skipping town for the day. I wouldn't mind some company. Wanna get out of here?"

"God, yes." She flung the door open all the way, not caring if he saw at her rumpled, slept-in worst as long as they could escape. "Give me five minutes to get dressed."

CHAPTER TWENTY-FOUR

Caitlyn leaned her shoulder against the passenger door and sighed, eyeing Will as he drove, tension she hadn't realized she was holding releasing. "How do you always know exactly what I need? I was just thinking about how badly I want to escape my life right now and poof, there you are with a plan to do just that."

Will shrugged, steering his Jeep down the winding road toward the main highway. "Just my natural genius, I guess. Though my sisters will probably want to take credit. They like to claim responsibility for the fact that I am a *sensitive man*." He jerked his chin at the road sign ahead. "What do you think? East or west? Vegas or Florida?"

"I appreciate the ambition, but I do have to be back for my lessons on Monday."

He grimaced. "Yeah, and I was only able to swing one day off. I guess it's just Grand Junction, then." He pointed the Jeep west.

Caitlyn leaned against the window, letting the chill of the glass seep into the skin of her arm even as the warm air from the vents blew her hair back from her face. They were only fifteen minutes from home and already she felt lighter, freer. No cameras, no comebacks, no one staring. Just her, Will, and the road disappearing beneath the tires.

She only felt bad that her messy life had spilled over into Will's and made him into a fugitive as well.

"I'm really sorry about all this."

"Did you arrange for those pictures to be taken?"

"Of course not."

"Did you want to be gossiped about from Sacramento to Savannah?"

"No, obviously, but—"

"Then it isn't your fault. I lost my shit the other night, but it was more because I found out about the first article from my ex than because of what it implied about us. I shouldn't have gone off on you like that."

"This is the ex-fiancé?"

"Yeah. It's no excuse, but it was definitely a trigger. Six months later and the sound of her voice still makes me want to spit nails."

Caitlyn studied his profile, the way his hair flopped over his forehead. "Are you still in love with her?"

He laughed, shooting her a look out of the corner of his eye. "Don't hold back, Caitlyn. Ask me anything."

"Sorry. It's the reality television. I feel like I have the right to everyone's secrets now." She said it flippantly, but it was a bald-faced lie and they both knew it. She'd asked him because he was Will, and even though they'd only known each other a few weeks—not even a month—she felt like she could ask him anything. They were just *easy* with each other.

And she knew she hadn't offended him with the question. Just startled him.

"No," he said finally. "I'm not in love with her anymore. I'm angry with her, but it's because it feels like she stole the life we planned right out from under me not because I'm harboring some secret desire to win her back. Honestly, I can't imagine getting back together with her now."

"Does she want you back?" *Because what woman wouldn't?* "Is that why she called when she saw you on TMZ?"

"No. Nothing like that. We have a... legal issue."

"Like an annulment?"

"No. We never got as far as a ceremony. But I did buy us a house. Which she now lives in. With my ex-best friend. And since I'm not going to get raise my kids there, it seemed reasonable to me that they should buy me out of my down payment. They disagreed. Now our lawyers are disagreeing. And it looks like they're going to lose, so she's trying to 'work something out' with me."

"So when you said she stole the life you wanted out from under you—"

"I pretty much meant literally, yeah. I moved in below you so I wouldn't have to be a twenty-eight year old living with his parents." He hooked his wrist over the wheel, surprisingly casual for one talking about his broken heart. "Hey, speaking of the chalet, did Les talk to you?"

"Les, the landlord? Last time I spoke with him he said he'd take care of Dale's bill. I haven't heard anything else. Why?"

"Apparently the insurance company is dicking him around and he's decided it's too much of a hassle to own a rental property. He called me to see if I wanted to buy the place. I figured he'd do the same for you."

"He might have. I had my phone off most of yesterday." Her head whirled with the heady idea of buying her place. She'd never owned anything. Never had anywhere that was entirely *hers*. Yes, her mother had lived in the same Upper East Side apartment for years, but Caitlyn had spent most of those years traveling and it had never felt like home.

When she'd first moved to Tuller Springs, she hadn't wanted to buy. She'd had the money, but she'd hoped she would buy her first house *with* someone—kind of like Will had before it blew up in his face. Now…

Daniel, Will… her love life had never been more complicated and her future more uncertain – so why was the idea of buying her place and slamming down some roots suddenly so appealing?

"Do you want to buy it?" she asked Will.

"Not particularly," Will admitted. "I can't afford it until I get my money back on the other house, and even if I could, the lower level has a little bit of a dungeon thing going on. Your apartment is all sunshine and happiness, but mine is like something out of an Indiana Jones movie—all doom and darkness. What about you?"

"I don't know. Maybe." She grinned. "Don't worry. I'd be a good landlord. I might even give you discounted rent if you teach me to ski."

His head whipped around, though the Jeep stayed steady in its lane. "Tell me you've been skiing before."

"A sport where I could break an arm? Not exactly encouraged for concert pianists."

"Oh, honey. You haven't lived." He grinned, all wicked promise, and for a moment she forgot they were talking about skiing. "I'll take you next week. You'll love it."

I'll bet I will.

Caitlyn was grateful most of Will's attention was taken by the road. She didn't think she could handle the full force of his sex appeal aimed at her right now. She squirmed in the seat, pointing the heater vents away from her—she was quite warm enough on her own. She forced her attention away from the mountain of solid muscle in the driver's seat and toward the sharp, familiar lines of the mountains outside the car.

Nothing to see here. Just two friends out for a drive. Nothing to see.

But so much to feel…

The woman sitting in his passenger seat was driving Will crazy. He'd been half hard for the last hour. Not that she'd been doing anything particularly seductive. Apparently all she had to do was sit there, with her legs tucked up under her on the seat and her auburn curls twisting over her shoulders and he wanted her.

Who was he kidding? All she had to do was breathe and he wanted her.

He told himself it was because she was off limits. Or because he'd been seduced by her music long before he met her. He could tell himself any number of reasons, make up a thousand excuses, but the truth was he wanted her. And there wasn't a damn thing he could do about it but wait.

She took the contracts she'd signed very seriously. Until the show was over, he had to keep his hands off. But that didn't stop him watching her out of the corner of his eye as they drove. She had a little half smile on her lips and her eyes were bright and open, with none of that guarded nervousness she'd had since the first TMZ spread hit.

This had been a good idea. A road trip to nowhere. Something to clear his head and chase the shadows out of her eyes.

"Do you think I'm too fragile to go bungee jumping?" Her fingers tapped out a quick, complicated rhythm against her thigh.

The question came out of the blue and Will laughed, until he realized Caitlyn wasn't smiling. "Wait, are you serious?"

"I'm an adventurous girl. Just because I've never done much of anything and I'm sort of shy doesn't mean I'm not brave."

"You already know I think you're brave. And of course you can go bungee jumping. And sky diving and whatever the hell else you want to do. Did someone tell you that you couldn't?"

She pulled a face. "I just feel like that's how the world sees me sometimes." He had a feeling *the world* was code for *that dickhead on the television show*. "Like I'm made of glass or something and I'll shatter at the first sign of strain. There are all these crazy adventurous dates on *Marrying Mister Perfect* and I never got to go on any of them. I'm not saying I wanted to jello wrestle on national television—"

Will choked, nearly swallowing his tongue at the mental image of Caitlyn, in a bikini, dripping jello. *Dear God.*

"I just don't want them to be right. I don't want to be the kind of girl who can only survive if you keep her up on a pedestal."

"You aren't that girl. They aren't right."

"Are you sure?" she asked, and there was such heartbreaking vulnerability in the question he had to do something.

"Positive. And we're going to prove it." He flashed her a wicked grin. "I have an idea."

The highway-side bar had a corrugated metal roof

and cattle horns sticking out of the door. Caitlyn eyed it dubiously. Will hadn't told her what his idea was, but this place looked like the kind of bar where the peanut shells were permanently stuck to the floor thanks to the help of bodily fluids she didn't want to think about. Not exactly her speed.

"I'm not much of a drinker," she murmured, her steps slow and reluctant as they approached the door and those long white horns, her sense of adventure tamping down somewhat. She might want to go zip-lining, but getting in a bar fight with a motorcycle gang was an experience she'd just as soon forgo.

Will grinned and snagged her hand. "We aren't here to drink."

There was no bouncer guarding the door at two-thirty on a Saturday afternoon. Will shouldered it open and held it for her as the stench of the place—sweat and beer and French fries, not *entirely* unpleasant—assaulted her nostrils.

"Then what are we—*Oh*."

The bar was built around three rings – two smaller ones on either side and a giant one in the center. And in the center of each ring was a massive mechanical bull. Two of them were silent and stationary now, but a woman was rocking back and forth on the smaller one to the left, laughing and flinging one arm back and forth.

It looked jarring and uncomfortable... and completely outside her comfort zone. And *fun*.

Caitlyn swallowed. "I'll have that drink now."

Will grinned.

"You hold on here."

"Here," Caitlyn echoed, squeezing with a white-knuckled grip.

"If you're falling, don't try to fight it, just let yourself slide right down to the pads."

"The pads," she repeated, nodding jerkily.

She was doing this. Caitlyn Gregg, child prodigy who might as well have *reserved* as her middle name, was straddling the padded back of a mechanical bull in a virtually abandoned honky tonk outside Grand Junction. She might have lost her mind.

She lifted her head and her eyes locked on Will, draped over the rail, a little smile quirking his lips as he watched. When he caught her gaze, he winked, broader smile flashing, and gave her a thumbs up.

The operator looked up at her. "You ready for this?"

Caitlyn grinned, feeling the start of something fierce and wild inside her for the first time in her life. "Absolutely."

The bull began to rock.

"I think we can safely say bull-riding is not one of your many skills."

"I was awesome," Caitlyn insisted as they crunched across the snow in the parking lot together, back to his Jeep.

She'd been terrible. Beyond terrible. She'd squealed and tumbled off the bull after about two seconds—when they still had it on the kiddie setting. The operator had actually said he'd never seen anyone fall off that fast.

But she'd done it. She gotten up there, wrapped her legs around the dang thing, and held on for dear life. Her mother would have a coronary if she knew.

Caitlyn felt like she could fly.

She wanted to fling herself into his arms and—

No. Not that.

Things with Daniel were unresolved and even in Grand Junction there was no guarantee that one of the eleven other people in the bar hadn't recognized them. They could even now be watched by a camera phone. But she felt like her skin would burst trying to hold all the emotion in her body and if she could just throw herself against him, he could absorb it all like a lightning rod.

Then he caught her hand.

And *wham*. Just that. Just his palm against hers, but she felt that skin-to-skin touch from her scalp to her toe nails, like a circuit connected making her a conduit for electric emotion. She was surging with it. No one and nothing else had ever made her feel this alive. Nothing and no one else had ever tried.

His grip was electricity, his hand the only thing tethering her down so she didn't float right away.

Will opened the Jeep door and she was forced to relinquish his hand. She rubbed her singed palm against her jeans as he rounded the hood and hopped in. He backed out of the parking space, teasing her about her bull-riding prowess—or lack thereof. She replied, barely aware of the words, just the effervescent tone.

Then they were on the highway, pointed back toward reality, and his hand slid across the divide, catching hers, resting their linked hands on the emergency brake, and the circuit completed again.

Just that. But it was everything.

CHAPTER TWENTY-FIVE

Miranda pushed herself up the last hill, breathing hard, feeling the muscles in her thighs straining with the ascent, each footstep a struggle. She hated running with a passion that she normally reserved for telemarketers and the incompetent. If not for the mental clarity that came afterward and the need to keep her body from becoming a saggy mess from too many hours in the editing bay, she would happily never run again.

The pavement jarred through the soles of her shoes and she glared at a woman loping the opposite direction on the path with long bounding strides as elegant and effortless as a freaking gazelle. Miranda mentally planned the gazelle's murder and slow evisceration until she realized another pair of footsteps were thudding in rhythm with hers.

She swung her head around to the runner in her blind spot and glared. "Are you stalking me?"

Bennett—another of the it's-so-easy-and-I-look-amazing-doing-it gazelles—arched a single brow. "I showed you this route. You know very well it's my regular Sunday run. I figured you wanted to see me."

She glowered at him—the gorgeous and effortless asshole Bennett—and realized he was right. Her subconscious was a piece of work. She'd been pissed this morning for no reason and needed to run, but not just anywhere. *Here*. Where she was sure to see him.

The show was going well. The ratings were through the roof, seriously sensational—*thank you, Elena*—though public sentiment was starting to shift against Daniel. She'd seen that coming. And it would only continue. She'd known it in her gut even as she'd fought against it, trying to force herself to believe that he was a nice guy and he and Caitlyn would ride off into the sunset together when all of it was over.

She knew that wasn't going to happen now. She'd seen the pictures.

Not the ones of Daniel and the women. No. It was the innocent little picture of Caitlyn and the man she said was just a friend. Her neighbor. She was just holding his arm in the shot, not even looking at him, her face shyly averted.

Miranda had seen that and she'd *known*. Her spidey sense had gone crazy. That same romantic spidey sense that had predicted Jack and Lou, and Marcy and Craig— though she'd been a little behind the ball on that one. The same spidey sense that had never made a freaking peep during Daniel and Caitlyn's season. Because they weren't really in love.

But if they didn't end up together, if there was no happily-ever-after, if love didn't conquer all, did that mean Bennett was right? Was Miranda part of what was wrong with society?

"I take it this isn't a truce," he said.

Miranda was panting too hard to give a decent response.

She stopped running, planting her feet. Bennett jogged a few more steps before he stopped as well, turning to face her with that patient, curious expression she'd used to love and now wanted to throw things at.

Nothing to throw here.

"Why do you hate my show?" she demanded. "I realize we aren't *you*. We aren't finding needy families and building them homes. Nor are we finding the next big dance star and giving them a shot at their lifelong dream," she snapped, rattling off two of his biggest hits, "but we're doing something worthwhile, aren't we? Isn't love worthwhile?"

His expression tightened. "If your show were about love, I'd be all for it, but it's not. Not as it is now. It's about pandering. Cheap entertainment."

"So it's not the show concept you disapprove of. It's me. It's the way I'm running it. Because I'm *cheap*."

He ground his teeth, getting in her face. "Miranda, would you stop twisting my words?"

"I'm so very sorry," she said with acid sweetness. "I'm sure you mean *pandering* as a compliment."

The words were even more biting because she was afraid he was right.

She was starting to feel, more and more, that although she'd had two seasons end in genuine love, giving her a sense of righteousness about what she was doing with the show, that Bennett *freaking* Lang might actually have a point about the exploitative nature of reality dating shows.

It was Elena that was killing her.

The delightful members of the press were eviscerating her. She'd been cleverly tagged the "Slutty Suitorette" on a variety of blogs and the damn name had even started trending on Twitter. She was a hashtag. Elena hadn't been alone in that Jacuzzi, but no one was calling Daniel a slut. No, it was only Elena who was dirty because she'd dared make out with a man she was dating.

It just didn't sit right with Miranda. The injustice of it.

"They know what they are signing up for," she said, but she could hear the defensiveness in her own voice.

"That isn't the point." Bennett held his tongue as a group of runners jogged past. When they were out of earshot, he took her arm and tugged her to the side of the trail. "When you started with *Marrying Mister Perfect*, you didn't want it to be just another dating show. Do you remember that? You weren't calling all the shots yet, but you still managed to make something real with Jack and Lou. Something that was about more than sensationalism and sex appeal. When you got promoted I was so incredibly proud of you, but what have you done with it? We have a responsibility to be better, Miranda. When a horrific accident happens, now the question isn't whether or not we have the footage, because there is *always* footage these days, the question is whether or not we should show it. Does seeing it benefit us? Is it right?"

"You're equating my show to a horrific accident?"

"Do you remember when we started fighting? Do you remember why?"

Her throat grew tight and her skin suddenly felt like it was stretching over her cheekbones, not quite fitting right. "I was working too much. You didn't want me to travel with the show."

He shook his head. "No. That was a blip. It was Marcy's father. You called me for advice on how to bully the hospital staff into allowing you unrestricted filming access inside the hospital. While your star's father was on the verge of death and she was going through the worst experience of her life, you wanted to make sure you could get it all on film."

"The audience loves that stuff. Everyone wants to see the picture of Jackie Kennedy after JFK. The human drama of it. The power of that moment. We connect with it."

"That moment doesn't belong to the rest of the world. It's hers." He grimaced, shaking his head with disgust. "There's no such thing as privacy anymore."

"I shut off the cameras," Miranda protested. "I almost got fired because I didn't film in the hospital and I missed several pivotal turning points in last season's romance because of it. Wallace pitched a fit. Hell, we had to have Pendleton explain why Darius was no longer around because we didn't even film her kicking him off."

"You still used the shot you got before you decided to take the high road."

She knew the shot he meant. Her cameras had caught last season's Miss Right and her favorite Suitor together in an unguarded moment. He'd comforted her, scooping her up and carrying her through the hospital corridors. The gorgeous image had become one of the iconic moments of the season. Powerful and raw. Real.

"I was nominated for an Emmy because of that shot."

"I know. That doesn't mean you should have taken it." He shook his head angrily. "I still don't understand why you do this. Why this show? You're so good. You could do anything."

"Because this is what I *want* to do," she snapped, temper fraying. "Because I want to believe in love. I want to believe it conquers all. This show may be ridiculous, but it's about love and *that isn't ridiculous*. People make fun of us because we're fluffy, girly television, but why does everything have to be war and backstabbing? Do you know how many shows there are about people solving murders? Not to mention the news with all the actual wars and death. Shows like *Marrying Mister Perfect* might be the *only* things on television that are actively trying to put love on the airwaves. And yes, sometimes people get hurt, but that's *love* and the way we do it may be cheesy and melodramatic sometimes, because we turn a microscope on a moment in people's lives when they aren't rational and clearheaded because they are *falling in love* and we're all idiots when we do that." She shook her head bitterly. "I certainly was."

She'd been an idiot to love him. The man who could never say it back.

"Miranda."

"No." She turned back toward the parking lot. "Enjoy your run, Bennett. We're done here."

"Miranda," he called, jogging after her. "The job I've been trying to get you to take. It's mine."

That froze her in her tracks. She turned, trying to keep her dumbstruck feeling from showing on her face. "What?"

"I'm retiring. Stepping down as EP of *American Dance Star*."

"And you want me to take over." It wouldn't compute. "You just told me you think what I do is shit."

"I told you I think you're better than what you're doing. And you are."

She couldn't parse through that right now. Her brain was entirely occupied by six little words.

Executive Producer of American Dance Star.

Holy shit. She'd dreamed of that job, never thinking she'd have a shot at it because no one could replace Bennett. She wanted his job with a greedy lust that was almost indecent. But... "Why? Why retire? You're young."

"Old enough," he said with a wry laugh. "I just don't have the stomach for this business anymore. And I certainly don't have the killer instinct."

He'd just been giving her shit about her killer instinct and now he wanted her to take over because of it? And the idea that Bennett Lang, who lived his job as much as she did was actually going to *retire.* "You can't be serious. What would you do with yourself?"

"I don't know yet. Find a hobby, maybe. Teach ethics to children who have zero understanding of privacy thanks to Facebook. Something." He shrugged. "It might not stick, but I hope it does. I need some time away."

Something hard and heavy shifted in her stomach. She couldn't imagine an LA without Bennett in it. "What do you mean time away? Away where?"

"I don't know yet," he admitted. "I guess I hoped you..." He trailed off. "It doesn't matter."

Her heart—which had stupidly lifted at his words—fell again. Of course he wouldn't say he wanted her to have some say in what he did. Bennett didn't put himself out there like that. And she was sick of being the only one out on an emotional limb.

"Are you only offering me this in an attempt to get me back in your bed?"

Anger at the suggestion flushed his cheekbones. "This isn't a casting couch, Miranda. You're the best for the job. I want you back but there are no conditions. You can pick one or the other or both."

"Or neither," she added.

His eyes narrowed further. "Don't screw up your career because you're mad at me. Take some time to think about it. Until the end of your season, if you want. But then I'd like an answer."

"To which job offer? EP of *American Dance Star* or

your mistress?"

"You weren't my mistress," he snapped.

Well, she hadn't been his lover. *Love* was in the freaking word and he wouldn't say it.

She just looked at him.

"Both," he growled.

"Thanks for the offers, Bennett. You've given me a lot to think about."

She waited for him to say something more—to tell her that he wanted more from her than a qualified producer and a willing bed warmer. To say he needed her mind and her heart and *her* as his equal in every way. But Bennett just nodded, albeit reluctantly, and turned back to his run.

Leaving her with her thoughts in knots and her heart in shambles.

CHAPTER TWENTY-SIX

"Oh Caitlyn, oh baby…"

Caitlyn watched herself making out with Daniel on the television, mildly nauseated. She couldn't help the sickening sensation that she was cheating.

Cheating with Daniel, the man she was still at least nominally engaged to, on Will, the man she hadn't done more than hold hands with on Saturday.

When did this become my life?

It didn't help matters when Mimi tilted her head to the side and asked, "Have you noticed that he calls all of you 'baby'? It's like his go-to endearment."

Caitlyn was going to explode.

Daniel was avoiding her calls—doubtless convinced that she would watch tonight's episode in Barbados, where they danced under the stars and made out like teenagers, and all would be forgiven. Will had been swamped with work—apparently the shots of the two of them in gossip rags all over the country had made Tuller Springs into a tourist destination and the mountain was doing better business than it had in years. Which meant more ski patrol hours, more lessons, and, for her, less time with Will.

He'd held her hand the entire way back on Saturday. Even when she dozed off against the window for almost an hour, when she woke up, he still held her hand, tucked safely in his. It was probably the single most romantic moment of her life, waking up with her hand in his like that—and that included the moment of Daniel's proposal.

They were so different, Will and Daniel. Even the way they talked about how they'd found their careers. Daniel's story was touching—a teacher changed his life by helping him overcome his dyslexia and now he wanted to do that for other children—but he'd told it so many times by now that it sounded like a line. There was nothing real left in the words. They'd been trotted out too many times.

But Will's story, it was just the story of *him*. A story of stumbling around and piecing it together and there it was, take it or leave it. He wasn't trying to impress anyone. He didn't *expect* anyone to be impressed or moved. He was the man he was. And she loved…

That.

Not him. Goodness, it was far too early to be thinking the L word about him.

Wasn't it?

She was simply tired of the image games. Tired of rehearsed speeches. Tired of being put on a pedestal.

And she was going to *explode* if she couldn't talk to someone about her crazy messed up life.

Caitlyn leaned over to the remote in Mimi's hand and punched the pause button, making the screen freeze with Daniel's hands grabbing her ass. *Lovely.*

"Will took me bull riding on Saturday."

"Okay." Mimi gave her a look. "Is that a euphemism for something?"

"No, like actual bull riding. A mechanical bull. I was awful. It was incredible."

"Okay." The cautious my-best-friend-is-a-crazy-person look stayed firmly on Mimi's face as Caitlyn stared at her, a little manically. The truth was bubbling up inside her, pushing, pulling, screaming to get out.

Five bajillion dollar lawsuit, here I come.

"Mimi, I have to tell you something. Something that I absolutely cannot tell you, but I'm going to explode if I can't talk to someone. Swear secrecy. You can't even tell Ty."

Mimi's eyes got huge. "Are you pregnant? Is it Will's? Or, oh my God, *Daniel's*?"

"Swear!"

"I swear, I swear! On my kids, I'll never tell a soul, I promise!"

Caitlyn's held breath whooshed out. And the all of the words chased that breath out on a rush.

"I won. Daniel picked me. He proposed and I said yes, even though I was panicking and I'm pretty sure the only reason I agreed to marry him is some sort of modified Stockholm Syndrome that happens during the show, but I did it, I agreed, and now whenever I try to break it off with him, he's changing the subject or dodging my calls and he wants to get married *on* the show, in front of the world, not later, but in less than two months when the live reunion special airs. And he said before that he just wanted to be a normal elementary school teacher from Indiana, but now he's living in LA and he wants me to move out there and he's been talking to my mother who's been talking to the LA Philharmonic about me being a resident artist or something and they both want me to get back into performing which sounds like *death*, but he isn't listening to me and I'm starting to wonder if he ever did or if he just built this image of me as the delicate flower who needed the sunshine of his support to flourish as a performer again or something—that analogy didn't quite work the way I wanted."

Mimi gawked, mouth open, eyes wide. "No wonder you set your house on fire."

"And then *Will*. Oh God, I am so freaking crazy about Will. But if I have a public relationship, then I can be sued for breach of contract for more money than I've made in my entire life. And I've told him that, but when he holds my hand all I want to do is jump on him and ride him like a mechanical bull—only for longer since I fell off after like two seconds. And of course he has no idea that Daniel picked me and wanted to marry me and that I, kind of, you know, *did it* with him, though it was only that one time and it wasn't very good and I hadn't even *met* Will yet, but now I feel like I cheated on him with the guy that I'm engaged to and every time I see an episode where Daniel is all romantic toward me and I fall for it like a sap because I was completely caught up in that crazy, stupid world, I am terrified that *Will* is going to see what an idiot I was and decide I'm not worth the trouble and dump me even though we aren't even dating because I'm still technically—I think, I'm not entirely sure—engaged to someone else."

Caitlyn fell back, deflated after all the words poured out. "So that happened."

Mimi blinked at her, bug eyed. "Do you have any more of that vodka?"

Caitlyn and Mimi sat side by side on the floor, propped against the couch, not far from where she'd lain on top of Will the other night when she'd felt like all of her erogenous zones were eagerly reporting for duty. The vodka bottle—not quite empty, but close—was wedged between their legs and they took turns refilling the glass tumblers Caitlyn had grabbed from her cabinet. The glasses had started out filled with ice, but it had long since melted and now they were sipping the sugary liquor neat.

"I wonder if this is what Daniel feels like," Caitlyn mused.

"Drunk?"

"No," she elbowed her friend. "He has all these women competing for him and he gets to pick which one he wants, but if he doesn't pick the right way at the right time or whatever, he could lose the one he really wants."

"*You* were the one he really wanted," Mimi reminded her.

They'd watched the remainder of the show in bits and pieces, pausing whenever Mimi had a question or Caitlyn had one of her dubious epiphanies. Now she rolled her head back to rest on the edge of the couch and stared at his face where they'd frozen it on the screen. He really was handsome. And earnest.

"Do you think he'll be sad when I break it off with him?"

"Didn't you already break it off?" Mimi slumped down more, blowing at her bangs and watching the neon purple strands flutter back down toward her face.

"Sort of. I think I'm going to have to be more firm. He's slippery."

"Did you love him?"

"Will?"

"No, Daniel. Wait." Mimi's hand slapped down on her knee. "You're in love with Will?"

"Shhhhh! He could be home." Her head swung around as she stared suspiciously at the floor. She knew he could hear her play. She'd never asked if he heard more than that. "I'm not in love with Will. I barely know him."

"You like him! You totally do!"

"Shhsht! We were talking about Daniel. And how heartbroken he's going to be when I break it off with him because he loves me. Though it never feels like he loves me. It feels like he has this idea of me and he keeps trying to shove me into that box."

"I can't believe he wants you to leave Tuller Springs," Mimi said indignantly. "*I'm* here. Clearly you have to stay."

"I would have left anyway if I'd gone to live with him in Indiana." She wagged her feet on the rug, distracted by her toes. "Do your toes feel weird?"

"No. But my lips are numb. Look." Mimi smacked her lips at Caitlyn and giggled.

They might have gone overboard on the vodka. A fact she was probably going to regret in about seven hours when her first lesson of the day arrived.

Mimi's cell phone rang and Caitlyn heard her answer it, as if from a great distance. "Ty! I'm drunk! Come fetch me."

"Your husband is going to think I'm a bad influence," she said when Mimi hung up the phone.

Mimi patted her arm, missing the first time, but managing a few good pats after she finally made contact. "He knows me better than to suspect anyone is the bad influence but me." She frowned. "Did that make sense?"

Caitlyn sighed, gazing at the undeniably pretty face on the screen. "Do you think he really loves me? Daniel? After that scene with Elena…"

She didn't have to say which scene. Mimi grimaced.

Daniel hadn't precisely trash talked the other girls, but he'd made it clear that Elena was the sex goddess and he felt nothing for any of the other women that could remotely compare to the pure passion he felt for her. No wonder Elena had always looked so annoyingly confident at Elimination Ceremonies.

But the moment that had really made Caitlyn's stomach churn was when Daniel asked Elena not to say anything to the others about his lack of sexual feelings for them. Their little secret.

"Was he lying about not having sexy feelings for me? I mean he lied to everyone. By omission. And yeah, he had to because of the rules of the show, but he asked Elena to lie for him too. Which is skeezy. Unless he was lying to her? But why would he do that?"

"That wasn't Daniel talking. That was Daniel's Little Friend. And men's penises lie."

"So his heart could love me while his penis loved only Elena?"

"Hey. You're hot. His penis may have grown to love you."

"You're right. He could have had a change of heart. He might really love me. And I'm being awful and unforgiving if he loves me, aren't I? I should give him another chance, shouldn't I?"

"If he truly loved you, he would never ask you to leave me."

"What if he came here? What if we bought this house and lived here forever?"

Mimi pursed her lips. "I don't think Will would like it."

"No. But what if Will doesn't really want me? We're just friends, you know. And he saw me when I almost set my hair on fire with the veil. Why would he want me?"

"Because you're *awesome*, obviously." Mimi slung her arm around Caitlyn's shoulders, a move that only worked because Caitlyn was three-quarters of the way to laying on the floor. "Don't worry about Will. Just worry about telling Mister Perfect there that you don't want to get married and move to Tinseltown. The rest will sort itself out."

Caitlyn nodded, the weight of Mimi's wisdom making her head feel heavy. It would all work out.

CHAPTER TWENTY-SEVEN

"Never again."

Caitlyn woke with a groan and her second Wednesday-morning hangover of the month.

She was still on the living room floor, though some kind soul had shoved a pillow underneath her head and set a glass of water and a bottle of aspirin on the floor in front of her—just far enough away that she wouldn't knock it over in her sleep. Ty probably. She didn't remember him coming to collect Mimi, but he must have at some point since her friend was not sprawled out beside her in a similar state of post-alcohol remorse.

Caitlyn groped for the water and the aspirin, grateful when her stomach didn't roil too much. It was mostly her head that felt like it was packed with cotton and acid.

Shower. Clean clothes. Tidy up the evidence of last night. Get some food in her stomach. Then she'd be ready to stagger her way through today's lessons. So long as everyone played very, very quietly. She didn't think she could take *fortissimo* today.

An hour later she was back to almost completely human—with a solid half hour to spare before her first student arrived. The pounding in her head had even reduced to ignorable levels. Thinking back, she decided she must have had less to drink than she thought --

probably as drunk on the idea of being able to finally spill the truth as anything else. She had a text from Mimi waiting—*Don't worry, even drunk I didn't tell Ty. Taking it to the grave. XOXO.*

Caitlyn felt a weight she hadn't been conscious of lift, but another remained. She remembered almost all of their conversation. And what they'd agreed she needed to do.

Twenty-eight minutes before her first student. There was time.

Caitlyn dug out the MMP cell phone and dialed.

He answered on the second ring, but then, of course he would. He thought she'd be back in love with him after watching last night.

"Sweetheart! Are you counting the days until our little getaway? I know I am."

The mid-season vacation they were supposed to take together. She'd completely forgotten it. He did sound excited. Which made her feel guilty for what she was about to say—and how completely emotionless she felt about saying it. Shouldn't she at least be sad that she was about to end their relationship? She wasn't sure she had ever loved him, but if he had truly loved her... if he still did...

She found herself hesitating, and blurting out, "My landlord is selling my place."

"Oh." It took him a moment to process that out of the blue declaration. Then, "That's great, sweetheart! You can probably get out of your lease early—"

"Actually, I was thinking I might put in an offer. You haven't seen Tuller Springs, Daniel. You don't understand how the mountains get into your soul. I really love it here. It's become my home."

"Honey." The endearment was low, patronizing.

"We've talked about this."

"Yes, but we never actually agreed. It's not a lot of money. Even if we did end up together and wanted to be somewhere else, it would make a great vacation home. Our own little ski chalet." Even as she heard the words leaving her mouth, she realized she was doing it again—bending what she wanted to fit around his plans. She didn't want Tuller Springs only on vacations. *But compromise is what relationships are founded on...*

"Do you even ski?"

"No, but I've been thinking about learning." An image of Will popped into her head, rugged and grinning as he raced down the mountain.

"Baby—sweetheart, I know this is a big change, but you need a clean break. The middle of nowhere Colorado? You'll only ever be a piano teacher there."

"That's all I *want* to be, Daniel." She let the edge into her voice, but he didn't seem to hear it.

"But there's so much more in you, baby. I see that. I see *you*."

"No. You don't. And I don't think you ever have." There was more in her—but it was bull rides and brownie bites and Daniel couldn't see that. He never would. He wanted her up on that goddamn pedestal so high she couldn't touch the world around her.

"Sweetheart..."

"I don't want to marry you, Daniel. I don't want any of it."

"Caitlyn..."

She could hear him getting ready to evade, getting ready to sidestep the objections that might get in the way of his plans. "I'm breaking up with you, Daniel. Now. We're done."

"Caitlyn, baby, don't be hasty."

"I'm not being hasty, Daniel. I'm being *me*."

She hung up, flooded by triumph, relief…and a guilt chaser.

He'd be fine. He hadn't loved her, and even if he thought he had, he'd get over it. He may be bummed for a day or two, but he'd bounce back. Stronger than ever. He was Mister Perfect, after all. And it wasn't her job to console him. She couldn't make them both miserable for the rest of their lives just to spare him the hurt in this second.

She had to pursue her own happiness. Even if that made her a horrible, selfish person that all of America would hate.

Sometimes a girl just had to do something for her own happiness.

Caitlyn reached for her other phone, dialing the recently programmed number.

"Will? I want to take you up on that offer. I want to learn to ski."

CHAPTER TWENTY-EIGHT

Caitlyn went down—again—with a thump, a groan, and a puff of snow. Will skied to where she had landed in an awkward heap, his little flicker of concern easing when he heard her self-deprecating laugh.

"I think we've found another thing that I'm terrible at."

"Everyone sucks at skiing their first time out. It's a rite of passage." He grabbed one of her flailing skis and helped her organize her limbs before she attempted to get vertical again. "You're actually doing pretty well." *Bald faced lie.* She had zero natural aptitude for the sport. "And look on the bright side, at least no one can see you falling on your face."

They'd had to wait until she was done teaching for the day before he could take her out on the mountain and in the evenings the bunny hill was all but abandoned. A ridge shielded it from the rest of the resort and gave them as much privacy as they could hope for on a ski slope.

Her skis now side by side, he reached down, his gloved hands catching hers as he levered her up onto her skis again, bracing her when she would have gone sliding off.

"When do I get those pole things?" she asked, jerking her chin to where he had stabbed his poles into the snow at the base of the bunny hill.

"When you can stay on your feet without them. Right now they would just get in your way and you'd probably ending up stabbing yourself with one. Or worse, me."

She shot him a disgruntled look—which would have been more effective if she hadn't looked so adorable. Her cheeks were rosy above the top of her scarf, eyes bright—and just a little cranky.

"My legs don't do what you want them to do," she complained. "I had this great image of myself flying effortlessly down the slopes. Instead I'm here in a dorky helmet on my ass half the time."

"You will fly effortlessly. Someday. In the mean time, you look fabulous in the dorky helmet and it's a fabulous ass." Even if it was hidden in the fluff of the hot pink snow pants.

She stuck out her tongue at him and he laughed.

"Come on. Try again." He coaxed her into position. "And this time, try not to lean back so far. It doesn't slow you down. It just takes away your control and throws you off balance."

"To slow down, make a pizza wedge," she muttered to herself.

"Exactly."

He released her and she began an awkward glide down the smoothly groomed slope. "That's better," he called. "Now try a turn. Weight on your inside ski and just glide around, nice and smooth."

She kept sliding down the slope—perfectly straight.

"Try a turn," he yelled again, louder. She'd done them before, but this time she just kept coasting straight for the edge of the slope.

"I can't!" she hollered.

"Make a wedge to slow down," he shouted, skiing over until he was right below her on the hill, reaching up to catch her.

And somehow she managed to turn. Uphill. Out of his reach.

She slid right off the edge of the neatly groomed bunny hill, into the buffer of soft, deep powder designed to stop the beginners before they made it to the tree line. She wasn't going particularly fast—though it probably felt fast to her—and as soon as her skis hit the deeper snow, they stopped—though her body kept moving forward, sending her tumbling into the snow bank with a shout. She landed with a spray of snow and a grunt.

Will cringed. "You okay?"

She twisted on the ground, tangled in her skis. "I have fatally wounded my pride."

"Pride is overrated." He reached down to gently rearrange her skis so she didn't damage her knees trying to get up.

"Says the Ski God who makes it look so *easy*," she grumbled.

"I've skied pretty much every day I could since I was four. It gives me a slight advantage." He reached down to help her to her feet, but this time when she took his hands, she yanked and he tipped to thump into the snow beside her.

When he dusted the snow out of his eyes, he saw that she was grinning. "You hadn't spent any time on your ass. Didn't want it to think it wasn't *fabulous* enough to visit the snow like mine."

"Happy now?" He gently brushed the loose snow from her cheek, with one gloved thumb.

Her gaze went soft, shifting to rest on his mouth and everything in his body tightened. They'd come this close to a kiss before and she'd always pulled away. No reason this time should be any different. She still had over a month of the show left.

Her eyes would slide to the side, a blush would creep up her cheeks, and he'd be left aching. He couldn't say she was a tease. He knew exactly what he was getting into with her, but the waiting wasn't getting any easier.

"Can anyone see us?" she whispered, never looking away from him.

"Not unless they climbed up that ridge over there with a telephoto lens." Will nodded toward the ridge, though he didn't take his own eyes away from Caitlyn and her mouth.

"If they're that dedicated," she murmured, "they deserve the shot."

She leaned toward him. Any second now. Her gaze would slide away first. But instead her lashes fell heavily to veil her eyes.

And...

Her lips were on his, soft as silk, sweet as honey, and more addictive than the rush of cutting the first tracks through fresh snow.

It was just a brush, a taste, a sweet little peck of a kiss. An invitation.

He took it from there. Deepening, coaxing, and she yielded to him with a soft sigh. They were both wrapped in too many layers of clothing. He'd never hated his gloves more, for keeping him from her skin. But God, the taste of her.

When he finally lifted his head, her cheeks were flushed and her eyes as lust-dazed as he felt.

"On second thought, I think I like skiing," she murmured.

He chuckled, the sound a little hoarse. "I'm glad to

hear it, but we should probably get up before we both freeze our fabulous asses off." He shoved to his feet and took a moment to steady himself before reaching down and tugging her up. Even bundled up, she was light and he put his hands on her waist—ostensibly to help her balance, but mostly because he liked the feel of her, even through all the padding. "You ready for one more attempt? From the bottom of the bunny hill it's a straight, gentle slope all the way down to the Lodge and after we return your rental gear you get the best part of your first day of skiing."

"Oh? Better than making out with the hot instructor?"

"I was thinking warming up with hot cocoa and massaging the aches out of your muscles in front of a fire, but I could be persuaded to consider other forms of heating you up and rewarding you for all your work tonight."

A tantalizing glint entered her dark blue eyes. "Which way to the Lodge?"

Caitlyn didn't know what had come over her. Sure, she was done with Daniel—which still felt amazing—but she could still get sued for having a relationship, so what the hell was she doing making out with Will in the snow?

She couldn't have felt less sexy during her first ski lesson. She'd looked like the Staypuff Marshmallow man, dunked in fluorescent food coloring and wearing a bike helmet, and she'd somehow managed to fall down every fifteen seconds—whether she was moving or standing still. It could have been an excruciating experience. By rights, perhaps it should have been. But the way he'd looked at her...

His eyes had tracked her, filled with affection and poorly banked heat, and she'd shivered—and not from the cold either—though snow seemed to have crept inside every article of clothing she was wearing and she wasn't sure she was ever going to warm up all the way again. Though Will was welcome to help...

By the time she'd gotten the courage to tug him down on the snow beside her and plant one on him, she'd felt like her skin was two sizes too small for her body and she was going to burst right out of it if she couldn't kiss him right that second. It had been perfect. So right she'd gotten chills. Though that might have been the snow.

But now, as she stood pouring hot water from the kettle over the instant cocoa powder in two mugs, watching Will arrange their damp winter wear over the drying rack he'd set up beside the potbelly stove, her nerves were back with a vengeance.

What did she know about seduction? A big fat nothing. That had been part of the appeal of going on the show—they would take care of all that for her, set up romantic scenarios that even she couldn't screw up and coach her through them. Now she was on her own and Caitlyn had never known what to do with herself in sexy situations.

She stalled as long as she could, stirring the powder, making sure it was perfectly dissolved. Will stoked the fire he'd set in the stove. She could already feel the warmth of it dispelling the winter's chill—but it did nothing to warm her frozen nerves.

"Caitlyn?"

She jolted out of her daze, catching Will watching her with a little crinkle of concern between his brows.

"Cocoa's ready!" she chirped, far too brightly—that wasn't sexy, damn it. She picked up the mugs to carry them over to the sitting area.

Will accepted his mug and settled himself on one end of the couch, his free arm stretched along the back in silent invitation. Was she supposed to just plop herself next to him? Curl up against all that gorgeous masculinity and make herself at home?

Her stomach jumped with nerves and she slid onto the couch—as far as she could get from him while still being on the same piece of furniture. He didn't react, simply sipped his cocoa and murmured something complimentary about the chocolate.

"Yeah, I spring for the good stuff with my cocoa," she babbled, unable to keep that freakish cheeriness out of her voice. "No expense spared on chocolate in this house."

She sounded like she was at a pep rally. If he made a move she'd probably start a freaking cheer in his honor and scare him senseless.

But he just sprawled in his corner of the couch, sipping cocoa, basking in the warmth of the fire, gazing up at the mountain and occasionally sending her a glance filled with warm affection... and something *much* hotter.

He sipped his cocoa, his gaze on her. "So...what made you decide to stop performing?"

Caitlyn jolted, glad she wasn't taking a sip of her cocoa because she would have given herself third degree burns on her esophagus. Alarm bells blared in her head, her sensual panic instantly morphing into agitation of a different sort. Was Will just like Daniel and her mother, only wanting her to be his performing monkey?

CHAPTER TWENTY-NINE

"Why do you ask?" she asked warily, hiding her face behind her mug.

Will shrugged. "You're amazing. I was just curious why you stopped."

Caitlyn's heart plummeted. He was just like them—

"Did you hate it?"

Wait... Daniel had never asked if she hated it. He'd just assumed everything about her old life was magical and she must be repressing her desire to return to it, with him on her arm.

"Was it the attention and spectacle that got to you?" Will asked. "Because, if so, going on the reality show was a weird choice."

He had a point... "No, it wasn't that. Being a famous Classical musician isn't like being Angelina Jolie. I can still go to the grocery store or the movies and no one knows who I am. It's only when I go places like Lincoln Center in New York that people would ask me for my autograph—and that part was actually kind of nice. They were music lovers and we could share that, you know?"

"So it wasn't the fame. The schedule?"

"I... it's complicated."

"Okay." Just that. So simple.

He leaned back and sipped at his cocoa, gazing out

the window, but she knew he wasn't ignoring her. He was waiting, letting her decide if she wanted to tell him or change the subject. She knew he would accept either choice without batting an eye. Which, oddly, made her want to tell him more.

"I told you my childhood was... pretty dysfunctional. My parents had a contentious relationship. Honestly, I'm not sure why they ever got married. But the one thing they could agree on was my music. My *gift*, they called it. And so, when I was very small, I threw myself into it because I thought it would make things better between them. When my career took off as a child phenom, I became a sort of bargaining chip between them. They started fighting again and my mom started cheating again—not even bothering to be discreet anymore—and when they got divorced, it was a good thing, I know that now, but at the time all I saw was that my stupid career had torn us apart. I blamed my success for everything that was going wrong and for a while I hated the piano with a passion—but my parents insisted I keep performing. My career was too important to throw away because I was going through a *phase*. So I performed—hating every second of it."

She paused, regrouping, and found Will watching her. Steady. Not judging. Just listening.

"How old were you?"

"Thirteen when they got divorced. I was pretty miserable for a couple years—what girl going through puberty doesn't want to be on display every night, right? I played, but I would dream about *accidentally* breaking a finger just so I could stop." She took moment to drink her cocoa, the chocolate deliciously soothing. "I was in San Francisco one day when I was fifteen, researching emancipation online so I could get away from my parents and stop performing. I was so ready to be done. And that night I had to play Rachmaninov. His Piano Concerto #3 in D Minor. It starts out all sad and aching and builds to this agitation and frenzy. Back and forth like that. Sad and wild. Then the finale starts with this driving angry explosion. All fire and passion, but it ends with the most gorgeous catharsis—almost triumphant—and as I played it all of that just poured out of me. I'd never played like that before. I was always technically brilliant—everyone said so—and I had a gift for musicality, but this was a depth of emotion in my music I'd never experienced before. I forgot about the audience and completely surrendered myself to it. When it was over the ovation went on for fifteen minutes. People were crying. I was crying. Hell, I'm pretty sure the conductor broke down at one point. It was an incredible experience. And I realized I'd been blaming the piano for everything I was mad at my parents about. I found my love of music again that night and it was my salvation."

She studied the chocolate bits sticking to the inside of her mug. "I kept performing after I came of age. I didn't want to lose that bond with the music. I met Mimi and we became friends, and when she married Ty and left the symphony to move to Colorado and have kids, I realized I was envious. I wanted that quiet life. I loved music, but I could take or leave performing. My public life had such a complicated history and sometimes I still felt like I was letting my mother control me when I played venues she'd always wanted me to play. I kept performing for another couple years—and there were nights when it was magnificent, but also times when it felt like drudgery and I just wanted to walk away. Then Mimi's son was born and I came to visit and we talked for hours about music and life and loneliness and what I really wanted and I realized I didn't have to be on stage to still have the piano in my life. It took another ten months to finish out my contracts and phase myself out of the life, but then it was over and I moved here and now…"

"Now you just play for me."

She toasted him with her empty mug. "An audience of one."

He caught the mug as she waved it, plucking it out of her hand and setting it aside with his. He reached for her, his long arms spanning the distance she'd put between them. "Come here."

"W-what?" And just like that, her nerves were back, jangling even more frantically than before.

"I promised you a massage," he said softly, gesturing to her tense shoulders. "I'd hate for sore muscles to ruin your first memory of skiing."

"I… uh…"

His fingertips grazed her shoulder near her neck, giving a gentle squeeze.

Caitlyn launched out of her seat like the couch had a built-in eject button. "You like Chopin?"

She fled to the piano, feeling safe only when her fingers touched the keys. She hadn't panicked like this with Daniel, but he hadn't made her feel this wild syncopation in her blood. It was too much. *Will* was too much.

He didn't chase after her—thank God—simply turning on the couch to watch her as she began to play Chopin's Prelude in B Minor. It was called the Heartbeat Prelude with its steady pulse-like repetition, but her fingers rushed through the notes too fast, making the heart race. He waited until the short piece concluded before strolling to the piano. She plunged into another Chopin, a nocturne this time, but she didn't know it as well and her fingers faltered on the notes. She broke off and fumbled in the wooden chest beside the piano where she kept the music. She almost tore the book when she found it, spreading it open on the piano's stand and reminding herself to breathe as Will perched on the piano bench beside her.

"Caitlyn."

She flubbed the intro again, unable to focus on the notes on the page in front of her.

Will didn't touch her, aside from his shoulder brushing lightly against hers. "Caitlyn, I was just flirting. We don't have to do anything."

She stared down at her hands, frozen on the keys. "I don't want you to stop," she whispered, before forcing herself to look up and meet his impossibly deep brown eyes. "I'm just no good at this stuff."

His lips quirked in that heartbreaker of a smile. "I beg to differ."

She bumped him with her shoulder. "You know what I mean. I never know what to do with myself or if I'm doing the right thing."

"Do what feels right. It won't be the wrong thing."

What felt right. It felt right to be with him. To have his warmth pressed along her side. She wanted his hands on her again, but couldn't imagine how to get from here to there. She didn't want to be the aggressor, but how to invite him to touch... She'd only ever known how to seduce with the piano.

His favorite.

Caitlyn struck the opening chord of the Pathetique. She was close enough to hear Will's indrawn breath and feel the slight shift in his body, angling toward her. He was taller than her, even sitting, but she didn't feel like she was in his shadow, so much as protected by his heat. His warmth seemed to wrap around her as the opening chords sang from the piano's strings.

She was breathless with anticipation, waiting for the first touch, the hairs lifting on her arms as she played. She'd never thought of the Pathetique as a particularly erotic sonata, but she was suddenly aware of the sensualism that soaked the opening minutes, building.

His hand whispered over the small of her back, not quite touching, just shifting the soft fabric of her shirt, and she held a fermata far longer than it warranted, the moment suspended in that almost touch. Her breasts already felt swollen inside her bra, the nipples furled into tight points. Tension coiled in her stomach, heat gathering between her legs—and he hadn't even touched her yet.

Then, right as she began the first falling run, his lips fell on the point where her neck met her shoulder and Caitlyn's head sagged back on a gasp. Thank God for muscle memory or her hands would surely have faltered. She kept playing, her focus splintered as the piece grew more rapid and intense, building to its own climax and Will's lips caressed their way up her neck.

His heat pressed against one side of her body, his arm curving around her, the lightest of touches gliding up her other side, from her hip, along the indent of her waist, teasing her ribs, flirting with the outer edge of her breast, then back down before he got to where she *really* wanted his hands, and then her fingers did fumble.

"That is very distracting," she whispered, barely recognizing the husky breathiness of her own voice.

He hummed against the skin of her neck and she nearly came right then. "Do you want me to stop?"

Stop? She wanted to compose a symphony for him. "No."

The word was barely audible, the unwritten pauses in the music growing longer. She was never going to make it to the second movement—which she had always thought was the most romantic part of the *Pathetique*, but what did she know?

His mouth reached the underside of her jaw, the curve of her ear. The soft tug of his lips on her lobe made her miss a note. Then another as he made a little *mmm* sound, as if he was enjoying this as much as she was. *Impossible*. It was too good. He'd be a puddle on the floor if he felt even half of the sensations shivering through her body.

His other hand came around, careful not to get in the way of her arms as she played, and rested gently just above her knee. Then he squeezed.

Just that. Just a little squeeze and Caitlyn's brain completely disconnected from her body. She turned her face toward him, only an inch, but it was all the invitation he needed. His lips were on hers, a low groan of need reaching her ears—*his? hers?*—and her fingers forgot how to play. She twisted toward him, one hand gripping his T-shirt at his collarbone while the other wrapped around the wrist of the hand that was still gently massaging her leg. His other arm curved all the way around her back, gripping her side—she'd had no idea a man putting his hand on the line of her waist could make her feel so *sexy*, but then everything Will did was sexy.

His tongue teased her lower lip and then slipped into her mouth and—oh Sweet Jesus, *this* was a kiss. Every stroke, every taste drove her higher until she was dizzy with the vertigo of it.

The hand on her leg roamed upward and why wasn't she wearing a skirt? Clearly she needed to be wearing a skirt! He stopped at the top of her thigh, centimeters away from where she wanted him most. They were both fully clothed, necking on her piano bench, but she had never been so turned on in her entire life. One touch would be all it would take to send her flying. One little touch...

He stood abruptly, eyes wild, and shoved the piano bench with her on it away from the piano with a grating scrape across the floor, so fast Caitlyn was forced to grab for it or go flying off. He grabbed both her knees, pushed them apart, and knelt between them so her thighs were pressed against his ribcage, his body between her and the keys. Drawing her down for another kiss, his hands were deft on the buttons of her blouse.

Oh my God. Oh my God. Oh my God.

Her brain was jabbering, but she *didn't care.* Then her shirt was open and he was looking at her and swearing worshipfully and he pulled down the cups of her bra *with his teeth* and *oh my God*, she was going to die.

But what a way to go.

CHAPTER THIRTY

His mouth was—okay, suction? *Good.* Teeth? Also, surprisingly, *good.* And that flicky tongue thing? *Sweet Mozart's Toes. Amazing.*

Her bra had somehow vanished, along with her shirt, and now she felt the brush of fingers against her lower stomach as he wrestled with the button on her jeans.

And what was she doing? Sitting there like a bump on a log. Or a lump on a piano bench, gripping the edges for dear life and forgetting that she had *hands* and she really ought to use them.

She got a fistful of the back of his shirt. "You're wearing too many clothes."

Will grunted something she could only assume was affirmative against her skin and then he was moving at warp speed. On his feet—

Oh no. Your mouth was doing such good work…

Whipping his shirt off over his head and—

Okay, this was good too. The man had muscles on his muscles—all sculpted and with just enough hair to remind her that he was a Man, with a capital M. He popped the buttons on his own jeans, but before he could shove them down, he looked up, his eyes landed on her half-naked self and that wildness—she was really starting to love that wildness—entered them and he lunged for her.

He lifted her, guiding her legs around his waist as her arms naturally found their way around his neck. His mouth sealed on hers and he spun them, about to set her down—

"Not on the piano!"

The sound he made was half-laugh, half-groan. He hitched her against him with a palm on her ass, shot a single, hopeless look at the steep steps up to the loft and then closed the distance to the couch so fast the fluffy cushions were a soft pressure against her back before she even realized what was happening.

His weight pressed her down deeper into them and she decided she didn't care about anything that was happening other than him.

She spread her legs, his weight settling into the cradle between them. She could feel the hard length of him and she undulated against it—for once not caring if it was the correct foreplay technique, because *damn, who cared? That felt amazing*.

Kissing his way along her throat, he lifted his weight off her just enough to slip a hand between them, pressing it flat against her stomach and sneaking beneath the unbuttoned waistband of her jeans. She almost whimpered when he found her nub, rolling it beneath one finger. His fingers slipped deeper and he moaned, "Jesus, you're so wet."

She had no idea what to say to that. *Hell yes I am, get down there and finish the job* seemed a little too forward somehow. So she just grabbed his wrist, held on tight, and pushed her hips up against his hand. He swore again, fumbling one-handed to shove down his own jeans, as his fingers worked her higher, his mouth against the underside of her jaw—

He froze, instantly utterly still above her. "Fuck. Fuck

fuck fuck."

"Will?"

"Do you have something?"

Something? As in I've got something for you right here, big boy? Because hell yes, she... "Oh...." *Crap.* Condoms. "I don't usually do this sort of..."

He took over the swearing. "I'm going to die." He jerked his partially lowered jeans back up his hips.

"Do you have anything downstairs?"

He shook his head. "Lately I haven't..." His expression firmed with resolve. "It's okay. Don't worry. I'll take care of you." His hand, still wedged inside her jeans, began to move.

Caitlyn squirmed. "I want to... Will... take care of you... *oh God...* too."

She reached for his waistband and he groaned, dodging. "Don't worry about me, darlin'. I've got you."

And did he ever have her. She was about to have the most shattering orgasm of her life. With Will. Only he looked like he was in more pain that ecstasy and she wanted him with her.

"Will, stop."

He went statue still. "Are you okay? Did I—"

She stroked her hands through the slightly sweat-damp strands of his not-quite-black hair. "I don't want to do this without you. How long would it take you to get a condom?"

"Lodge convenience store. Eight minutes roundtrip if I take the Jeep. Seven and a half if there's no line."

She almost laughed. Her brain was barely functioning, but she should have known a man would know how to calculate the distance between him and sex down to the second. "Well, get going, champ."

His fingers moved one more time, driving a hard

235

gasp from her lips that he caught with his, dragging her into a long drugging kiss. "Just marking my place," he murmured as he disentangled himself from her and the sucking depth of the couch cushions.

He didn't bother trying to find his shirt, just grabbed his ski jacket from the drying rack and threw it on over his bare chest. Caitlyn didn't bother covering herself. She'd never felt sexier in her life. She raised both arms above her head, arching her back and watching her man stomp his feet into his boots.

He looked at her once, groaned and adjusted his jeans before walking—stiffly—to the door. "Six minutes. Tops."

Six minutes.

Six minutes when normally her brain would intrude and her doubts would surface and she'd be a gibbering mess of insecurity by the time he got back. But tonight was different. She was different with him. He made her feel like there was no right or wrong. No adequate or inadequate. No worry about being good enough. Just want and need and *yes*.

She lay sprawled in semi-sexual abandon, gazing up at the mountain, feeling drunk on Will and so absolutely *perfect* she couldn't imagine how the moment could be any better. Or rather she could. It would be better in four and a half minutes when he got back.

This was right. Everything had finally fallen into place.

She shimmied out of her jeans, debating for a while about whether or not to take off her panties, then remembered the *teeth* thing with her bra and decided to leave them on. She adjusted her position on the couch, trying to find the sexiest possible recline.

It wasn't a very long couch, she realized. Long

enough for her to lay on comfortably, but Will was a fair bit taller than she was. Either his feet or his head were going to be hitting the end. That wouldn't do. She could go up to the loft and wait for them on her bed up there, but she didn't want him to break something in his rush up the steps when he got back... and really it felt wrong to change the venue. This was where they had started. This was where she wanted to finish this.

In front of the fire...

Caitlyn hopped off the couch, grabbed the cushions and pillows and began arranging them into a nest on the floor. She grabbed her favorite velvet-soft throw and threw it over the entire cushy pile. *Not exactly a bear-skin rug, but not far from it.* Perfect.

She smoothed her hair, debated running to the bathroom for a quick teeth brushing, but decided there were more important things than chocolate breath.

Lights dimmed. Candles lit. The Pathetique and a carefully selected classical playlist drifting softly from the stereo.

Caitlyn heard footsteps on the stairs and rushed to arrange herself in her Rose in *Titanic* sprawl on the pillows as the door opened.

Will stepped in, already shedding his jacket, and his eyes sparked with something wicked and promising as he drank her in. "You've been busy."

He tossed the condom box on the floor beside her nest, kicking off his boots. She eyed the Costco-sized box. "You're planning to be."

He grinned, shucking his jeans and boxers in a single move that left her mouth watering. "I figured better safe than sorry. I have a feeling this might be a long night."

Caitlyn wet her lips, eyeing all that lithe, muscular masculinity with unmasked anticipation as he came down to kneel over her. "Sounds perfect," she whispered, right before he caught her lips.

And it was.

CHAPTER THIRTY-ONE

Caitlyn woke the next morning in her own bed, with only a note for company. Will's absence wasn't a surprise—he'd warned her before they fell asleep that his classes started earlier than hers and he'd try not to wake her when he left.

During their talks last night between more athletic activities, she'd learned that his classes began even before the mountain opened some days, especially on Fridays and weekends when they had more tourists, whereas Caitlyn's students were almost all in school and her schedule tended to be heaviest during lunch hour and after school let out.

She had a handful of homeschooled students who filled in the gaps—many of them with parents who drove them in from hours away for the privilege of taking lessons from the great Caitlyn Gregg—but her early mornings were typically her own. She'd experimented, her first year, with having before school lessons and discovered that both she and her students hated the early mornings.

Her first lesson on Fridays wasn't until eleven and it was only quarter to nine, so she didn't leap out of bed right away, taking a moment to enjoy the pleasant, sensual soreness in her body. She had a dopey grin on her face even before she reached for the note he'd left.

You were amazing. Encore tonight? XO Will.

It was simple, no overflowing outpouring of romance, but it still made her heart race. And yes, he'd just signed it with a "kiss" but she was already feeling the dizzy potential for the L word.

Not that she was going to rush into saying it. She'd learned her lesson about rushing into things with Daniel. She had all the time in the world with Will. They weren't on a nationally televised commitment schedule. They could take their time, enjoy one another, learn one another, and if she was falling head over heels for him... well, she could take her sweet time about telling anyone that.

She *couldn't* tell anyone about him until the show ended anyway. Just a few more weeks now and she'd be free. Free to be with Will and shout it from the rooftops. No more paparazzi. No more talk of LA or comebacks. Just skiing and playing the piano and Tuller Springs.

Heaven.

Caitlyn bounced out of bed, tied on her short green Chinese silk robe, and scrambled down the steps. Will—prince among men—had tidied up their nest already and left another note on the café table, along with a cooling to-go cup from Java Hut and a paper bag she found held one of their giant chocolate croissants. She flipped open the second note.

No expense spared on chocolate in this house. If you haven't had Java Hut's choco-croissants, you haven't lived. And after last night's acrobatics I figured you could use the fuel. XO Will.

She sat at the table, eating her croissant, drinking her lukewarm coffee and gazing out at the mountain, wondering which of the little figures zipping down the slopes was Will.

This was it. The life she'd always wanted. Right here in front of her. Now she just had to hold onto it.

"Will."

He looked up, expecting to find his four o'clock private lesson and instead found Tria standing next to the giant ski school sign, both arms wrapped tight around herself, either out of her nerves or an attempt to keep herself warm. Her blonde hair was still pixie short, just the edges of it sticking out from beneath her bright red hat. She hadn't changed.

He'd expected the sight of her to hit him hard. He'd managed not to lay eyes on her in the last seven months—no small feat in a town the size of Tuller Springs. He'd thought his heart would leap or ache or *something* when he saw her again, but there was no melodramatic reaction from the organ in his chest.

"I'm working, Tria."

"I know and I wouldn't be here, but you won't take my calls."

"Because we're supposed to be communicating through our lawyers. Anything you have to say to me you can say through them."

"This isn't about the money," she snapped, and it was the uncharacteristic sharpness that caught his attention. "I convinced Andy to sell the house."

It may have been the first time since The Wedding That Wasn't that it hadn't been "we" between her and Andy.

"Our real estate agent says the market has dipped and we're going to take a loss and when she starts talking about equity I have no idea what she's talking about. I'm not sure where we're going to find the money, but we'll pay you back. We'll do all that. But I need you to forgive Andy."

The bark of harsh laughter burst out of his mouth.

Tria's expression turned pleading. "He misses you, Will. You guys have been best friends since you were eight. He loves you. We both do."

"Then maybe you should have thought of that."

"Do you think this was easy for us? Do you think I just woke up one day and thought, *Hey, I think I'll break Will's heart?*"

"You aren't actually trying to make me feel sorry for you because cheating on me with my best friend was *so hard* on the two of you, are you?"

Her anger deflated. "No. I just want you to stop hating him. Hate me if you want. I deserve it. But Andy's having a really hard time. I tried giving you time to cool off. I thought eventually you'd come around on your own, but now…"

He didn't want to know. He really didn't. But… "What happened?"

Tria grimaced. "He messed up his knee again at a competition last week. He's out for the season. Thank God he had insurance this time."

Will scrubbed a hand across his face. "He's an idiot."

But that wasn't new. He and Andy had been inseparable since they were eight years old. Both addicted to the rush of fresh powder and both resisting the siren call of snowboards when all of their friends had begun switching over. Will had preferred Alpine events, the few times he'd competed, but Andy had gone nuts for moguls.

Andy had skipped college, choosing instead to try his skis on the competitive circuit. He'd been good—and he'd always considered himself too good to lower himself to teaching—but he hadn't been good enough to win the cash purses and sponsorship money to really be able to support himself as a pro athlete. He'd been nineteen when he blew out his knee for the first time and he'd never come back all the way after that, though to hear him talk the next season was always the one where he was going to dominate. Andy was a big talker. And a big dreamer. It had always been part of his charm, even when Will wanted to shake some sense into him.

"He's Andy," Tria said with a shrug.

"I always thought you had more sense than to fall for his bullshit," he heard himself saying.

Only when shock played briefly over her face did he realize it was the first time he'd even implied a question about why or how she and Andy had gotten together.

"He's a child," she acknowledged cautiously. "I know that. But I love him."

"And you didn't love me."

"Of course I did. I *do*. Just not the way I love him." She wrapped her arms tight around her middle again, her breath fogging the air, but he had stopped feeling the cold—he was iced from the inside out. "I couldn't marry you. It wouldn't have been fair to either of us."

Fair. As if she had ever cared about fair. As if agreeing to marry him when she had feelings for Andy in the first place—even if she hadn't known they were reciprocated—was *fair*. As if waiting until he'd bought her a freaking *house* to tell him that she was having second thoughts was *fair*.

His face must have shown some of his thoughts, because she stepped forward. "Will..."

A woman wearing rental skis made her way awkwardly toward the Ski School sign. "I have a lesson to teach."

"But Andy—"

"He's your problem now."

CHAPTER THIRTY-TWO

Caitlyn's last lesson finished up at six-thirty. Barely five minutes later, a knock sounded on her door and her heart rate went from allegro to vivace. *Will.*

She all but danced over to the door, flinging it open.

"Surprise!"

Holy Hadyn.

"*Daniel.*"

He reached for her and she stumbled back, dodging his embrace, which he took as an invitation to enter her apartment.

"You can't be here! What if someone sees you—"

"It's all good," he beamed. "The network arranged it. We were supposed to have our getaway next weekend anyway, but I pulled some strings and convinced them that it would be better for us to have a quiet weekend in. Just the two of us, here in good old Tuller Springs. I know how upset you were on our last call that I hadn't seen where you live."

"That wasn't why I was upset."

He waved his hand in a *close enough* gesture, turning to survey her apartment. "This is cute. Very rustic with all the wood. I can see why you like it so much, sweetheart. It's so homey."

Caitlyn couldn't seem to get her brain working at a proper speed. Her ex-fiancé had just shown up at her apartment, thought he was staying the weekend, didn't seem to think he was an ex, and her new... whatever Will was... would be here any minute since she'd sent him a text earlier agreeing to the *encore* he'd suggested in his note this morning.

Daniel seemed to have completed his survey of the apartment and turned to her, extending his arms. "Sweetheart, it's so good to see you in person."

Caitlyn backed away from his approach. "Daniel, we broke up." *And I had wild no holds barred sex with someone else.*

He dropped his arms, but his smile stayed determined. "You wanted to take a break. I get that."

"I don't think you do, because I don't want a break. I want a break-*up*. I want out, Daniel. No more wedding. No more us."

His smile faltered. "You don't mean that."

And as soon as he wasn't smiling, guilt surged. "I'm sorry, but I really do."

"Why?" he asked, more peeved than heartbroken. "The least you owe me is an explanation."

He wasn't wrong, but if she knew one thing about Daniel it was that explanations were invitations for him to argue himself into getting his way—usually when you didn't even realize you were arguing. Sometimes it felt like the only thing she *did* know about him was how persuasive he could be. Maybe she could start there.

"We got engaged too quickly. You don't know me and I certainly don't know you. I don't even know which Bond you most like."

"I think I know you better than you think," he argued, "and we owe it to ourselves to give this a shot. Our compatibility tests were off the charts. And James Bond? No problem! I'm most like Daniel Craig in looks—there aren't many blond Bonds—but I think I have more of Sean Connery's attitude—"

"Oh Christ. I didn't mean which one you *are* most like. Which one you like the most. Do you even hear yourself?"

"Give me a break, Caitlyn, I just misheard you. I'm not perfect, no matter what they call me."

No, you just think you are. "Why do you want to marry me, Daniel?"

"I love you."

Somehow she managed not to yell *you don't even know who I am!* "And Marcy? Did you love her?" He'd certainly professed his undying love to her on national television in the last season, even bursting into tears when she'd broken it off with him. He wasn't crying now. But then, she might not have been the one he really wanted. "What about Elena?"

His earnest, persuasive expression faltered. "Okay, I know the stuff with Elena looked bad and the press coverage of our love life hasn't exactly made things easier, but we knew this was going to be the most difficult part going in. If we could just get past this, it's going to be good for us in the end."

"*How?*"

He blinked, taken aback by her outburst. "It's necessary. For the show."

"Oh, I get that. I see how making our lives a sideshow raises ratings. What I don't see is how you running around devoting all your time to publicity is good for *us*."

"The show—"

"Will you shut up about the damn show! I am not the show. You keep saying it's good and it's necessary for the show, like that's supposed to make me feel better, as

247

if what's good for the ratings is automatically good for us. How? How do a few extra viewers do us a single bit of good?"

"Caitlyn, sweetheart, I realize you're upset—"

"Answer the question, Daniel. How? Is it all about making you a bigger celebrity?"

"Both of our careers can benefit—"

"God, you haven't been listening at all, have you?" She flung up her hands, almost feeling strange that there were no cameras rushing in to capture her histrionics. This was Daniel. There were always cameras when there was drama around Daniel. "I don't want to be a celebrity. I don't want the kind of career that benefits from notoriety. I don't care how many people watch us or talk about us. I went on the show to find love. I was looking for *you*, or who I thought you were, and it's become increasingly clear to me that you can't say the same."

His face was blank with shock. "Caitlyn."

"Do you know what I saw on the last episode? It wasn't you. It was me. I know that girl I became on the dates with you. I recognized the woman with the slightly glazed expression in the designer clothes. That was who I was when I was performing, making excuses for my unhappiness, telling myself it was just jitters or nerves or the price I had to pay for my art, when really I was miserable and letting other people tell me what I wanted out of life. I let you tell me what I wanted, Daniel, and I shouldn't have done that. I am twice the idiot for letting it happen again, but I fought too hard to get away from that trap last time and I'm not going to let myself fall back into it with you."

"Caitlyn, whatever you want—"

"Stay right there." She climbed the stairs to the loft,

using her hands for balance as she scrambled up them. The Rock of Ages was right where she'd left it, tucked in the back of her nightstand. She popped the box open and looked at it one last time, searching for a sliver of doubt, but she didn't feel a single shred of regret. It was time to get rid of the damn thing.

She snapped the box shut, climbed down, and walked over to Daniel. Taking his hand, she put the ring box into it and pushed his fingers into a fist over it. He looked so confused she felt horrible… but the relief that it was really, officially over was so immense her guilt couldn't touch it.

"I hope you find what you're looking for, but I'm positive it isn't me. I'm sorry, Daniel."

She almost said she should have said no when he proposed, but that would have embarrassed him on national television and she didn't think she could have done that to him. She could have told him as soon as the cameras stopped rolling, but she hadn't been sure. Once it was done, it was so much harder to undo. Part of her wished she'd left early like Sidney had, leaving the field open for Samantha and Elena, but there had never been a moment when she thought *No, this is the wrong guy for me*. Not until she was home with his ring on her finger, weighing her down like an anvil.

"You'll reconsider," he said softly. No one had powers of denial like Daniel. "Take all the time you need to think about things. When you're sure—"

"I'm sure. And I think you should go."

He didn't resist when she guided him to the door. The network would have arranged transportation for him, but she asked anyway. "Do you need a ride anywhere?"

"No. No, I'm good."

And then the man she had once agreed to marry walked out of her life. She would see him again at the reunion show, but the fairy tale was over.

Thank God.

Caitlyn closed the door and pressed a palm flat against it. She could have handled that better. She could have been kinder. Gentler. She'd lost her temper when he'd kept trying to talk her into agreeing with him without ever listening to her. But she doubted there was ever a good way to break up with someone. The best that could be said was that it was done. They were done.

A whisper of sound drifted up from the apartment below. The deck door opening. She'd never heard Will moving around down there in the past, but she'd never had reason to listen either. Now she was attuned to every subtle creak and thud. He'd be taking off his gear, stripping down and jumping in the shower to warm up and wash off the sweat of the day.

The image of him in the shower, warm water running in rivulets down the muscles she'd familiarized herself with last night, made her breath quicken with anticipation. How long before he dried himself off and came up here to kiss her senseless?

And what was stopping her from going down there and kissing him senseless? He wasn't Mister Perfect, picking between a bevy of Suitorettes and always the one in control. Caitlyn could take the initiative too.

Do what feels right. It won't be the wrong thing.

For once she trusted that was the truth. With him.

Caitlyn darted out of her apartment before she could lose her nerve. Her feet were light on the stairs, her knock a rapid staccato to match her racing heart. She rocked anxiously from foot to foot. *Do what feels right. Do what feels right.*

The door swung open and she did what felt right. Up on her toes, one hand behind his neck, drawing him down as she stretched up, lips to lips, then a rapid accelerando, a rush of lust and momentum. His arms came around her and he lifted her against him, giving her a better angle on the kiss, though he broke it to murmur, "Hello, there."

"I missed you." She framed his face with her hands, bringing their mouths back together for that perfect resonating chord of want that only he seemed to be able to strike.

He didn't bother trying to speak again, backing into his apartment, her feet dangling off the floor as he carried her pressed against his chest. She had only the vaguest sense of his apartment—smaller than hers and darker, like he'd said, but none of that mattered when they fell onto the luxurious softness of his duvet.

He was still wearing the T-shirt and jeans he wore under his snow gear when he taught. He hadn't instantly stripped down as she'd envisioned. "Take off your clothes," she ordered as soon as he laid her on the bed. "I haven't seen you naked in *hours*."

He laughed, obediently tugging off his shirt. "I think I like this new aggressive side of you."

So do I. She'd never seduced anyone before, or been the aggressor in any sort of sexual sense. She'd never felt like she *could*, but this was Will. And with Will everything seemed possible. Even being aggressive and naughty. She unbuttoned her own blouse, reveling in the way his eyes locked onto her fingers. "Why are you still wearing your pants?" she purred.

"Just slow I guess." Then he stripped them down his legs and he was naked and oh *my*, she had a feeling being the aggressive seductress was going to be very,

very good.

CHAPTER THIRTY-THREE

For the next two weeks, Caitlyn had to resist the urge to pinch herself. Every moment the show had tried to force and fabricate with Daniel seemed to happen naturally with Will. He was funny, spontaneous, and romantic, turning even the most ordinary moments into so much more. The evening he'd found her in the chalet's shared laundry and boosted her up on the machine... She'd never think of the spin cycle the same way again.

It wasn't all sex either—though she had *no* complaints in that department. He seemed to have an instinctive awareness of when the media speculation and increasing tide of reporters and lookie-loos into Tuller Springs were getting to her. He'd traded shifts again one Saturday to steal her away for another directionless drive. *Playing life by ear*, he'd said, and she'd slipped off her shoes, tucked her feet beneath her on the passenger seat, and felt all the cares of the world falling farther and farther behind as their little bubble of contentment rolled down the highway.

She would play for him sometimes, often inviting him up to her apartment at the end of the day by playing the Beethoven Pathetique as soon as she heard him moving around downstairs. He would knock on her door before she made it to the second movement, without fail.

Everything felt lovely and *real*. No elaborate cinematic dates. They weren't even allowed to be seen together in public or tell anyone they were seeing one another—which seemed to be harder on Mimi than it was on them. They were both perfectly content to stay in and just be together, but Mimi was fair to bursting under the pressure of the secret. Only Caitlyn's repeated reminders of the dire consequences kept her mouth shut.

They spent most evenings together and most nights, though Caitlyn was grateful for the time away from him on the evenings he would spend with his family and on Tuesdays when she watched the show with Mimi. She worried he would get sick of her—and those times apart, even if it was only a day, gave their reunions a desperate, eager edge.

She woke up every morning dizzy with happiness. Life would have been perfect... if not for that lingering sliver of doubt, nagging at her like a splinter beneath the skin.

She dreaded Tuesdays.

Will thought Daniel had dumped her.

Every week the fear grew worse that he would see something or hear something and realize just what an idiot she'd been over Daniel and despise her for it. She couldn't tell him how foolish she'd been without risking a lawsuit, but she hated the idea of him discovering she'd accepted Daniel's proposal by watching the show. She had to tell him about the engagement—and the end of it—but she was haunted by their conversation about vow breakers.

Would he put her in that category? Would he think she was just like his ex-fiancé?

By unspoken agreement, they both very carefully avoided the details of their previous relationships. She had the excuse of a nondisclosure agreement, but Will's face would turn to stone whenever she alluded, even accidentally, to his broken engagement.

And then it was Valentine's Day.

A Tuesday, so normally one of her nights away from Will when Mimi would keep her from going pyro-girl while watching the show, but Ty had brought out the big guns in the Wonderful Husband competition, even hiring a sitter and making reservations, so Caitlyn was on her own.

Things were still too new with Will to expect that they would necessarily celebrate the holiday together— they hadn't defined whatever it was that they were doing together or said anything about feelings, and it wasn't like they could be seen in public together anyway, especially not on a night like Valentine's.

Tonight's episode was the last exotic date before the Meet-the-In-Laws dates. Spain. Pouring wine on the brazier. Daniel talking to her for the first time about what their life would be like after the show. Caitlyn wasn't sure she wanted to see that. And she sure as hell didn't want Will seeing it. Or finding out about it from his sisters, who she knew watched the show.

She wished for a giant eraser to rub out the entire event from her past. When other people made romantic mistakes, they could walk away without having to relive them on national television. Not for the first time, she wondered what had possessed her to sign on for this.

Mimi had been enthusiastic and the producers were beyond persuasive—*unique opportunity, wonderful journey to find your soul mate.* And she'd wanted to believe it all. She clung to that dream of the fairy tale romance as hard as only a girl from a broken family could.

Last week had been the episode with the lie detector

test and Caitlyn couldn't help but wonder what her results were. Had the test been able to tell that she was lying to herself? Daniel hadn't opened them. He'd decided that he wanted to trust the women and didn't need the results—dramatically burning them in front of the Suitorettes before the Elimination Ceremony.

But now Caitlyn was dying to know. What would have happened if he'd read them?

Lies and illusions. The show specialized in them. And tonight was a doozie. Spain. The flamenco show and the first time Caitlyn had told the cameras she thought she might really be falling for him.

Dread turned her blood to sludge.

Caitlyn went through her Valentine's Day lessons on edge, her usual smiling rapport with her students feeling forced. Some of them had brought her Valentines and she let each of them raid the basket of chocolate hearts she'd kept beside the piano all week, telling herself it was a holiday for kids and greeting card companies and nothing more.

Then the roses arrived.

Her heart began a drum roll in her chest as she accepted the delivery and plucked the tiny envelope from the spear amid the blooms. They were gorgeous. Extravagant. And she shouldn't have received them. Some enterprising reporter could track the purchase back to Will—

Except the card wasn't one of Will's little notes, the ones she'd begun to find tucked into random places around her apartment.

It was from another man.

Be my Valentine? I miss you so much. Love, D.

"Shit."

In three weeks she had to fly out there for the live

reunion show. She'd been avoiding thinking about him, worried enough about Will's reaction that she'd let herself forget about Daniel. Forget his impressive ability to pine when he thought that was what he was supposed to be feeling.

The flowers sat on her café table, dwarfing it with their massiveness. There must be four dozen of the damn things. *Overcompensating, Daniel?*

She couldn't even toss them in the dumpster because one of the many entertainment reporters who had taken to visiting the town might find them and make an entire front page story out of it. *Suitorette Trashes Roses!*

But if Will saw them…

He would know. The jig would be up. A veil might be a gag gift but eleven million roses on Valentine's Day sent a certain message. A message like *I agreed to marry that idiot.*

Caitlyn stared at the Blooms of Doom. "Shit," she said again, as if repetition might help.

Right on cue, she heard the first creak and thud of Will downstairs. Her fingers flexed. On any other day, she would force herself to wait a minimum of sixty seconds before rushing to the piano and playing the *Pathetique*. But this was a Tuesday. And Valentine's Day. And an invitation on Valentine's *meant* something — even a musical one — and if he did come upstairs, like Dear God she really wanted him to, then he'd see the Blooms of Doom.

He might come up anyway. She was pretty sure she'd mumbled something about not spending the evening with Mimi when he'd slipped out of her bed at the crack of dawn this morning. God, why couldn't she remember what exactly she'd said? It was possible she'd *already* invited him and he was even now showering — *do not get distracted by thoughts of him showering, Caitlyn Marie Gregg!*—and getting himself spruced up to come upstairs.

He could not come upstairs.

She would cut him off at the pass. Go downstairs. And if he had no intention of seeing her on Valentine's and she completely embarrassed herself, so be it. As long as he didn't see the Blooms of Doom.

She wasn't ready for her house of cards to come falling down just yet. One more night of happy. Please God, give her that.

Will dropped the plastic Walgreens bag on the counter and began stripping down, intent on grabbing a quick shower and making himself presentable, but keeping one ear open for the Pathetique. His response to that song was downright Pavlovian. Instant hard-on and instant disregard for everything other than getting to her as fast as possible.

He didn't hear the music and even though he desperately needed a shower and shave, part of him was disappointed. Did she not remember her sleepy invitation for him to come over tonight? Or maybe he was in the doghouse for forgetting Valentine's Day. He'd completely spaced on the holiday—though he supposed he should have noticed an increased number of idiot teenage boarders trying stupid tricks to impress girls and needing to be med-evaced during his ski patrol shift.

He wouldn't have even known he'd screwed up, except Claire called him to bitch about the fact that Don had the audacity to suggest they try a romantic holiday dinner *with* their children, since they'd both forgotten to arrange a sitter in advance. Will had lied and told her he had a ski patrol shift for night skiing to get out of being conscripted as babysitter—and then made a frantic last minute run to Walgreens to raid the novelty candy aisle.

He'd sent a belated Happy Valentine's text to Caitlyn before driving home. No response.

She didn't seem the sort to get pissed about stuff like the proper way to observe couple holidays, but his sisters were proof that perfectly rational females could turn psychotic with very little provocation on the infamous V-Day.

He'd just pulled on a pair of dark slacks and a blue sweater Laney insisted made him look like a stud— according to her friends, because *ew*—when a tentative knock struck his door.

Caitlyn didn't usually come to him—though the memory of the last time she had was enough to get him half-hard. He smoothed a hand through his still-damp hair, grabbed the heart-shaped box of chocolates and went to open the door.

He had a momentary flicker of concern that it might not be her—*Jesus, if Tria has the gall to show up today*—but when he opened the door it was all Caitlyn, wearing one of the skirt-and-blouse outfits she taught in and nervously twirling a lock of red hair around one finger. He thrust the chocolates at her. "Happy Valentine's."

"Oh!" She took the candies, cradling them like they were more precious than gold—which made him feel like even more of an ass for the rush job. Especially when he noticed the price sticker still clinging to the back.

"Crap." He reached out and peeled the sticker off, crumpling it in his hand. "Sorry. I almost forgot about Valentine's entirely. Bad boyfriend?"

Her expression of shock made him replay what he'd just said. *Smooth, asshole.*

She blushed. "I… I didn't… uh… get you anything either."

"Friend," he amended, too late. A slow flush crept up from his collar. "I guess we haven't talked about—a little presumptuous—"

"No," she cut him off. Then she launched herself at him. Will grunted, catching her and staggering back into the apartment as she kissed the living daylights out of him.

Somehow he managed to shut the door and get them to the bedroom. The chocolates landed somewhere in the middle of the living room. The stud sweater didn't last any longer than her sexy little skirt and blouse. Then she was kneeling, tugging at his belt buckle.

Okay, so *boyfriend*. Good word. *Very* good word.

Half an hour later he was back in the shower. This time with company.

"I know we can't officially be together," he said, enjoying exactly how together they were at that moment. "It just sort of popped out." She snickered and he swatted her bottom, which only increased her laughter. "The *boyfriend* thing. I mean if you aren't ready…"

She shut him up with a hand over his mouth, then replaced it with her lips. "I liked it," she said when they both came up for air. "And I love that you said it first. Remind me to send your sisters a thank you note for putting you in touch with your feminine side."

"I'll show you my feminine side," he growled.

She squealed, laughing. "Or maybe a nice fruit basket. When we're able to tell people."

And there it was, his stupid heart catching air

because she alluded to a future... to a time when there would be no restrictions and they could just be together. Open. Honest. The sneaking around felt wrong—like he was making it with someone else's girl, even though he knew she was only his. He'd never really cared about advertising his relationship status before, but it would be nice when they could be public about it. When he could put his arm around her in town and everyone would know she wasn't that *Marrying Mister Perfect* girl. She was his.

Soon.

CHAPTER THIRTY-FOUR

"Wow. That is a shit ton of roses."

Caitlyn grimaced at the first words out of Mimi's mouth when she showed up on Wednesday to watch the DVRed episode. "Will you take them? They're from Daniel and I need to get them out of the apartment before Will sees them."

"The ex is trying to drown you in flowers, huh? Sure, I'll take 'em off your hands. I can tell Ty they're from my secret admirer. Keep him on his toes." She held up the grocery bag she'd brought, bulging with Ben & Jerry's. "Chunky Monkey or Phish Food? When I saw in the promos that this episode featured Elena in a bikini, I thought we might need reinforcements."

"Bless you. Open both." She waved Mimi toward the television. "I'll get spoons."

"You know, I'm starting to see why these shows are so messed up," Mimi said, wagging her spoon thoughtfully. "If you only saw the pieces he was with you, it would be the perfect romance. Or the pieces with Samantha. Though Elena's segments would look more like a porno. But it isn't until you see them back to back that you realize what a dick he is."

"I don't think he's a dick." Oddly, now that she was

no longer engaged to the man, she felt much more inclined to defend him. She could almost feel sorry for him. "You don't know how persuasive the producers can be. They're in your ear twenty-four-seven talking about exploring opportunities and going with the moment. It can be hard to get a sense of how you feel about a person when you're constantly being told it's possible to love everyone."

Mimi considered that for a moment, then shook her head, hot pink streaks sliding through her black hair. "Nope, I'm pretty sure he's a dick. None of the producers made him tell both you and Samantha that you'd make the perfect mother to his children. That isn't the kind of thing you just throw around on a date."

"I'm not sure he even wants kids," Caitlyn admitted. "He thinks he does, but I get the sense he's pretty confused about what he really wants right now. I think being Mister Perfect has really gone to his head."

Did Will want kids? It was the kind of thing they hadn't really talked about. She knew he had wanted them with Tria, but did he still or was he leery of making that kind of commitment with another woman? He'd said he was her boyfriend—which still gave her little shivers just thinking about it—but that wasn't exactly wedding bells and baby booties.

Caitlyn wasn't sure where they were heading, but she didn't have to be. They didn't have to work out all the details by a certain date. No love-on-a-clock here. Things could develop between them at a slower pace— though the chemistry sure wasn't slow.

But right now, she would live in the moment. And the moment was good.

As long as she didn't look at the *Marrying Mister Perfect*-shaped ax hanging over it all, waiting to fall.

CHAPTER THIRTY-FIVE

Will stepped out of his post-work shower and tipped his head as a shriek of feminine laughter carried down from the apartment above. Another Tuesday night. Mimi would be up there, watching *Marrying Mister Perfect* with Caitlyn. He was almost tempted to turn on the television and see what was so funny, but he'd avoided the show so far and didn't want to break his streak now.

His sisters would be watching. Only two more weeks until the live reunion show, according to Caitlyn. Was this the episode she got voted off?

Another burst of laughter filtered down to him. Mimi, by the sound of it. Caitlyn's laugh was quieter, like she wanted to hold the amusement close to herself rather than releasing it all into noise.

Most other Tuesdays he'd either picked up an extra shift or had a family dinner to attend, but last week had been Valentine's and this week he was on his own, straining for a trace of Caitlyn's laugh. He liked Mimi, liked that Caitlyn had someone to watch with. He wasn't jealous of their time together but he realized he was a little jealous of their friendship.

When was the last time he'd laughed like that with a friend? Probably before the Wedding That Wasn't. With Andy.

Shit. He really had cut himself off from the world.

While Caitlyn had been throwing herself out there in the biggest way, he'd been burrowing into his cave and become a full-on hermit. He wasn't ready to call Andy and make amends—not even close—but he was overdue for some male bonding.

His sisters would be watching *Marrying Mister Perfect*. Which meant Dale, Bryan and Don would be free to grab a beer at the Lodge pub.

Will reached for the phone.

"Mrs. Gregg, I know I've only known your daughter a short while, but feelings can develop very quickly in a journey like ours and if she's the one standing beside me at the end of all this, I just wouldn't feel right if I didn't have your blessing before I got down on one knee. Would you give me the honor of your permission to ask your daughter to be my wife?"

Another Tuesday, another train wreck.

It was the night of her Meet the In-Laws Date, when she showed Daniel around Manhattan and took him to meet her mother. Caitlyn sat with Mimi on the couch, watching with unmitigated dread as he gave her mother almost the exact same speech he'd given Elena's papa and Samantha's parents—though there hadn't been any such speech with Yasminda's parents. Spoiler alert.

"He's smooth," Mimi commented.

Caitlyn's stomach churned.

Watching the episode had been nauseating on several levels. It wasn't just that he seemed to have the same level of sincerity when he was talking to each of the parents and gazing soulfully into the eyes of each hopeful Suitorette. It was the way they looked back at him.

Elena, with that knowing *I've got you, chico* look of

hers that was both sexy and possessive. Yasminda with desperate adoration. That was bad enough, but it was the way Samantha looked at him that was the worst. Hopeful. Yearning. With that first little flicker of faith, as if he'd given her back a dream she'd almost stopped believing in.

"I think I might be sick."

"Milk," Mimi suggested. "Soak up some of the sweetness."

They'd been binging on the leftover Valentine's candy and now it wasn't sitting well in her stomach. Caitlyn went to the Keurig and brewed herself a cup of coffee instead of the milk. She had a feeling she wouldn't be sleeping tonight anyway.

The episode kept playing behind her.

Her mother's joyous permission granted. The laughing. The hugging. Their return to where Caitlyn was waiting. The one-big-happy-family cheer of it all.

"I need to tell Will about Daniel."

Sudden silence behind her. Mimi had hit pause.

"What did you just say?"

Caitlyn waited for the cup to finish brewing and wrapped her hands around it before turning and facing the music. "I haven't told Will that Daniel proposed. And I accepted. And then broke it off."

Mimi's jaw hit the floor. "I thought you told him when you told me!"

Caitlyn shook her head miserably. "He didn't seem to care about the show—he was my reprieve, you know? My support system. And then we started—you know—and it never seemed like the right time to tell him—it's not like he ever asked about it or anything. But now... He called me his girlfriend last week. Or rather, he called himself my boyfriend, but my heart about stopped, Mimi. It was so freaking hot."

"Oh sweetie. You've got it bad."

"I have to tell him."

"Yes, you do."

She would. She took a sip of her coffee, but it did not find her stomach to be a hospitable environment. "I'm definitely going to be sick."

"To football!"

A roar went up in the pub and Will added his voice even though he'd never really been that obsessed with the game. The Guys Night Out that had started when he called his brothers-in-law to meet him at the Lodge pub had snowballed until half the married men in Tuller Springs were huddled around the bar, celebrating all things testosterone with more gusto than selectivity. So far the toasts had covered a variety of sports, trucks, lawn-mowing, hunting and steel-toed boots. Laney's husband Bryan seemed to be leading the charge on most of the toasts—which was particularly entertaining since Will happened to know Laney was the better shot in their marriage and could probably run circles around him in most of the sports he'd mentioned.

Will and Don had retreated to one of the booths, but they still joined in whenever another toast erupted from the group at the bar.

Don raised his beer in one massive fist as a bellow for motorcycles rang out, grinning in his mild way. He was a dead ringer for an action hero, but the man was mellow as the Buddha. He nodded toward Bryan, three sheets to the wind at the bar. "He's gonna make a good dad."

Will's head snapped around. "Do you know

something I don't know?"

Don shook his head. "Just a hunch. I'm guessing they just found out it's a boy."

Will twisted in the booth to study his other brother-in-law. Bryan's smile was of the dopey, shell-shocked and euphoric variety that both Don and Dale had worn when their wives were expecting. "Why haven't they said anything?"

Don shrugged. "First trimesters are tricky. And... you know."

Will frowned. "I know?"

"They probably didn't want to rub their happiness in your face after the Tria thing."

Will stiffened at the suggestion that his sister might not feel like she could admit she was happy because he was so miserable. "That was months ago."

"Yeah," Don agreed. "And this is the first time you've done anything remotely fun that wasn't a mandated family activity."

He was tempted to argue. His work was fun most days. And Caitlyn was certainly fun, but he couldn't admit he was seeing her yet. Two more weeks.

He couldn't wait until he could tell people.

It was funny, when he'd been with Tria he'd never really been possessive or cared much about telling everyone that they were together, but with Caitlyn he couldn't wait to shout it from the rooftops. Maybe because he couldn't. Or maybe because something inside him knew this was different.

"How did you know Claire was The One?"

If Don was startled by the touchy-feely question, he didn't show it. "She told me I was never going to meet another woman as amazing as she is." He shrugged. "She's usually right about stuff like that."

Will blinked. "You knew Claire was The One because she told you she was?" That sounded like his sister.

"Yep." Don took another pull of his beer.

Caitlyn wasn't going to tell him. She wasn't arrogant like Claire. All of her confidence seemed to be reserved for her music.

Though maybe she was trying to tell him with the Pathetique.

Everything felt right with Caitlyn, but then everything had felt right with Tria too and he'd been wrong about her.

"Did you guys know that Tria and I weren't going to make it?" he asked Don—and realized he'd definitely had more to drink than he thought. He'd often wondered if his family had thought he was an idiot for proposing to her in the first place, but he'd never said the words before.

Don studied him for a moment, taking another swig of his beer as he considered the question. "No one knew," he admitted. "Probably would've been easier for your sisters if they didn't feel guilty for not seeing she was going to hurt you."

Will frowned. He'd never thought of it that way. He'd always just seen his own stupidity in not seeing the truth. It had never occurred to him that his sisters would feel bad for not protecting him. They'd always been his romantic advisors and when he'd needed it the most, they'd all been wrong about Tria together. It was comforting in a way. Making him feel like less the fool.

"I was completely blindsided," he admitted. And that had hurt as much as the betrayal. That he'd been so wrong. That he couldn't trust his instincts anymore where women were concerned. The fact that Caitlyn had been through her own nasty break-up was probably the only reason he felt like he could trust himself with her. They were both walking-wounded, romantically speaking.

"We all were," Don said. "But better to find out now than five years down the road with two kids."

Another cheer went up from the bar and Will turned to look at Bryan where he was attempting to crowd-surf with limited success. Will still wanted that—the house, the kids, the dopey grin, though maybe he'd skip the crowd-surfing.

He might be rushing things with Caitlyn, but he'd always liked going fast—on the slopes and in life. For the last seven months he'd forgotten he was the guy who threw himself into things. But Caitlyn had reminded him who he was and he wasn't going to screw things up with the girl who could do that.

It was after midnight, but Caitlyn was still awake when she heard the heavy *thud* on her landing, followed by the world's softest knock. She hadn't been able to sleep—her mind too busy spinning in circles, trying to find the words to say what she needed to say to Will. She climbed out of bed and scrambled down the loft steps, padding across the dark apartment to the door where she could faintly hear a male voice sing-songing *"Caaaaaitlyn"* ever so softly on the other side.

She knew even before she opened the door that he was drunk. She just wasn't prepared for how adorable he was drunk.

Will listed against the doorjamb, peering up at her through the hair that had fallen into his eyes, blinking slowly and smiling blearily. "Hey, you're awake," he told her, still whispering.

"Couldn't sleep," she admitted—not sure why she whispered back. "Is everything okay?"

He nodded tipsily. "My brother-in-law was sort of celebrating, but not really because they can't tell me because I'm not as happy as them."

Her eyebrows went up. "Am I supposed to understand what that means?"

He shook his head, grinning like a fool. He really was too cute when he was hammered. "I made you something. It's a romantic gesture. I'm an enlightened man." He stumbled a bit on the word *enlightened,* but managed to get it out. Nodding triumphantly. "I read romance novels."

"You do?"

"I do. My sisters made me start because *girls know stuff,* but they're actually really good."

"I'm sure they are." She had no idea why they were talking about romance novels.

"Do you want to read one? I'll get you one from downstairs." He swayed suddenly away from the doorjamb and she had a terrifying vision of him taking a header down the stairs.

She reached out, catching his arm and tugging him into her apartment. "I'm not sure you should be navigating any stairs right now, champ."

"You think I'm drunk," he declared, with the careful authority of extreme inebriation.

"I do." She got him into the apartment and kicked the door shut.

Will swayed, his head wobbling and eyelids seeming too heavy. He paused and she wondered if he would remember what they were talking about, then he nodded. "I might be drunk."

She bit back a laugh.

"But I made you a present."

He waved the CD-shaped case he held in one hand and she leaned back to avoid being hit on the chin with the present. "Thank you."

Mix Tape had been written in uneven Sharpie across the front of the case.

"'s a mix tape," he slurred.

"I gathered."

"Cuz you always provide the soundtrack—and don't gemme wrong, that Pathetique gets me hard as a freaking rock—but I wanted to supply the tunes tonight." He waved the CD again and she caught it before he could give himself a black eye.

"You should listen," he told her, making uneven progress toward the couch where he flopped down, long legs sprawled out in front of him.

She went over to the stereo, popping out the current CD and sliding his into the slot. "Out of curiosity, how drunk were you when you made this?"

"Pretty drunk," he admitted. His head had drooped against the back of the couch and his eyes were closed. "s'my Caitlyn playlist. Just burned it to a disk. Easy." He opened his eyes and lifted his head with effort. "C'mere."

She grabbed the stereo remote and crossed to curl on the couch next to him. He hummed happily and wrapped both arms around her, pulling her snug against his chest. "You smell nice," he rumbled.

"You smell like a brewery," she said, trying not to laugh.

He nodded very seriously. "I might have had a couple beers." Then his eyes seemed to focus on hers and he grinned goofily. "Hi, Caitlyn."

"Hi, Will."

"I made you a present."

"You gave it to me already."

He nodded, eyes falling closed as he sagged deeper into the couch. For a second she thought he might have passed out, then his arms tightened around her and he rumbled. "Middle school playbook. Mix tape is guaranteed kiss, maybe even second base."

She smothered a laugh. "You hoping to get lucky, sport?"

"Hell yeah, I'm bringing out my A Game tonight. Mix tape is good stuff. You should listen."

She lifted the remote and hit play. *Knock Three Times* began to play and she laughed as the singer begged his neighbor to knock on the ceiling if his feelings were reciprocated. "It's very us."

"It gets better," Will assured her.

Caitlyn cuddled down deeper into his arms to listen. And it did get better. The second song was from Norah Jones—*One Flight Down*—and her internal organs liquefied in the heat of the slow, sultry song.

Will had been silent for so long she was certain he was out cold, but when she lifted her head from his shoulder she found him watching her, with eyes steadier than his level of inebriation should have allowed.

"You use music to express how you feel," he said, only slurring a little. "I'm expressing myself."

And a yearning Jason Mraz song about wanting to be more than friends began to play.

Oh Holy Haydn.

She knew she should tell him the truth about Daniel, but he was drunk and so damn sexy and she just wanted it to last a little bit longer. Just one more night. Or maybe seven. She could put it off just a little longer.

The man was using the sexiest songs on the planet to

tell her how he felt about her. No pedestals in sight. Only the burning heat in his eyes and his arms strong around her.

Go with the moment, Caitlyn. She heard the words in Miranda's voice—and for once the reality television advice had never sounded better.

She sank into the moment and his arms.

CHAPTER THIRTY-SIX

"I chickened out again," Caitlyn said in lieu of hello as soon as Mimi answered the phone.

Mimi groaned dramatically. "Cait. You've got to tell him. Like, yesterday."

"I know. But Mimi, he made a mix tape. I literally cannot hear it without wanting to pounce on him like a tigress."

"You know I normally support tigress pouncing, but you *have to tell him*. The finale is less than two weeks away. You do not want him to figure it out when it's a headline the next morning."

"Right. I know. I just..." Caitlyn sank down onto the couch, staring blindly out the window with the phone pressed to her ear. "What if he hates me when he finds out?"

"He isn't going to hate you."

"What if he does? His ex jilted him. I jilted Daniel."

"It isn't the same."

"Isn't it?"

"Caitlyn." Mimi put on her I-am-the-boss mom voice. "You are braver and stronger and more deserving of love than you give yourself credit for. Man up, own your awesome, and *tell the man*. If you want, you can start by telling him you're in love with him."

"Mimi! I'm not. It isn't... we aren't defining things.

We're taking it slow. Letting the relationship grow at a natural pace."

"And I'm sure all of that sounds awesome when you're rationalizing, but if you feel the need to confess your undying love for the boy downstairs I fully support that plan. When are you telling him?"

"He has to work tonight and he has a family thing tomorrow. Right after that. I promise."

"No chickening out."

"I won't. I promise." And this time she meant it. She was running out of time. If she didn't tell him soon, the rest of the world would.

"Will, I would like to officially apologize for almost setting you up with the Mister Perfect chick. Though I didn't *actually* set you up so I don't know why Julia gets to be all *I told you so* about it."

"You dodged a bullet," Laney piped in.

Will rolled his eyes in the general direction of his three sisters as they sipped their hot cocoa at the kitchen table and each cast an indulgent eye over their collective husbands and offspring cavorting outside in the snow. He gave Laney an extra look, trying to figure out if she was hiding a baby bulge with her baggy sweatshirt—but she so often wore baggy sweatshirts he couldn't tell.

"What are you three blathering about now?" He'd come inside to grab a carrot for the snowman Hailey was trying to will into existence through stubbornness alone, but at the mention of Mister Perfect his ears pricked up.

In the last week, Caitlyn had been jumpy, popping Tums like they were going out of style and occasionally starting to say something and then breaking off and blushing. At first he had been concerned her awkwardness had something to do with the idiot he'd made of himself with the mix tape fiasco, but she seemed to love the CD—if the amount she was playing it and the fact that she always jumped him when the second song came on were any indication. And over the last few days it had become obvious it was something about the show's conclusion that was upsetting her. She jumped a mile whenever anyone mentioned it.

He'd fought back his curiosity and managed not to ask. She'd tell him when she was ready. Her past was just that—her past. He planned on being her future.

Only one more week now. He'd more or less avoided learning the gory details of the show, but he knew that much.

His sisters hadn't broached the topic again since for all they knew he'd stopped seeing Caitlyn. They hadn't been caught together in public again since the infamous TMZ photos—which he was never going to live down.

"The girl we were going to set you up with. Caitlyn." Claire explained. "She's one of the final two on *Marrying Mister Perfect*. So it's a good thing you steered clear."

Laney nodded sagely. "Everyone thought that Samantha was a lock to win it all and Elena was going to go far because all men think with their dicks, but Caitlyn was the dark horse and well, there you go. Dodged a bullet."

Not for the first time, he felt like his sisters were speaking in girl code and hadn't given him the decoder ring. "I'm not following. Why do you keep saying I dodged a bullet? What does it matter if she was in the top two?"

"The sex dates."

Laney shushed Claire. "The final two are always both

completely hung up on the guy. For, like, *ever*. I mean, they legitimately expect to marry him. That is some seriously *massive* emotional baggage they're carrying around."

"And the sex dates," Claire insisted.

Laney rolled her eyes. "Yes, Claire, the sex dates."

"What are the sex dates?" Will didn't know much about the show, but he knew it was on primetime network television so he figured it would have to be within the bounds of FCC regulations.

"Overnight dates," Laney explained, taking pity on him. "In these super sexy foreign locales. The cameras fade away and everything is left to the viewer's imagination, but it's pretty obvious they're getting it on."

"Even if they say they're good girls," Claire put in. "What happens in the Fantasy Suite doesn't always stay in the Fantasy Suite, if you know what I mean."

If Caitlyn was nervous about him finding out she'd gone all the way with this Mister Perfect ass a few months ago, that would certainly explain her recent squirrely behavior. He tried to tell himself he didn't care—he'd known she wasn't a virgin when they first hooked up and he sure as hell wasn't one himself. He was trying to be enlightened, squashing down his caveman jealousy.

"So you're saying because she may or may not have slept with this guy months ago, that I should avoid my very nice neighbor because she must have massive baggage?"

"They're saying that," Julia confirmed. "I'm saying you should avoid her because she's engaged."

"Excuse me?"

"You don't know that for sure," Laney immediately

argued, while Will recovered from the verbal sucker punch.

"Why else would he be here?" Julia countered. "You've seen the pictures. And the flowers! They're engaged. Mark my words."

"There are, like, a thousand reasons why he could be visiting the runner-up."

"A zillion red roses?"

"Decoy flowers!"

"Hey!" Will shouted. "Could someone please explain to your poor brother what the hell you're talking about?"

This time it was Claire who took pity on him. "Some pictures came out yesterday of Mister Perfect here in Tuller Springs. It's pretty obvious that he was going into her place when they were snapped."

"And on Valentine's Day, Monica at the Lodge said she saw some guy delivering the biggest bouquet of red roses she'd ever seen to Caitlyn's door. Does that seem like the kind of thing you do for the runner up?"

White noise fogged his brain.

There was an innocent explanation. There had to be.

But why wouldn't Caitlyn tell him that this Mister Perfect guy had come to see her if it was perfectly innocent? And why would she hide a flower delivery? If there even were flowers—Monica at the Lodge wasn't always the most reliable source, though she was enthusiastic with the gossip.

Flowers, photos, sex dates...

Why the hell *had* she been wearing a veil that first night they met? She'd said it was a gag gift, but her eyes hadn't quite met his when she said it. Had they? Or was his memory playing tricks on him?

"Are you going to take that out to them? Will?"

He looked down, surprised to find himself holding a carrot. Hailey. The snowman. "Right. Yeah. Of course."

And then he was going to get answers. It was time he and Caitlyn had a little talk about Mister Perfect.

CHAPTER THIRTY-SEVEN

"Excuse me, Caitlyn?"

Caitlyn slowed and turned toward the sound of the hesitant female voice. She supposed it was too much to ask to sneak out to buy a half-gallon of milk and some Wheat Thins without being stopped by someone who'd seen her on television. Especially this week of all weeks.

The Finale and live reunion special would air on Tuesday. She'd be flying out to Los Angeles for the taping in just a couple days. And she hadn't had a chance to say anything to Will. Time was running out, but she was so terrified of losing him as soon as she told him, she just kept hoping he would love her enough to look past it, kept waiting for him to say the words.

The woman who'd stopped her was petite and pretty, with elfin features and big blue eyes. The kind of waifish beauty big strong men loved to protect.

"Photo or autograph?" Caitlyn asked with a smile that was only slightly forced. She tried to be nice to the fans of the show, but the constant attention was exhausting. She'd never had this kind of notoriety when she was performing. Sure, she'd sign the occasional autograph, but it had never been this constant barrage.

"Sorry?" the pretty waif asked.

"Would you like your photo with me? Or can I sign something for you?'

"Oh, no, no. I'm Tria. Tria Mathers? Perhaps Will mentioned me? I was…. We… that is…"

The ex.

This was her. The woman who had broken Will's heart. The woman he still couldn't think about without having his face harden into a stone mask.

Tria. She was lovely. Precious. A gorgeous little pixie.

Caitlyn hated her.

"I don't…" What the hell was she supposed to say?

"I know you two are friends." The tips of her blonde hair stuck out from beneath her hat as she gazed up at Caitlyn in the parking lot, earnest and wide-eyed. "I saw the picture on TMZ. I thought you might be more than friends when I saw how he was looking at you, but now… I guess you're with that TV guy. But it's Will I was hoping you could help me with."

If the woman said she wanted to win him back, Caitlyn was going to go for her throat like a badger. "Help you."

"I know this isn't any of your business, but Will and my, uh, my boyfriend Andy—"

"The one you jilted him for."

Tria swallowed visibly. "Yes. They were best friends their entire lives and I killed that. I know I don't deserve Will's forgiveness and maybe Andy doesn't either, but we would both do anything in the world to earn it." Tears glistened in her baby blues. "Will has every right to be angry, but I hate that what we did turned him into this angry, unforgiving man. He was never like that before. Will is the warmest, sweetest, most wonderful guy I've ever met and I hate the idea that he's festering with bitterness because I was a stupid cow."

Caitlyn eyed the distance to her car. "I don't know

what you expect me to do."

"He won't even listen to me. I thought maybe if you talked to him… just sort of gently… the next time you see him…"

Her pleading his ex's case. That was bound to go over well. Tria looked tearful, but determined. A determined little pixie. "You're one of those people who has to fix everyone else's problems, aren't you?"

Tria's grimace was self-effacing. "Guilty. I can't stand when things are unresolved."

Just like Will. How angry he must be to leave this unsettled. "I'm not going to get in the middle of it, Tria. Sorry."

"It isn't for me. It's for him. And Andy."

"You may be right." As much as it burned to admit it. "It may be better for the whole world if we can just forgive and hug it out. But you can't force that and I'm not going to push him. He's still that warm, sweet guy."

"Just not with me," Tria whispered.

"Yeah, well, can you blame him? You broke his heart." She didn't expect Daniel to forgive her. When she finally realized they were broken up for real. If he ever did.

For all she knew he was still planning the wedding.

Shit. She needed to tell Will. D-Day was looming.

"I've gotta go, Tria. Good luck."

The perfect little blonde pixie watched her walk away.

Will's Jeep was parked in front of the chalet when she got back from the store. He must have finished up the Hamilton Family Fun Night early.

Perfect. She would put away the milk, play the

Pathetique, and then confess everything. Nondisclosure be damned.

It would be fine.

Caitlyn put away the milk. Popped a handful of Tums. Sat at the piano. Stared at the keys. Flexed her fingers. Petted the silky ivory. Put her hands back in her lap. Went to the cupboard for more Tums, grateful she'd sprung for the value sized container. Back to the piano.

A knock rattled the door in its frame. "Caitlyn? It's Will. I know you're home."

There was a note to his voice. Brusque. Hard. She'd only heard him sound like that when he was talking about his ex.

Oh God. Someone must have seen her talking to Tria. Trust the Tuller Springs gossip mill to get the news to Will in less time than it took her to drive home.

Caitlyn rushed to the door, pulling it open, explanations ready on her lips, when his first words sent her thoughts scattering to Timbuktu.

"Did you agree to marry him?"

Oh shit.

CHAPTER THIRTY-EIGHT

The way her face fell would have been comical, if it hadn't been tragic. It was true. She was engaged. Will resisted the urge to rub his chest where his heart used to beat.

"How did you... who told you that?" she whispered, horror and shock and something that almost looked like relief all flashing across her face.

"Does it matter? You're engaged?"

"Not anymore," she whispered, and the words seemed to echo in his head, confirming it.

"But you were. When we met.... The veil." *God, he was such a fucking idiot.* It had all been right there and he hadn't seen. He hadn't wanted to see. "Jesus."

"Come inside, please." She ushered him in the door and his feet moved of their own accord, shuffling numbly along. "I've wanted to tell you. They had me sign all these nondisclosure agreements, that I won't leak anything about the results of the show, but I had to tell you. I'd already decided that I would risk the lawsuits because I needed you to know."

"Did he send you flowers? On Valentine's Day?" His voice seemed to be coming from far away, some distant island.

"Yes. I'd broken it off, but he—"

"And you hid them. That's why you came

285

downstairs. To keep me from seeing."

"Will, please…"

"And he came here. To see you."

"It was weeks ago. Before you and I even kissed. I gave him back his ring."

"Did you sleep with him?"

The flicker of guilt on her face was another mule kick to the gut. "I didn't even know you then," she whispered.

Later he would feel guilty for making her feel ashamed. Later. Now he wasn't feeling anything. Just the low buzzing in the back of his brain like a hive of angry bees.

"I broke it off with him as soon as I realized there was something real between you and me. It's *over*, Will."

"You're right. It is."

But he didn't mean with that guy and from the look on her face she heard the distinction in his voice.

Horror. Hurt. The glimmer of tears. "Please, Will, don't do this."

And then the words came, the ones that had been swarming in the back of his brain with the bees. "When Tria explained that she was leaving me because she'd just fallen in love with Andy out of the blue and you can't control your heart, do you know what I promised myself? I swore I would never be that guy. I would never do to someone else what they did to me. But you just went and made me that guy without even telling me."

"I didn't mean for it to happen like this."

"No. Of course not. No one ever does."

"I made a mistake when I agreed to marry him and I made another one when I didn't tell you sooner, but when was I supposed to say something? It always felt like it was too late or too soon. I screwed up. I get that you don't want to be that guy and you're pissed at me for that, but it wasn't just about you." A rosy flush of anger spread across her face and neck. "Would you rather I made myself miserable for the rest of my life just so I could always keep my word to someone you've never even met? I wasn't going to do that. Especially when it was a promise I made in haste, without thinking things through, swept away in the moment, completely outside my usual reality. People make mistakes! Especially on reality TV. But we try to correct them and now you're punishing me for figuring out that you're the one I want? I'm not Tria!"

"This isn't about her."

"Everything is about her with you!" she shouted. "Do you still love her?"

"Don't be ridiculous."

"That isn't an answer." Angry tears swelled in her eyes. "She came to see me today. Did you know that? She's worried that you're turning into a bitter bastard because you can't let go of your anger for her."

"That's none of your business."

"That's what I said. Of course, that was before you decided I was just like her. You can't forgive her, so how can you forgive me, right? But when you hold onto anger like that, the only person you make miserable is yourself. You don't forgive people for them. You do it for you. So you're not festering under the weight of all your regrets. I know I screwed up. I'm *sorry*. So damn sorry. I'm sorry for Daniel and for you and for Elena and Samantha—"

"Caitlyn, calm down."

Her breath was coming too fast, almost hyperventilating. "Would you even have let me get this close if I'd been completely available? If we'd been able to have a normal relationship and tell people, would you have even wanted me? Did you like that it was all behind closed doors? You didn't have to tell your family about me. It was never real for you, was it? No commitment if no one knows."

"You aren't making any sense. You need to calm down."

She went to the piano, bracing her hands on it, forcing herself to breathe. "I made a mistake."

"So did I." He'd fallen completely in love with another woman who was only going to break his heart.

She looked up, hope in her eyes.

"Goodbye, Caitlyn."

She flinched as if he'd struck her. He didn't stay to see her cry.

Caitlyn sank to the floor as soon as the door clicked softly shut behind Will. It should have slammed. If this was really the end of their relationship, shouldn't there have been a cymbal crash? There had been screaming (hers), hysterics (also hers), tears (her again). The least he could have added to the equation was a good door slam.

She sat on the floor and stared at the grain in the floorboards. Shouldn't she be sobbing? Shock. That's what this was. Disbelief. What had just happened? Was he really gone?

A little whimper escaped her lips, but she didn't have the strength to get up and go after him. What would she even say?

I love you.

The words shuddered through her, and then she did

begin to sob. Stupid, gulping sobs.

Ugly crying. Blotchy faced with a freaking fountain running from her nose.

Of all the regrets she could have, out of everything she'd stupidly said, the one thing that burned was the fact that she had never, not once, told him she loved him.

Caitlyn dragged herself over to the phone, dialing. It only rang once.

"Hello?"

"Mimi?" Her voice quavered, hitching.

"Where are you? What's wrong? Oh shit, you told him, didn't you? Are you home? I'm coming over. Don't move. I'm coming."

Caitlyn whimpered something affirmative and curled up to wait. It wouldn't always hurt this much. Time healed. She told herself that. Over and over.

It won't always hurt. Heartbreaks fade.

But the words felt like a lie. Will Hamilton was never going to fade from her heart.

CHAPTER THIRTY-NINE

Will was righteous and pissed. Then he was righteous and depressed. Then he was righteous and drunk. Then he was drunk and depressed. Then he was unconscious.

By the time he hit hungover and stupid, it was Friday morning. And Caitlyn was gone.

He tracked down her friend Mimi, who glared at him like he'd taken up seal clubbing, but when he opened with, "I'm an idiot" Mimi grudgingly informed him that Caitlyn had flown out to Los Angeles early to clear her head and do a dozen spa treatments to try to reduce the puffiness of her eyes before she had to appear on national television.

Will felt like even more of an asswipe with the confirmation that he'd made her cry.

Even though her friend was all in favor of his rushing out to Los Angeles to grovel, Mimi didn't know where Caitlyn was. The show was intensely secretive about things like that, so unless she answered her cell phone, he was shit out of luck.

She didn't answer her cell phone.

He left messages. He begged. He groveled.

Then he called for the twelfth time and heard the ringtone seeping through the ceiling of his apartment. She'd left the phone behind.

The woman he—okay, yes, he was pretty sure he was

ass over ears in love with her—was about to be reunited with the so called *perfect* guy she had once been engaged to and Will had completely fucked up the send-off. He couldn't even remember half of what he'd said to her. He just remembered the angry bees in his head and feeling like she had betrayed him and lied to him—and yes, she'd definitely lied, and not about the little things, but she hadn't had a choice and—God, he just needed to see her. It would all be better if he could just *see* her.

He'd have *I'm sorry, Caitlyn, I love you* written across the sky in Los Angeles—but that would probably only get them both slapped with a lawsuit for ruining the ending of the goddamn show.

He had no freaking idea what to do.

So he went to his sisters.

"You ready, hon?"

A strange sense of déjà vu came over Caitlyn as she looked into the mirror and met the reflected gaze of Miranda Pierce. Standing over her shoulder, the producer wore a black headset mashed down over her sleek, razor-sharp platinum bob.

Caitlyn wasn't wearing a fancy gown this time. The stylists had agreed on a simple sea-foam green cocktail dress and heeled sandals. Nothing too bridal.

"Sorry you won't be getting your wedding."

Miranda arched a single sculpted eyebrow. "Did you want to get married on national television?"

"No," she said with absolute conviction.

Miranda shrugged. "Well, there you go. Besides, the occasional dramatic break-up is just as good for ratings as the sappy happy endings. Marcy and Craig are still going strong. Jack and Lou are breeding like bunnies—

we're leading with an ultra-sound photo of the twins. It was about time we had a romantic failure. We can't win 'em all. And it would be boring if we did."

Lucky me, the poster-child for romantic failure.

Miranda glanced down at her ever-present tablet. "You know the drill. We'll save you for last. The girls en masse will get to rip him a new one and then Elena gets her turn and then we'll bring you out."

"Can I speak to Elena? Before the show?"

The producer shrugged. "I don't have any objections to that, but ultimately it will be up to her. She might not want company."

"That's fine. I just… can you ask her?"

Miranda smiled, the professional smile that never made it all the way to her eyes. "Absolutely. You sit tight."

Caitlyn sat, her mind blissfully blank. After the last few days of thinking things over—Will, Daniel, the show—she felt like she had come to a few decisions. Now she just had to be brave enough to act on them. No matter what Mimi said, or how adventurous Will had encouraged her to be, she wasn't exactly known for her bravery.

Five minutes later, Miranda reentered the dressing room. "Miracle of miracles. She'd love to see you. Just hang on a second until we can clear the hallway and then we'll sneak you down there."

Caitlyn nodded.

It was funny, the little things about the show that had already begun to fade from her memory. Being held in a room so the wrong people didn't bump into one another. The pleasantly dictatorial demeanor of the producers and cast wranglers, telling them where to be and what to do. The ubiquitous psychologists, waiting in the wings to talk to them about what had happened and coach them into opening up on camera more.

She wouldn't miss it. Not one bit of it.

Elena's dressing room was three doors down and an exact mirror image of hers. The Latina beauty was sitting at the vanity when Miranda opened the door, but immediately rose to face them. She planted her hands on her curvy hips and arched her long neck in a look that could have been haughty or combative, but Caitlyn now recognized it as Elena bracing for impact. She'd taken a lot of hits in the last few months. The Slutty Suitorette.

"Hi," she said awkwardly.

Elena nodded. "Hey."

"I'll just leave you two alone. No cat fights off camera," Miranda said, though the joke fell flat in the tense room. "Just knock on the door when you're ready to leave, Caitlyn."

And then they were alone. The two women who had made it to the end of the Epic Journey Toward Love that was *Marrying Mister Perfect*.

She was still stunning. Samantha might have been the most beautiful, but Elena trumped everyone on sheer sexual magnetism. *Salma Hayek, eat your heart out.* She tossed her long black hair, eyeing Caitlyn guardedly.

Elena had always been impatient, impetuous and blunt. Caitlyn took a page out of her book.

"Did you love him?"

"Did you?" Elena countered after a minute pause.

"I thought I did," she admitted. "Or that I might. I was never sure."

"I was," Elena said. And the tension suddenly left the room. Her defensive posture eased and there they were, just two women who'd been stupid enough to date the same guy at the same time. "I threw myself into it completely. I was absolutely convinced that he was the one. I told myself it was true love. I can be very persuasive – even when I'm only fooling myself."

"Do you still?" Caitlyn asked softly. "Love him?"

Elena hesitated. Then finally… "No. I hated you for a little while," she admitted, then shrugged. "It was easy to blame you for every time he lied to me. But eventually I wised up and became grateful you'd taken the bullet for me. I would have married him." She grimaced with distaste—somehow making even that expression seem sensual. "I was that sure. And what a nightmare that would have been." She nodded to Caitlyn's bare left ring finger. "You've called it off?"

Caitlyn nodded. "A few weeks ago."

"Brave," Elena murmured. "If you wanted him, though, you'd have my blessing. No hard feelings."

"I wondered if I owed you an apology."

Elena's face—always so revealing—clearly displayed her surprise. "Oh, *querida*, *no.* You don't owe me anything. I made my own mistakes."

"They haven't been kind to you. In the press."

"The Slutty Suitorette? My father is appalled. He's barely speaking to me now. I suppose I could have predicted that, if I'd been thinking."

"Why did you do it?" Caitlyn asked. "I've always wondered. Why play the villainess?"

"Why play the tramp, you mean?" Elena shrugged again, but that edge of defensiveness was back. "I thought he would be worth it. I never dreamed he would pick someone else. Mister Perfect." She gave a low, humorless laugh. "You know sometimes I wonder if I even knew the difference between falling for Mister Perfect and falling for Daniel. I'm pretty certain *he* didn't know the difference—and that was the really dangerous part. But I figured it out too late. I doubt I ever would have figured it out if he hadn't rejected me. You're smarter than I am."

"I don't think that's true."

"No? You figured out the secret. It's easy to think he's your last and only shot at happiness. That if you don't want Mister Perfect, or if he doesn't want you, you'll never find anyone. They encourage you to think that. But it's a show. It's a lie. It's not your life. And love isn't one guy selecting the best possible girl from a bunch of desperate candidates like the world's most fucked up job interview."

Caitlyn's heart clenched, thinking of Will and what she'd thought love was and everything she'd thought she had with him. "What is it? Love, I mean."

Elena snorted. "Hell if I know. Let me know if you figure it out, okay?"

Caitlyn smiled a little, feeling that same macabre kinship. Survivors of the same natural disaster. "Deal."

Will waited until all three of his sisters had seated themselves at his kitchen table before he asked the ten million dollar question.

"Am I still hung up on Tria?"

Claire and Laney exchanged a glance.

Julia hummed a sympathetic noise. "Only you can say what your heart feels for her—"

"I'm not in love with her. That isn't it." He tried to remember exactly what Caitlyn had said. "Am I being a dick, clinging to anger and resentment to avoid real relationships?"

"Well..." Julia hummed.

"You have every right," Claire said, dripping sympathy. Though she was usually the first one to tell him to get his head out of his ass. His family had been babying him. Letting him wallow. *Shit*.

"Who said that?" Laney asked, cutting right through to the juicy part with her keen gossip radar.

"Caitlyn."

"*Marrying Mister Perfect* Caitlyn?" This from Claire.

"Oooh, did she tell you if Daniel proposed to her?"

"Focus, Julia," Laney snapped, "Will is having an emotional breakthrough." Both she and Claire glared at their middle sister.

"Caitlyn *is* my emotional breakthrough. Mister Perfect did propose. She said yes. Then she broke it off. Because of me. Of us… There was an 'us.' But when she told me that she'd jilted Mister Perfect for me, I lost it. I yelled. I was a fucking moron and now she's gone.

"Typical guy," Claire shook her head.

"Help me fix it," he pleaded.

His sisters had all descended on his apartment within fifteen minutes of his call, arriving en masse since Laney had swung by to pick up the others, which was both wonderful and terrifying. Now he just needed them to wave their magic wands, give him invaluable girl advice like they had since he hit puberty and show him the magic gesture that would make it all right.

It had to be all right.

"Um…" Julia and Claire exchanged a glance, for once looking at a loss for genius girl advice.

"You do realize she's on television, like, *right now*," Laney said. "The Finale and Reunion Special air tonight."

Shit. She was with *him*. Right now. Mister Perfect could be pleading his case. Probably being fucking perfect.

He swore.

Claire shoved him toward his couch. "Sit. We'll watch with you. Moral support."

"You'll watch with me so you can feed off my love life like emotional vampires."

"Like I said," Claire said cheerfully as Laney turned on his television. "Moral support."

He could have kicked them out, but the truth was, he really could use the moral support – even if it did come with a certain dose of emotional voyeurism. His sisters were dramatic pains in his ass, but they were his and they loved him and they wanted him to be happy and right now he needed all the voices he could find petitioning God to send Caitlyn back to him. So he sat with his sisters and prayed at the altar of reality television for the woman who seemed to have become the love of his life.

CHAPTER FORTY

The lights burned down, as warm as a tropical sun. Caitlyn sat stiffly, as far away from Daniel as she could get on the cozy little love seat, her hands folded in her lap. They weren't shaking. And for once her stomach was fine. It still felt strange, knowing this was being broadcast live to millions of households in America, but she'd found her center. All of this didn't seem to matter so much anymore.

"I don't see a ring," their host, Josh Pendelton, said gently, oozing empathy and charm. "We all watched that romantic proposal, we saw that very happy couple on the screen, but now I understand things have changed. The airing of the show can be hard on our couples. We've seen it before. Are you still together?"

"We broke it off," Caitlyn said, soft, but firm.

Daniel cleared his throat. "Josh, may I say something?"

"By all means, Daniel," Josh smiled, debonair and always composed. "The floor is yours."

Caitlyn wasn't sure what to expect. Some manifesto on Daniel's part? But she supposed she should have seen it coming when he turned to her and reached for her hands. She let him take them, though his grip felt unnaturally hot.

"Caitlyn. I still love you."

She almost sighed. *Of course you do*. The man didn't know what he felt. She opened her mouth, started to shake her head, but he plowed on before she could refute his claim.

"I've missed you, sweetheart, and I've never wanted anything as much as I want you back. You're it for me."

The nausea was back. Lovely.

"I know I made mistakes." His eyes flicked to the side, where the other Suitorettes were sitting. Several necks craned as everyone turned to stare at Elena—who was probably planning a voodoo doll with Daniel's name on it. "But I still believe we're meant to be together. I still want our life together." He pulled something from his pocket. A ring box. A very familiar ring box. *Well, shit.* "I love you, Caitlyn. The one thing I did that wasn't a mistake was picking you."

Ouch. She hoped Elena kicked him in the balls later. "No, but it was my mistake to say yes."

A gasp rippled through the crowd and Caitlyn winced. Okay, yes, that had come out much more harshly than it had sounded in her head.

Here was Mister Perfect. Still handsome. Still romantic—if in a generic, non-specific way that made her feel like she was just filling a role. Perfect Fiancé. Not Caitlyn.

But he was offering her that life again. That tempting life. Husband. Children. Happily-ever-after.

Bird in the hand.

From the look on Daniel's face, she knew she could name her terms. On national television, no less, so he couldn't renege. She had no idea where she stood with Will. They hadn't exactly left things in a good place. He was still nursing wounds from being jilted. He might never want to get that close to another woman. Taking a chance on Will might very well blow up in her face and leave her heartbroken and alone.

The choice had been so hard before. She'd been so panicked. So unsure.

It was ridiculously easy now.

"Daniel, I'm sorry. You're a good guy, but I can't marry you. In the last few weeks, I've started developing feelings for someone who has been a great friend through this entire process." *Use the jargon, Caitlyn. Always a process, never a nightmare.* "I don't know if he feels the same way or if anything will come of it, but it wouldn't be fair to you to pretend my heart isn't otherwise engaged."

"Would this be Will Hamilton? The man you were photographed with a couple months back?" Josh asked, smoothly taking back the reins of the show.

"No comment," Caitlyn murmured.

She had a thousand things to say to Will, but she wasn't going to say them on national television. Her love life wasn't their business anymore. The rush that accompanied that thought was practically orgasmic.

She may have screwed things up with Will by not being up front about things with Daniel, but he was still the only man she could imagine marrying and she was going to win him back. It was her turn to woo him.

Miranda moved through the darkened studio. The show had finished airing hours ago. Caitlyn was on her way back to her hotel, several of the other Suitorettes were either on their way to the airport or to a bar. Another successful season… but she didn't feel satisfied. Just tired.

The dual specters of *American Dance Star* and Bennett

Lang had hung over her for the second half of the season, the decisions providing equal parts temptation and dread. She didn't know if she could take over Bennett's job—even if it was her dream job—without being reminded of him every second of every day. And on the romantic side, if he was retiring, she wasn't even sure how their lives would go together—if there was even a hope for them as a couple.

She still couldn't escape the feeling of inequity. Like he wanted to be her adored mentor rather than her partner.

She reached for the last light switch on the set, only to see a figure moving up on the love seat where all of tonight's drama had taken place. A very familiar, muscular blond figure.

Miranda sighed. Daniel had had a rough night. The Suitorettes had taken him to the carpet for leading them on—which admittedly was part of the show. Then Elena had torn him a new one for treating her like a disposable sex doll—which admittedly, he deserved. And then Caitlyn had practically laughed in his face when he tried to re-propose to her. Poor guy.

This is what rock bottom looks like, champ.

She tucked her tablet under her arm and climbed the risers up to the main stage area. Daniel looked up, his pretty face contorted in confusion, muscular back bowed.

"I don't understand what happened."

She was reminded of the first audition tape she'd seen of him. Wholesome, laughing, unspoiled. Poor guy. "You bought into your own image."

His head lifted and he blinked up at her. "What?"

Miranda sank down onto one of the set couches, slipping her heels off her aching feet and tossing her tablet onto the cushion beside her. "I could tell you that Caitlyn just fell in love with someone else. That you were a pebble on her road to true love or whatever bullshit. Or I could say that it was the pressure of the show—being apart for months on end while it's airing and not being able to comfort her when she had doubts. I could tell you that it wasn't you, it was her, but I'm feeling particularly honest today so I'm gonna give it to you straight, Danny Boy. It's you. You started out as a nice guy—the guy all of America wanted to date, the one every mother in America hoped would meet her daughter—and then you drank the reality show Kool-aid, started reading your own press clippings, bought into your own hype and became a royal, first class, grade A douche."

His chin rocked back like she'd socked him and Pretty Boy glowered at her. "Is this supposed to be comforting?"

"I'm not here for comforting. Go to a club after this and five girls will line up to comfort the hell out of you all night long. I'm giving it to you straight—which is a rare commodity in this town so you should take it as the manna from heaven it is."

His mouth tightened in anger. "So I'm a douche."

"You are. But the good news is you might not be an irredeemable one. You were a genuinely great guy when you came on the show the first time. And then the fame changed you. It happens to a lot of people—some more severely than others."

"I'm not famous," he said, but something about the way he said it convinced her that he knew it was a lie as much as she did. And that he would lap up every drop of attention that came his way.

"Sure you are. You're famous for being the one

everyone wants—which is a dangerous kind of fame. Society is busy screaming about how men are assholes and here you are—a unicorn. The One Good Guy. But the second you buy into that crap, you stop being the One Good Guy and become just another brand of asshole. As soon as you believe you're God's Gift to Women, you aren't anymore. Catch-22."

He grimaced. "I used to teach that book."

"To second graders?"

"High school. I taught high school for a year before I moved to fourth grade. I never taught second."

She shrugged. "Until they're old enough to go on the show, they don't exist to me."

"And you think my reality is skewed?"

"I never said mine wasn't." Miranda liked her glass house. "I just answered your question about how this happened. You became an ass. The kind of man that a sensible girl like Caitlyn would never choose to spend the rest of her life with. It took her a little while to wake up and smell the asshole, but when she did she had a big strong fire-fighter on hand to make sure she got her happily ever after."

"And that leaves me where?"

"Single and unemployed in Hollywood. Don't worry. It happens to the best of us."

His head snapped up at that. "They fired you?"

"Of course not, dummy. I'm amazing. I can write my own ticket." Literally. *American Dance Star* was waiting. If she wanted it. "Believe it or not, you turning into a dick on national television and then getting jilted was great for the ratings because we were able to spin it. Everybody's happy."

"Except me."

"Well, yeah." *And Elena.* She'd taken a beating in the

court of public opinion and Miranda still felt bad about that. Not that Daniel seemed to care. "Were you really going to be happy engaged to Caitlyn? You barely know her. And honestly? Right now you barely know yourself. Maybe figure that out before you go running into marriage with the first gorgeous, smart, sweet, stable girl to come along."

"I know who I am."

"The teacher who doesn't teach anymore. Mr. Perfect who got jilted on national television because he wasn't so perfect after all. A self-professed country-boy living in LA. Yeah, you sound like you've got it all figured out."

"So I'm changing." He sulked. "People change."

"They do. And I always hope it's for the better, but how often does that happen?" Miranda gathered up her tablet and her shoes. "Just do me a favor. As you're changing and growing and finding yourself in LA, don't go on Dancing With the D-List. Have some freaking self-respect and stop chasing fame."

She left him there. Security and his driver would make sure he got home all right. Or wherever he wanted to go after he left here. He wasn't her charge anymore, but he wasn't going to toss him out into the night either. He'd been a good Mister Perfect, in his own way. Good for ratings, anyway.

She ignored the little shiver of guilt that she'd done that to him, ruined him somehow by picking him as Mister Perfect. He'd been her call. Corn-fed country-boy school teacher. How could she have known he'd turn into Fame-zilla?

"Miranda."

That voice. Raspy sex and sin. *Shit shit shit*. She turned slowly, adjusting her grip on her heels and her tablet. "Bennett. How did you get in here?"

"I pulled some strings to get an invite to the taping—"

And someone is getting fired for not warning me you were in the building.

"I wanted to watch your finale. I'd never seen one of these reunion deals before."

She didn't dare ask him what he'd thought of it. She didn't have the emotional energy to take his critique tonight.

"I guess you're here for your answers," she said instead.

"Yes and no."

She didn't know what to make of that. Was one of the offers no longer on the table? Which one?

"I've been thinking about what you said. About the show being the only thing on television that glorifies love."

"I didn't say it was the only thing, just that it's not a bad thing to do."

"Will you let me finish?" he asked, his lips quirking in a way she hoped was promising. If he was giving her that smirky smile, maybe...

No. She wouldn't get her hopes up. "Is this the moment when you tell me you've been wrong all along and beg my forgiveness?"

His expression tightened.

Nope. Not that moment.

Strange. She was so good at orchestrating the romantic futures of others, and yet could never seem to get the romantic moments in her own life to play quite right.

She folded her arms defensively around her middle, awkward with all she was carrying, but she managed it.

"Sorry. Go ahead."

"You said we're all idiots when we're falling in love."

"That certainly sounds like something I would say."

"Miranda. Shut up."

"Fine," she muttered.

He took a deep breath, like he was about to dive underwater. "You want me to treat you like an equal, but we'll never be equals."

Irritation spiked hard. "Go fu—"

"You're a thousand times better than me."

Wait, what? She'd been working up a good head of steam, but the words slowly penetrated and her jaw dropped.

"I never deserved you. The only thing I had to offer—my experience in this business—was the one thing you kept throwing back in my face. I freaked because I've never needed anyone the way I needed you and you didn't need me back."

"I *loved* you," she said, the words echoing in the empty sound stage.

"But *why?* When you said the words, all I could think was that I'd pulled one over on you and any second you were going to wake up and realize what a mess I am. I've been divorced three times, Miranda. I'm a decade older than you. If you didn't want what I could give you as a mentor, I couldn't figure out why a woman like you would be with me. Do you have any idea how terrifying that is?"

"As terrifying as calling you from Italy to tell you I loved you without any guarantee that you would *ever* say it back?"

"You've always been better than me. Braver. Hell, that girl on your show tonight was braver than me. But if she can do it, the least I can do is man up and say I've wanted you back every second of every day and I understand why you won't take me because you're too good for me, but I love you."

Sound receded as everything slowed. "You don't say that."

"I know." He stepped forward, suddenly in her space. She swayed back, but there was a camera boom and she could only stand there as he loomed over her. And it was probably the hottest moment of her life.

"You never say that," she whispered, his face so close. "Not with anyone."

"I never meant it with anyone else." He groaned, swiping across her cheeks with his thumbs. "Shit, baby, don't cry."

Was she crying? "You said yes and no."

"What?"

"You said yes and no. Is the job no longer available?"

He snorted. "Of course you want to know about work when I'm trying to have a romantic moment." But he was grinning as he said it. "Yes. The job is yours if you want it. And if you don't... The show was good tonight. It was... sincere in a way I wasn't expecting. I'll be honest, I'm still not in love with it so I'm hoping you'll take the *ADS* job, but if *Marrying Mister Perfect* is what you want to do, I'll try to be better about understanding why. If you'll have me. Can you forgive me, Miranda?" His lips quirked, that sexy almost-smile. "I was an idiot, but someone very wise told me we're all idiots when we're falling in love. Probably me more than most since I came to it so late in the game."

She narrowed her eyes, which still seemed to be leaking from the edges. "Don't start making cracks about your age again."

"It is a substantial difference. You could easily find someone closer to your own—"

"Stop. You're the King of Reality Television, Bennett Lang. You aren't supposed to be insecure. I *love* you, you idiot. Even if you are decrepit and ancient."

"Hey."

"And I don't need you to prove how worthy you are with job offers."

"That isn't why I—"

"In fact, I can't imagine working at *American Dance Star* without you." But *with* him... that would be a whole new adventure. "Are you sure you want to retire?"

His eyebrows arched. "You mean co-produce? You want to try living together *and* working together?" he asked skeptically.

She looped her arms around his neck, her tablet resting against one shoulder blade as her heels bumped against the other. "So we're living together, are we?"

"I just assumed—you said—look, I suck at this stuff—"

"Relax, Romeo. I can see I'll have to teach you about milking a romantic moment." She went up on her toes. "You're supposed to be kissing me now."

And he did.

Maybe she wasn't so bad at her own love life after all.

CHAPTER FORTY-ONE

The silence from the apartment upstairs was killing him. It had been two days. Two days since the finale aired and he'd been given a second lease on life when he saw he might still have a chance with her. But she hadn't come back.

He was going nuts missing her. They'd had a rash of freakishy warm weather, melting the snow so it was like skiing through a slushee and he came home soaked to the skin every day. It was miserable. Or maybe he was just miserable.

Thursday. His day off. Leaving him far too much time to think. Taking advantage of the Sucker Spring weather, he spent the morning working on the engine of the Thunderbird—mostly as an excuse to be out in the parking lot, watching for Caitlyn's arrival. She had to come back today, didn't she?

His sisters had argued for hours about what exactly he needed to do and say to convince Caitlyn he wasn't a complete waste of genetic material. About the only thing they'd agreed on was that he needed to find some way to get closure on the Tria and Andy situation.

They might be right.

Didn't mean he had the first idea how to go about doing that.

Normally if he and Andy had a falling out, one of

them would invite the other to go skiing and they'd forget about whatever was bugging them on the slopes. But the dumbass had gone and wrecked his knee. Suggesting they get together for anything else just felt too weird. Especially when he wasn't even sure he wanted to see the man who had once been his friend.

Shit.

Maybe he could get closure by talking to him on the phone. He could manage that much.

He went inside, wiping the grease off his hands, and dialed the number he'd set up for the house when he and Tria moved in, a weird mix of aggression and a sense of inevitability rising up as he listened through the first ring.

"Hello?"

"Tria. I'm calling to talk to Andy."

"Oh. Um. Andy's at PT. I was about to go pick him up, but I'm sure he'd love—"

He wasn't there. Off the hook. "Right. Bye, Tria."

He hung up. And stood staring at the phone. He'd been ready to talk. Ready to have it out. Now the fact that Andy had thwarted him in his attempt at resolution was just another nail in the asshole's coffin.

He was barely aware of grabbing his keys and storming out to the Jeep. He was three miles down the road to the physical therapy center in the next town over before he even realized where he was going.

Andy might not even be there. Tria was going to pick him up. They might be gone already. His ex-fiancé and the asshole who had—

Andy was sitting out front in a wheelchair, his injured leg propped out straight in front of him, face tipped up to soak in the unseasonably warm sun.

Will slammed the Jeep into park, launched himself

out of the driver's side and stalked up to him.

"Will, hey…"

His fist slammed into Andy's face, knuckles splitting against teeth. They both swore, Will cradling his hand and Andy spitting blood.

"Feel better?" Andy said, gingerly testing his teeth with his tongue to see if they were all still attached.

"Not really. I kind of feel like a dick for punching a guy in a wheelchair."

"Even if I deserved it? I was surprised you didn't come after me months ago."

Andy's nose was bent in two places—once from where he'd done a facer into a chairlift pole and once from a brawl they'd gotten into with some boarders when they were seventeen and stupid. He'd always been able to take a hit and keep on kicking.

"Even then."

"I'm sorry," Andy began and Will cut him off.

"Stop. I don't want to do that. I can't do that yet."

"I want to apologize. I have this whole speech. I've been rehearsing it for, like, months."

Will just stared down at him. Andy. Still the same old loveable screw-up. "You love her."

Andy winced. "Yeah."

Yeah, well, I loved her too, asshole. It would have been easier if he hadn't. If it had just been a stupid infatuation. If he'd just gotten carried away in the moment. But he hadn't. He'd loved her. It may not have been the same kind of down to the bone connection he felt for Caitlyn, but he'd really loved her. "Well, you got the girl," he rasped. "Your stupid love story ripped out my fucking heart."

"I know," Andy said hoarsely. "I hated myself this year. Tria says I'm trying to kill myself. Taking stupid chances because if I get hurt, I deserve it, right? We both deserve it—"

"Shut up."

Andy swallowed audibly, but his mouth snapped shut.

Will stared down at his friend, absently rubbing his knuckles. He didn't want Tria anymore, but what they'd done still burned like acid. The two people he'd trusted most outside his family had each put a hand on the knife and stabbed it into his back. He was justified in being angry about it. Justified in holding a grudge. But maybe justification wasn't enough.

Maybe it was time to loosen the stranglehold he had on his anger and make room for something else in his heart. *Someone* else.

"Look. We're not going to hug it out and be best buds or anything, but I'm gonna work on not being so mad at you and you need to knock off the stupid risky shit. I'm the one who gets to be pissed. You're the one who got the girl. So keep her, you idiot. You broke my fucking heart. Fine. Now make it worth it. Make her so happy I'm happy for you even when I want to knock your teeth in. Understand? Don't waste this."

Andy nodded jerkily, jaw working.

Will turned away—and saw Tria, standing in the crook of her open car door a few feet away. He hadn't even heard her pull up. He didn't know how much she'd seen and heard, but he'd had about as much closure as he could take today. He jerked his chin at her, wordlessly, and walked back to his car.

It wasn't exactly a bundle of puppies and rainbows, but it was a start.

Now if only Caitlyn would come home.

CHAPTER FORTY-TWO

The driver helped her unload her bag. Just the one bag this time. She'd been in LA less than a week. She could have managed the roller-bag herself, but her hands were full. Gerbera daisies. Giant happy flowers. Will had said they were his favorite.

She'd never brought a man flowers before. But then she'd never tried to woo anyone either. Never ridden a bull... never fallen in love... Will was just a font of new experiences.

The door flew open when she was still five feet away from it. Will stood framed by the doorway, wild and dark and gorgeous, like Heathcliff on the freaking moors.

"I heard the car," he said, without moving from the doorway, his eyes drinking her in just as greedily as she was doing to him. "How was your trip?"

Behind her, she felt the driver hesitate, probably trying to figure out what the hell to do with her suitcase now that she'd frozen into a statue, but she couldn't tear her eyes off Will.

"I told everyone in America that I was falling for you."

"I saw."

He didn't move, and her hopes, which had been so high when he ran to greet her, began to waver. Was he still angry about the lying? She was ready to grovel. She'd come prepared to woo, damn it.

Caitlyn hitched up her hopes and the flowers. "Are you going to let me in?"

He blinked, glancing around as if suddenly realizing he was blocking the door. If he heard the double meaning in the words, he didn't show it. "I spoke to Tria," he blurted. "And Andy. Worked some things out."

And her hopes took another nosedive. "What?"

Was he getting back together with his ex? She'd suspected he might still be in love with her. A shiver of dread worked down her arms. His eyes locked on the slight movement.

"Shit, you're cold. Come inside."

It wasn't cold out with the sun beating down. The temperature in the parking lot would have suited Los Angeles, but she didn't argue as Will reached past her to take her bag from the driver, trading it for a tip and ushering her into the dark, windowless foyer and up the stairs.

She unlocked the door and it was the most natural thing in the world for the two of them to go inside together. Sometime in the last two months her place had started to feel like *theirs*. At least it had to her. She was terrified that they weren't on the same page at all. They'd had one fight—and it had been a doozie—and then she'd had to go. She'd been such a mess she hadn't even remembered to bring her cell phone.

Will set her bag down next to the door. "Who gave you the flowers?"

She blushed, awkwardly shuffling the bouquet from one hand to the other. "Um, I got them for you actually. I know it's silly, but you said you like them and I thought, why are girls the only ones who get flowers, right?"

For a moment he didn't react, then a smile broke out over his face like sunshine bursting into her heart. "Don't move," he said. "I got something for you."

Please God, let it be another mix tape. She'd bought a portable CD player and listened to the mix non-stop on the flight.

He was out the door before she could blink, leaving her there, still holding the flowers. He was gone less than a minute before he burst back in, holding a rectangular package, like a department store shirt box. "Happy Independence Day."

"It's March."

"Independence from the show."

He thrust it at her and they awkwardly exchanged — flowers for box. He barely looked at the daisies, watching her intently, something a little manic in his expression — which was making her insanely nervous. She felt like something massive must have happened while she was away.

"You said you talked to Tria?"

He nodded jerkily. "Yeah. Well, mostly I talked to Andy. And punched him. It was good. Not the punching. The talking."

He was babbling. Will never babbled. She was the babbler in the relationship.

He jutted his chin at the package. "Are you going to open it?"

Almost afraid to see what was inside, Caitlyn moved to the piano, resting the box on the top as she peeled off the ribbon holding it shut. Will followed, hovering nearby, but just out of touching distance.

She pulled off the box top.

Sheet music. Beethoven's Pathetique Sonata. Her throat closed.

"I know you already have it. Look inside."

She pulled back the cover and there, on the first page, taped right over the first note on the page, was a ring.

It wasn't the Rock of Ages. There was nothing showy or flashy about it. It was delicate, a small stone in an intricate, almost antique-looking setting. Lovely.

A ring.

Caitlyn swung to gape at Will.

"You can say no," he said, the sentence so fast it almost sounded like one word. "I know we haven't known one another that long and you're probably sick of guys proposing to you. But that's when you had me. From the first note. You asked me if I believed in love at first sight and I think I joked about it, but you had me from... okay, not from hello, I'm not gonna say that, but from the very first second I heard you and saw you and touched you and kissed you. Every single first dug another hook into my heart and the seconds and thirds just drove you deeper. Even that freaking ridiculous wedding veil. And I know I freaked out about that perfect guy and this is probably the last thing you want to hear right now. My sisters told me this was a dumbass plan. They said I should apologize first and let you breathe. Did I remember to apologize? I don't care about the show or you making me the Other Man— though I wish you'd told me and you have to tell me stuff like that in the future, if we have a future—"

She'd never seen him spaz out like this. It was kind of adorable. Her big strong fire-fighter completely losing his shit. "So you forgive me?" she interrupted, needing to hear him say those words.

"God, yes! Nothing to forgive, but I would forgive

you anything."

She almost laughed at his colorful choice of words, but didn't want him to think she was laughing at him. Not when he was so adorably earnest. And completely unraveled.

"Shit. I'm not doing this right." He dropped to one knee—and her urge to laugh evaporated as her heart swelled in her chest. Wow. Just seeing him down there... that had to be one of the hottest sights on earth.

"Will..."

"I know I'm screwing this up. I had this whole speech planned and then I got distracted and I don't know which parts I said, so let me just repeat. I love you. Please marry me. Or tell me you're not ready to answer yet because it's too soon, I get that, I'm rushing it, I always rush things, but I mean every word. And I'm so sorry. I could cut off my tongue for making you cry."

"Don't. I like your tongue."

His eyes filled with fragile hope. "I don't want to pressure you. I don't want you saying yes when you aren't sure, because we've both been bitten by that before—"

"Will." She bent and pressed a palm to his cheek. "You can stop talking now."

"Caitlyn..."

She set her lips over his, shutting the poor man up with a kiss. When she pulled back, she lingered to whisper the word against his lips. "Yes."

He sucked in a breath. "Are you sure? Because I know it's fast—"

"It's perfect," she whispered, looking into those gorgeous eyes with their sinner lashes. "I think I needed something fake so I would know the real deal when it came along. You're it, Will. You're my fairy tale. I don't know when I fell in love with you—though I suspect it probably had something to do with all the chocolate you kept feeding me." He chuckled and she grinned. "I came home with a whole elaborate plan to woo you and propose to *you*, so you'd know for sure I wasn't saying yes for the wrong reasons like last time."

"Oh. We can do that too. I'm very open to being wooed."

She laughed, feeling the fizzy champagne delight in her blood that only ever seemed to happen when she was with him. "I love you. Now get up here and kiss me properly."

"Yes, ma'am."

He stood, bent her over the piano, and kissed her—very *im*properly indeed.

Her hands were shaking when he slipped the ring on—and it was perfect.

EPILOGUE

Caitlyn lay on the couch in the circle of her fiancé's arms, twisting her hand from side to side to admire her ring—his grandmother's, which he had never given to Tria—from every possible angle.

Her fiancé. It sounded... *heavenly*. The rightness of it settled around her as perfectly as his arms.

They lay in the shadow of their mountain and she wondered how soon she could broach the idea of buying the chalet. They could remodel it—combine the two apartments, turn the downstairs into guest rooms and a storage area, though they'd have to keep the bathroom down there since it was so much bigger than the one upstairs and she had a real affection for that spacious shower of his. *Very* fond memories.

She bit her lip. And his thumb immediately reached up to rub the spot.

"What?" His voice rumbled through his chest against her back.

After what he'd gone through with Tria, she couldn't ask him to buy a house with another fiancé, but she'd promised no more lies. She shrugged, settling for the middle ground. "I like it here. Of course I'll like it anywhere with you."

"If I ever get that money back from Andy and Tria, we should put in an offer on this place," he said—just like that. So easy and casual. And Caitlyn about melted. He trusted her. That was so freaking hot.

"I actually have a little nest egg put by," she suggested tentatively. "From my performing days. If we wanted to put in an offer on this place, we could."

"How big a nest egg?" he asked, his hands sneaking under the hem of her shirt. "Am I about to become a kept man? Used shamelessly for my sexual prowess?"

"Maybe," she purred, shifting to give him better access, the better to show off his sexual prowess. "I was thinking I might do the occasional performance too."

"I thought you hated that life," he murmured, his mouth finding the good spots on the side of her neck.

"I wouldn't be touring. Just the occasional thing—Colorado Symphony, if they'll have me. Maybe see if there are community orchestras in the area. I don't miss the life, but I do sometimes miss playing with other musicians. Would you mind?"

"I suppose it would be greedy to keep all your music to myself," he said, against her collarbone as he slid her shirt aside. "I guess I can share you with your adoring fans. As long as I get you all to myself every night."

She turned in his arms so she could kiss him. "Deal."

It was some time later, both of them sprawled on the floor with Caitlyn wearing *only* the ring when they spoke again.

"My mom will want to plan the wedding." She traced a pattern across the muscles of his chest. The man was a freaking work of art.

"My sisters might give her a run for her money." He smoothed a hand down the length of her flank.

"I suppose we should tell people now," she murmured, strangely reluctant to share their little bubble of happiness with anyone else.

"Not just yet." Will spoke against her skin, waking up her utterly satisfied body for more. "You'll meet my family and I'll meet yours, but tonight… you're mine."

"Every night. And every day. Every song and every breath and all the moments in between."

She'd found her happily ever after, and she wasn't letting go.

ABOUT THE AUTHOR

Winner of the Romance Writers of America's prestigious Golden Heart Award, Lizzie Shane lives in Alaska where she uses the long winter months to cook up happily-ever-afters (and indulge her fascination with the world of reality television). She also writes paranormal romance under the pen name Vivi Andrews. Find more about Lizzie or sign up to receive her New Release Newsletter for updates on upcoming Reality Romance books at www.lizzieshane.com

WANT MORE LIZZIE SHANE?
DON'T MISS THE REST OF THE SERIES:

MARRYING MISTER PERFECT
(Reality Romance, Book 1)

ROMANCING MISS RIGHT
(Reality Romance, Book 2)

FALLING FOR MISTER WRONG
(Reality Romance, Book 3)

PLANNING ON PRINCE CHARMING
(Reality Romance, Book 4)

COURTING TROUBLE
(Reality Romance, Book 5)
Coming in 2016

CPSIA information can be obtained at www.ICGtesting.com
Printed in the USA
LVOW08s2129010416

481786LV00003BA/317/P